Escape to Retribution Bay

Aussie Heroes: Retribution Bay

Claire Boston

BANTILLY
PUBLISHING

First published by Bantilly Publishing in 2021

Escape to Retribution Bay - Aussie Heroes: Retribution Bay

EPUB format: 978-1-925696-85-1
Print: 978-1-925696-86-8
Large Print: 978-1-925696-87-5

Cover design by Mayhem Cover Creations
Edited by Ann Harth
Proofread by Teena Raffa-Mulligan

About the Author

Claire Boston fell in love with romance and romantic suspense at eleven when she discovered her mother's stash of Nora Roberts novels. Like Nora, she writes series set around families or groups of friends with a guaranteed happy ending.

She loves travelling and learning about new cultures and interesting vocations which she then weaves into her writing.

When Claire's not at the computer typing her stories she can be found creating her own handmade journals, swinging on a sidecar, or in the garden attempting to grow something other than weeds.

Claire lives in Western Australia with her husband, who loves even her most annoying quirks and is currently learning how to knit. You can find her complete book list on her website www.claireboston.com/books.You can connect with Claire through Facebook and Twitter, or join her reader group

(http://www.claireboston.com/reader-group/).

Also by Claire Boston

Romance
<u>The Texan Quartet</u>
What Goes on Tour
All that Sparkles
Under the Covers
Into the Fire

<u>The Flanagan Sisters</u>
Break the Rules
Change of Heart
Blaze a Trail
Place to Belong

Romantic Suspense
<u>The Blackbridge Series</u>
Nothing to Fear
Nothing to Gain
Nothing to Hide
Nothing to Lose
Shelter
Shield
Harbour
Protect

<u>Aussie Heroes: Retribution Bay</u>
Return to Retribution Bay
Trapped in Retribution Bay
Escape to Retribution Bay
Secrets in Retribution Bay

Non-fiction
<u>The Beginner Writer's Toolkit</u>
Self-Editing

Dedication

To Michelle Diener, my Nullarbor road trip buddy.

Chapter 1

"You imbecile! Get her into my office." Tan's low snarl made Tess Lim cringe and she changed her trajectory, heading towards a table she'd already cleaned, rather than into the kitchen where Tan was. Her hand shook as she sprayed cleaner and wiped the surface. Calm down. She hadn't raised Tan's ire.

Her feet desperately needed a rest but if she sat down, even for a minute, Tan would be angry.

The restaurant door opened, and two police officers walked in. She glanced towards the kitchen. Tan normally dealt with them, but he was nowhere to be seen. Tess swallowed hard and forced a smile. "Can I help you?"

"We've got a takeaway order for the station," the taller one said.

She hadn't heard the sizzle of food cooking in at least half an hour. As far as she knew, all the kitchen staff had gone home already. She'd been waiting for the last table of diners to finish, and they had just left. "One minute, please." Had their order been forgotten? That would make Tan even angrier.

As she approached the kitchen, Tan strode out carrying a paper bag. He smiled widely in what Tess thought of as his customer smile. "Officers. How has your day been?"

"It'll be better after we've eaten," the short one said.

Tess couldn't smell any food. How long had their food been sitting in the kitchen? Or was there even food in the bag? The way Tan carried it, just by the top, made it seem as if it wasn't particularly heavy.

She tore her gaze away before anyone could notice her looking. She'd learnt not to show any interest in Tan's affairs. Tess did a final lap of the restaurant checking each table was set ready for the next day. When the police left, she'd tell Tan she was finished. Her aching feet could make it. Soon she'd be home, and flopping on her bed, and wouldn't move until morning.

"You done?" Tan demanded.

Tess flinched. Tan stood at the restaurant entrance. Arms crossed, he pinned her with the scowl he reserved for her. Behind him in the car park, the police were getting into their patrol car. "Yes, Tan." She gathered the cloth and spray bottle and hurried towards the kitchen, keeping her head bowed.

"Leave them on the bench," he said.

Odd. Normally he insisted she return everything to its proper place. He handed her a yellow envelope. "This fortnight's pay."

She bowed. "Thank you, Tan." The packet was thin despite the fifty-hour weeks she worked. The rest he said he sent to her parents back in Singapore or kept for her food and board, but if that were true, her parents had never mentioned it. Still, after eighteen months, she had almost ten thousand dollars saved, but only because she had no opportunity to spend it between university and work.

"You can walk home tonight. I have business to attend to."

No, not another hour on her feet! She forced a smile,

trying not to think of the cold, dark streets. "Yes, Tan." She shrugged on her thick puffer jacket, her muscles already tense, and retrieved her bag from under the counter, her fingers automatically feeling out the lining to ensure the cash she saved was still there. She hadn't opened an Australian bank account, and didn't trust Tan not to steal it from the granny flat she rented from him.

Tan pointed to the front door. "Leave that way. I'll lock it behind you."

She stepped into the dark night, zipping up her jacket and shivering as an icy breeze brushed past. Rustling trees lined the streets like boogey-men. She could do this. She'd walked home in the dark before. All she had to do was pretend to be one of the daring female pirates she liked to read about, or one of those intrepid women who had come to Australia and thrived, despite its strangeness.

Buoyed by the thought, she avoided the puddles left by the rain and was halfway across the car park when she reached into her jacket pocket for her phone. Empty. Damn it. She'd left it charging in the kitchen. She couldn't survive without her phone. It was her safety net, and her connection with the world. But Tan wouldn't like her returning.

She stayed where she was a moment, debating. She sighed. What would Da Lim do? She smiled at the thought of her rogue ancestor. Da would do what it took to get what she wanted. The journals of her exploits in Australia had sparked Tess's desire to leave Singapore and study here. Da wouldn't leave without her phone.

Though Tess's stride wasn't as confident as she would have liked, she retraced her steps and knocked on the front door. Tan didn't come.

Probably hadn't heard her.

She'd go around the back and use her key. Her steps faltered and her skin prickled at the car parked in the alley behind the restaurant. Tan didn't like to be disturbed if he had others in his office, and he'd been angry before she'd left. Tess hesitated. The phone was on the bench right next to the door. If she was quick, she could reach in, grab it, and leave with no one noticing.

She listened at the door, but couldn't hear any voices. Slowly, she turned the key and pushed the door open a crack. No one talking. Her phone was right there on the bench. She reached in, pulled the charger from the socket, and tucked it and her phone into her pocket. As she eased the door closed again, a cry made her freeze. "I'm sorry," a woman sobbed. "It's not my fault. I didn't know he would talk."

Tess's skin heated, fear racing through her veins. What was going on? The woman sounded terrified. Every instinct shouted at her to close the door and leave, but that wasn't what Da would do. She would help those less fortunate than her, and strive to make the world a better place. That was the person Tess wanted to be. She hated scurrying away at the slightest sign of conflict. Bracing herself, she inched the door open wider and gasped. An older woman sat tied to a wheeled office chair, her face bruised, her dark hair full of grey. Tan and his new driver, Salvatore, stood over her, Tan holding a gun to the woman's head.

What on earth?

"I warned you what would happen if either of you talked," Tan said.

"Please! I never thought Roger would. He promised me. I thought he loved me."

"Obviously not enough."

The cold venom in Tan's tone made Tess shiver. This man was far more dangerous than Tess had suspected. She had to call the police.

The woman struggled against the ropes, glancing wildly around, and her eyes met Tess's. They widened.

"Help me. Call—" The gunshot's echo exploded in the stainless steel room and red sprayed from the woman's head, coating the newly mopped floor. She fell back, her head twisting towards Tess, the life fading from her eyes.

Tess shrieked, and Tan whirled around. He swore and raised his gun, pointing it at her.

Tess ran.

Her feet pounded the bitumen as she rounded the corner of the restaurant and cut across the car park. Dirt sprayed beside her and a pop chilled her core. They were shooting at her!

Only a few more metres and she'd reach the tree-lined footpath. She pushed herself harder and ducked behind a tree as the bark exploded next to her and a second pop followed the first.

What was she doing? She couldn't stay here. Though her fear wanted to override her feet, wanted her to pull her arms over her head and crouch down and pray she could disappear like she had when she'd had nightmares as a child, it wasn't possible.

This was a nightmare, but she was wide awake.

She pushed off the tree and ran, her breath coming in gasps, weaving around the trees so Tan couldn't get a clear shot.

Usually the streetlights were spaced far apart, leaving too much darkness between them, but tonight they seemed much closer together, illuminating her when all she wanted to do was hide.

A car roared to life behind her. She had to get off the road.

Up ahead was an alley between two houses. Her arms pumped as she urged herself faster, the weight of her laptop banging against her back. She charged down the path as the headlights illuminated her. Her lungs burned, and she couldn't breathe.

Think.

She knew this neighbourhood. The next house had a dog which barked whenever she walked past. On cue, deep woofs sounded on the other side of the fence and the thud of feet as the dog raced along with her.

Tess glanced behind. Salvatore raced down the alleyway after her, his bulky body slowing him down. Fear made her fly.

Think.

The car must have gone around the block, which meant it would come for her from the right. Directly in front, bushland separated her from the highway, and to the left, a bend in the road led around into a cul-de-sac.

The bushland was filled with deadly Australian snakes and spiders which could kill her.

But she faced certain death if her pursuers caught her.

She dashed out of the alley and turned left, sprinting across the road and into the dark trees. A narrow dirt path led to the cycle way which ran along the main highway. Perhaps in the dark, Salvatore wouldn't see it.

Another glance behind her. Salvatore ran onto the street. He looked right, and she ducked low to the ground and behind a tree. Her skin vibrated with tension as her eyes strained to pick out movement in the darkness. How many venomous creatures were watching her right now? Was a snake winding its way towards her, or a spider lowering itself on its web?

She sucked in oxygen, her breath loud to her ears, but she didn't dare move.

A car roared down the road, the throaty burble identifying it as Tan's Mustang. She froze in place. "Where is she?" Tan shouted.

"I don't know," Salvatore yelled back. "Might be in the bush or around the bend."

Tess curled into a ball, picturing Tan looking into the bush. Around her she felt beady eyes watching her from the dark, waiting to jump out and strike her. She bit down on a sob.

"No. She's terrified of snakes. Check the front yards, I'll sweep the streets." The car roared off again.

Tess stayed where she was, trying to breathe quietly, trying to calm her heart rate. She needed to move. After they'd searched the front yards of the houses, they'd search the bush. Tan knew she wasn't athletic enough to jump a fence into a backyard.

She peered through the bush towards the highway. At this time of night, the traffic was intermittent. She could run across the road into the next suburb, but more bushland lay on the other side, and she wasn't sure if there was a path through it. Did buses run this late at night? They must. Tan had let her go to an end of year university celebration last year as long as she was home by midnight, and she'd caught the last bus.

Tess didn't dare check her public transport app yet. The light would be a beacon straight towards her. Tan drove past after going around the cul-de-sac, and Salvatore was several houses away, searching. This was her chance.

Slowly she shifted, crouching still, and slunk down the path. It had rained most of the day, so the leaves were damp, softening her steps. As soon as she reached the highway verge, she moved away from the path so she wouldn't be seen.

No cars. She dashed across the dual-carriage way and climbed over the concrete divider in the middle of the highway. She stayed there for a moment, waiting for a car to pass. Thank God there wasn't a lot of traffic at this time of night.

Crossing to the median strip, she eyed the bushland for a path through. Up ahead was an intersection, but it was a couple of hundred metres away and she was too exposed here. Tan might leave the suburb and check the highway.

The very thought chilled her bones, so she dashed into the bush. Just a couple of steps in, enough so she could crouch and hide behind a tree while she checked the transport app.

What she wanted was the next bus anywhere, but the farthest she could go was preferable. Home. If she left the country, Tan couldn't hurt her.

She typed in the airport and discovered a bus would go past the nearby shopping centre in about half an hour. Now to get there.

She'd turn left at the traffic lights up ahead. Tess was about to stand when she heard the burble of Tan's car. She froze, eyes on the highway, and the Mustang crawled by, going far below the speed limit. Searching for her.

Her pulse raced as he pulled up at the red light. How far would he go before he doubled back?

She glanced through the bush. The streetlights gave enough light to illuminate the shapes of trees, and it was maybe twenty metres until she'd reach the street. The lights turned green, and Tan continued straight ahead.

Tess had to do this. She would face her fears. She would channel Da's courage. One of her university friends had laughed, saying there weren't as many snakes in the city as tourists believed. She'd said vibrations scared them off, but Tess couldn't risk stomping in case Salvatore crossed the highway too and heard her.

Staying crouched, she stepped carefully through the bush. Something soft and sticky covered her face. She shrieked and ran, swiping the spider's web away, not caring about where she was going. Bursting free of the bushland, she stopped under a streetlight, running her hands over her face and then her body to make sure no deadly redback clung to her clothing. She shivered and kept brushing her hair and her clothes.

Exhaling slowly, she scanned her surroundings and then checked the app. She was on a street parallel to the road Tan would turn down if he came this way, but she enlarged the map to find the least obvious way to get to the shopping centre.

One which avoided as many roads as possible.

She had a bus to catch.

Almost there. She'd been forced to hide twice on her way to the shopping centre because cars had driven past. Now the bus stop was only a few hundred metres ahead across the deserted car park. Her skin crawled at having to cross such an open field with nowhere to hide. She glanced down the road and her heart jumped. That was her bus.

Her fear of missing the bus overrode her fear of the open ground and she ran, her feet slapping through puddles, her backpack pounding into her back. She lifted a hand and waved, yelling as loudly as she could.

The bus didn't stop.

Tess's steps slowed and she panted, staring at the red tail lights of the bus as it turned the corner and out of sight.

She hunched as nausea flooded her. What now?

She stood in the middle of an open car park in plain view of anyone driving past and had missed her last chance to get to the airport.

First, she had to hide. The shopping centre behind her was the most obvious place. She'd walked past its loading bays on the other side.

She jogged back the way she'd come as the rain that had been threatening all night, started to fall.

Faster. By the time she reached the loading bay, her black pants stuck to her legs around her ankles and her hair was soaked. She should have bought a jacket with a hood.

The loading bay's ceiling overhung, providing shelter from the rain, and she tucked herself behind the dumpster at the back and took out her phone. The airport was still her best bet. A quick search told her it would take four hours to walk there, and the last plane left in half an hour.

She kept searching.

No buses, no trains, no hire car places open. Not even a taxi could get to her in time.

There was no leaving the city tonight.

Should she go to the police?

Would they even believe her? Those cops were good friends with Tan. Salvatore had probably already cleaned up the evidence.

But maybe she could call anonymously.

Over the patter of the rain on the roof, a low burble caught her attention, and she tucked her phone into her pocket. Then it rang, the sound terrifyingly loud, and her fingers fumbled to switch it to silent. Tan was calling.

She wanted to be sick. Quickly she held down the button to turn off her phone. At the entrance to the loading bay, the mustang crept past. She held her breath and curled into a ball, praying it wouldn't stop. The car turned, its headlights illuminating the loading bay.

The rain came down harder, the sound like thunder on the roof making it impossible to hear anything else.

Was Tan getting out of his car?

Was he walking towards her?

Tess didn't dare move.

After a long minute, the light shifted as the mustang backed up and drove away.

Tess exhaled. She was safe.

For now.

Chapter 2

Ed Stokes sighed and closed his eyes, leaning his head against the cold glass window. Windscreen wipers swished through the splattering rain. Mornings sucked. He especially hated getting up before the sun. It was a particular type of torture, which was why he'd delayed waking as long as possible. With no checked baggage, he only needed to be at the airport thirty minutes before departure.

His head thumped against the glass as Sheridan drove over a bump. "You're not going to sleep on me, are you?" his house mate asked.

"Maybe." Ed yawned. Hopefully, all this rain wouldn't delay his flight.

"I swear you're allergic to mornings," Sheridan said. "You'd never cut it as a shift worker."

He shuddered. "Lucky I'm not one." He'd discovered from an early age that anything too physical didn't match his strengths, much to his family's disappointment. A farm boy who didn't want to farm was unfathomable in his father's mind. Ed rubbed his chest. Not that his father had judged him for it; he just hadn't understood. Ed would give anything to be able to try and explain it to his dad again. But that would never happen. He couldn't believe his parents had been gone for three months.

He blinked away the tears. "We there yet?"

Sheridan laughed. "Almost." He turned into the airport drive. "I really appreciate you lending me your car while you're gone."

Ed shrugged. "I won't be using it. Better you drive it than it sits in the long-term car park for a fortnight. Cheaper for me too." He grinned.

"I would not have coped on public transport," Sheridan said. "Seriously, who would think a little mechanical problem would take two weeks to fix?"

His friend had never lived in the country, particularly not somewhere like Retribution Bay, which perched on the north-west peninsula of Western Australia. There you had to wait for everything. "Couldn't have you breaking down," Ed said. "Otherwise you'd never do my share of the work while I was away."

"Might not anyway. The software roll out is going to be a killer. You're a lucky bastard to get out of it."

Ed agreed. It would be a long, tedious process. He'd have to thank Amy and Brandon for the timing of their wedding.

Sheridan pulled into the drop-off zone of the airport, slamming on the brakes as a young Asian woman ran in front of the car. Her eyes widened, hands hitting the bonnet. She was drenched, water dripping from her long dark hair and clothes, backpack sagging, but the terror in her brown eyes turned to relief when she met Ed's gaze, almost as if she was expecting to see someone else.

"You OK?" he called.

She took a breath before nodding, raising a hand in apology and running away.

Ed rubbed his shoulder where the seatbelt had bitten in. "She's in a rush."

"I think she took two years off my life," Sheridan said.

The rain continued in a steady, pouring stream. No point waiting for it to let up. He'd get soaked. Damn it. "Pop the boot so I can get my bag." Ed shoved open the door.

"Yep. You'll call with your arrival time?"

"Sure." More than once. If he didn't, Sheridan would forget to pick him up.

He shut the door, ducking his head against the rain, and swung his backpack over his shoulder. He stepped onto the pavement, under a shelter, and waved as Sheridan drove off.

Ed shook off as much water as he could before entering the airport building. The terminal was packed, most people dressed in high-visibility gear which marked them as fly-in, fly-out workers. There were always a dozen or more flights heading out early to one of the remote mine sites. He glanced at the departure board to check his flight details, and his heart sank. Every flight had the word CANCELLED next to it.

They had to be kidding.

He walked up to a couple who were staring at the board. "Is it the weather?"

The man shook his head. "Baggage handlers have walked off the job. They're striking for at least twenty-four hours."

Shit. The wedding was in three days. He rubbed a hand over his hair, brushing out more moisture. He should have considered the possibility. The last time he'd flown home, the baggage handlers were having go-slow days to force negotiations for better working conditions. He pulled out his phone and found an article about the strike. Workers weren't ruling out the possibility of a second day of action. If that happened, he'd never get to the wedding on time, and he had the rings.

Though Brandon hadn't been much of a brother, Amy was relying on him, and she'd never let him down.

He couldn't disappoint her.

What were his options?

The drive was close to fourteen hours if he only stopped long enough to fill up with fuel. If he booked a flight for tomorrow, and it was cancelled, there would still be enough time to get there before the wedding, though he'd never done such a long drive by himself. The airline counter had a long line of very angry looking customers, so he opened the app he used to buy his flights and checked availability. Both flights tomorrow were fully booked.

He sighed. There goes that idea. Looked like he was driving.

He stepped out of the airport into the wintry morning air and moved towards the car park. Where had he—shit. He'd loaned his car to Sheridan and couldn't go back on his promise. Sheridan needed Ed's car to take his grandmother shopping once a week, as well as to get to work.

Ed went back inside and scanned the hire car counter. Each company had long lines in front of it. Ed checked the board again. Several of the flights were to destinations which were only a four to six-hour drive away. The companies were likely to run out of cars.

Quickly, he typed his details into his phone. He tapped his foot as he waited for the options to come up. Not a lot. All the people who arrived at the required one hour before departure had snapped up the cars. But there was a small camper van that would be perfect. He could pull over at rest spots and nap for an hour or two when he needed to. He clicked the button to hire and filled in all his details. Then he wandered over to the relevant counter. They had one line for pre-booked vehicles which was significantly shorter. While he waited, he called home and despite the early hour, Darcy answered.

"My flight's been cancelled," Ed told him. "I'm

driving up, so won't be there until tonight."

"What happened?" his brother asked.

"Baggage handler strike. No flights until maybe tomorrow and they're all booked."

"That sucks. Drive safely, OK? If you get tired, stop and rest."

"Yeah, I will. See you when I get there."

At the front of the queue next to him, he noticed the girl they'd almost run down. Water puddled on the floor below her. Her black pants and black leather shoes made him think she'd just finished work, and her thick blue puffer jacket had stopped being water resistant hours ago. She twisted her fingers together and bounced on her toes, glancing over at the entrance doors. "I need your driver's licence, Miss," the man behind the counter said.

She handed it to him.

He frowned. "This is a Singapore driver's licence."

She nodded. "That's where I'm from."

"Then you need to have an international driver's licence."

"I don't have one."

Ed missed the man's response, as it was his turn at the counter. He showed the woman his receipt, and she smiled. "Where are you travelling to?"

"Retribution Bay."

"Holiday or business?" She typed details into her computer.

"Holiday. My brother's getting married on Saturday."

She gave him a sympathetic look. "Then this strike has come at an awful time for you."

He nodded. Next to him, the man at the counter called for the next customer. The woman who'd been trying to hire a car was in tears. Maybe she was desperate to get somewhere too. "Hey." He touched her arm, and she flinched, spinning away from him. He smiled his most amiable smile. "Where are you headed?"

Recognition sparked, but she didn't say anything. This close, he saw scratches on her face as if she'd been attacked by a tree.

From her point of view, he was a stranger who'd almost run her down. "I'm driving to Retribution Bay, so if you need a lift north, you could come with me. I'll be going past Geraldton, Kalbarri and Carnarvon." He held out his hand. "I'm Ed."

She hesitated and then shook it, her touch light. "Tess."

"Sir, if you come this way, I'll take you to your car."

Ed glanced at the customer service woman. "Be right there." He smiled again. "Do you want to come?"

She looked over her shoulder again, and then nodded.

Concern filled him. She was worried about something. What if she was a criminal on the run? Still, she was smaller than he was, with a light bone structure, so she wouldn't overpower him. This time, his smile was forced. "Come on."

They followed the woman outside, and another employee brought the van around. Ed's heart sank. The website images didn't do the car any justice. It was old, like twenty years old, and had scratches all over the bumper. The sunroof was popped open and as the customer service woman opened the passenger side door, Ed noted water dripping from the gap. The driver thumped the roof, and it closed.

Inside, the seats were grey with miscellaneous stains on them, and the back was tiny. Would it survive the twelve-hundred-kilometre trip?

"It's all we have left," she said apologetically, and handed him a clipboard. "Mark any scratches on this."

He almost laughed and circled the whole damned vehicle. Instead, he walked around, circling and recording the myriad scratches and dents the car had in the bodywork. When he was done, the woman opened the sliding side door and explained how the bed folded down.

Tess gasped.

"We won't be needing it," Ed said, but took note anyway. Tess could share the driving after they left the city, and they'd be in Retribution Bay by nightfall. He didn't care if she didn't have an international licence.

The woman explained the rest of the features—a term which she used generously considering the cooking facilities consisted of a tiny portable camp stove with a single butane bottle, a plastic tub for a sink and a five-litre container of water. Thankfully, he wouldn't be using any of it. The only useful things were a couple of towels, one which he handed to Tess so she could dry herself. The customer service woman handed him the keys, and he threw his backpack in the back. Tess stepped back, clinging to her bag, so he shut the sliding door. "Thank you." He shook the customer service woman's hand.

He climbed into the car. "Ready?" he asked Tess.

She nodded, some doubt on her face. He agreed completely. Turning the key, the engine kicked over and growled, the sound loud in the cab. He sighed. At least it started. He pulled out of the pickup area, flicking on the windscreen wipers, which stuttered twice before sweeping into action.

Tess was silent next to him.

"You want to drive the coastal road or Brand Highway?" He turned the temperature to hot and switched on the fan. It blew out a gust of stale air before settling into a steady blow with a ticking sound behind it. Seriously, this car must have been hidden at the back of the yard for a decade.

Tess held her hands up to the heat. "Whichever's faster."

They were about the same, but the Brand was more direct from here, and in this car that would be a good thing. Ed rubbed his eyes. He would kill for a coffee. He'd planned to buy one and something to eat, after he'd arrived at the airport. They'd stop on the way out of the city.

The headlights weren't great, but they had only about an hour before the sun would be up, and the streetlights illuminated the road.

He settled into his seat. He was going home.

Chapter 3

Tess clutched her bag to her chest and stared straight ahead, every muscle in her body tense. What was she doing? Ed was a complete stranger. The area they were heading was sparsely populated and easy to disappear in—or made to disappear. She shivered and rubbed her hands together, holding them up to the heater, hoping the warmth would soon seep through her soaked clothing.

Exhaustion made it difficult to think clearly. She hadn't slept all night, constantly alert for the sounds of Tan returning. She hadn't dared turn her phone back on to make an anonymous call to the police in case the light from her phone attracted attention.

She glanced at Ed. Maybe she could call the police now. But what if Ed freaked out and kicked her out of the car?

No. It would have to wait until she was out of the city, perhaps when they stopped for petrol somewhere and she could call from the toilets.

Her eyes closed of their own accord and a flash of the woman's dead eyes lit up her vision. She jerked and forced her spine straight. She couldn't fall asleep. Not until she was out of the city, not until she knew whether Ed could be trusted.

"You OK?"

She nodded. "A little tired."

Tess's mother would be horrified by the situation Tess had got herself into. She could practically hear the panic in her mother's voice, the admonition for getting into a car with a complete stranger. She wouldn't understand why Tess hadn't gone straight to the police and would demand Tess return home.

"I get that. Mornings suck. Before you go to sleep, you'd better tell me where you're headed," Ed said.

His voice was loud above the whirr of the heater. Where was it he had said he was going? "Ah, Retribution Bay."

"Holiday?"

She nodded. Was it a holiday destination? She vaguely knew where it was on the coastline, but her interest in Western Australia revolved around the pearling industry in Cossack and then Broome, which was further north.

"My sister works on a whale shark tour boat," he said. "I might be able to get you a discount if you haven't already booked."

A kind offer, but she couldn't swim, and she wasn't getting into the water far from shore where tiger sharks also roamed. "Thanks. I'm not sure what my plans are yet." She grimaced. Who went on holiday without at least some plans? "I, ah, am meeting friends. They're organising something."

A street sign pointed to the highway she'd crossed only a few hours earlier. She hunched down and turned her face away from the window, almost expecting the glass to explode with a bullet. She trembled. Was Tan still looking for her? If not him, then he'd have others still searching the streets. She was too much of a threat, and Tan didn't like threats.

"I'm going to stop for coffee and something to eat at the service station up ahead," Ed said.

"No!" Fear gripped her. What if Tan was filling up his Mustang?

"I'll only be a minute."

Not here, not somewhere Tan or any of his friends might see her. She cleared her throat. What was a reasonable argument? "Can you wait until… ah… we get out of the city?" she asked. "So we don't get caught in rush hour?" Everyone always complained about the traffic congestion.

Ed sighed. "Yeah, all right. Good point."

She sighed and relaxed her hold on the arm rest, studying the man. Mid-twenties, maybe twenty centimetres taller than her, lean but not overly muscled. His light brown hair was almost blond, and it was his easy smile and the concern in his brown eyes which had convinced her to go with him. He hadn't been angry when she'd run in front of his car, he'd been worried. He reminded her of the guys in her Australian history class, easy-going and friendly. The type of person she'd hoped to meet coming here. The type of guy her parents would like if he was Singaporean. Her mother had warned her not to date Australian men. She didn't want Tess to stay in Australia.

"So have you migrated here?" he asked. "I heard the guy at the counter say you had a Singapore driver's licence."

Right. "I'm studying at the University of Western Australia."

"Cool. That's where I went. It's a great campus. What are you studying?"

He was making conversation. She could manage this. It would be an awkward drive if they didn't speak. They were out of the built-up area and bushland lined the road. Some of the tension left her. "A bachelor of science, majoring in biochemistry and molecular biology," she said. "With an extra unit of Australian history."

"That's an interesting combination."

And one her parents didn't know about. "I discovered one of my ancestors worked in Australia as a pearl diver in the late nineteenth century. I thought while I was here, I could search for more information about her." Da had been a rebel, and someone the rest of the family didn't talk about, but she'd found reference to her while going through the family history, desperate to find anyone who had felt as suffocated by duty as she did. Da Lim had given her hope.

"I thought most of the pearl divers of that era were male."

A burst of energy swept through Tess at a chance to discuss her favourite topic. "There were some female divers, but Da pretended to be male to protect herself." She couldn't imagine the strength Da must have had. The secret would have weighed on her every second of the day.

"That's brave," Ed said. "My family can trace its ancestors back to England. They arrived on the Retribution, the ship which gave Retribution Bay its name. It crashed on a reef in the gulf during a cyclone, and my family set up a sheep station in the area."

Tess straightened, excitement simmering. These were the stories she loved, people overcoming obstacles to make something of themselves. "When was that?"

"Ah, sometime in the 1870s. My great, great-whatever grandfather, Reginald had just married and was taking his bride, Lilian, north to start their life together. I don't envy Lilian. By all reports she was one of the few women on board, and the journey was tough."

Da was in Australia around then as well. "Were they coming from Fremantle or from England?"

Ed pursed his lips. "I don't know. There were

convicts on board, but I assumed they came from Freo."

How could he not be interested in such a fascinating story? Her family was filled with ancestors obeying the rules, except for Da.

"If it interests you so much, you can always come out to the Ridge and look through the old trunks we've got in the shed."

She gaped at him. "You have trunks from that period?"

He shrugged. "I'm not sure when they're from, just that they've been there forever. Mum was starting to go through them before..." Grief crossed his face.

She had the urge to reach out to him. "Before what?"

"Before she died." He cleared his throat. "Mum and Dad died in a car accident a few months ago."

Tess gasped. "I'm so sorry." The pain must be so raw still. As much as her parents frustrated her, she couldn't imagine life without them. "Do you have more family in Retribution Bay?"

"Yeah. Two brothers and a sister. I'm heading home for my eldest brother's wedding."

Oh. That was lovely and tragic at the same time. His parents would miss it.

What family did the woman who'd been shot have? How much would her death affect those in her life?

Tess clenched her teeth. She had to say something, do something to give the woman's family closure.

The sun was edging over the horizon in the east, and they were well and truly out of Perth. The rain continued to pour, putting the windscreen wipers through a workout they hadn't had in decades. Tess's jacket was drying, but the car smelled wet and foisty. Hopefully, by mid-day they would be far enough north to leave the rain behind and be able to dry out. All she had were the clothes she wore, her laptop, and her cash. She opened her backpack to check the damp hadn't got inside and breathed a sigh of relief at her dry computer.

"There's a roadhouse up ahead," Ed said. "It's far enough out of the city that we don't have to worry about traffic. Mind if I stop for coffee and food? I skipped breakfast thinking I'd get something at the airport."

"Sure." She hadn't eaten since last night either, and there was little chance Tan would search for her here. She closed her eyes. Should she call the police now? She couldn't keep running forever. No. They weren't that far from the city and if Ed overheard, he might leave her here.

What about her parents? She cringed. She did not have the energy to deal with them now. Her parents wouldn't believe her, or they'd see it as proof she shouldn't have come to Australia. But they'd sent her to stay with Tan. Did they know what kind of person he was? The couple of times she'd brought up her concerns about Tan's controlling ways, her parents had told her not to be ungrateful. Tan was doing her a favour by letting her stay, and if she didn't like it, she could come home.

Which wasn't an option as far as she was concerned. She daydreamed about using the money she'd saved to find her own apartment, or a room at one of the university colleges. She had enough to pay for a semester of accommodation, and if she found a job which paid her properly, she'd be able to afford her final year as well.

But to do that would be a major betrayal in her parents' eyes and they would stop paying her university fees. Those, she couldn't afford on her own.

"This will do," Ed said as he pulled into a service station. "You ever had Australian roadhouse food before?"

She shook her head as she unbuckled her seatbelt.

He chuckled. "Then you're in for a treat; meat pies, egg and bacon sandwiches, Corn Jacks and Chiko Rolls.

It's likely to repeat on you until lunch."

Tess frowned as she ran after him into the building. He spoke as if that was a good thing. Sometimes she couldn't quite understand Australians.

Still, she enjoyed trying something new, and she was starving.

What were Chiko Rolls?

***

Ed shook the rain from his head and made a beeline for the coffee counter. No one was waiting. "Your largest latte, please." He glanced over his shoulder at Tess. "You want one?"

She smiled and nodded, pulling the elastic band from her long hair and running her hands through it. Her smile brightened her face, taking some of the worry from her eyes, and she looked less the damsel in distress. He told himself not to be concerned about her twitchiness. He was a stranger, so of course she'd be a little uncertain. He'd hope his sister, Georgie would be as cautious in a similar situation. Did she still have the pepper spray he'd bought her?

Ed cleared his throat and turned back to the server. "Make that two." He joined Tess at the bain marie with its selection of fried food. What could he eat while driving? The Chiko Roll or Corn Jack were the obvious choices, but his stomach hadn't woken up sufficiently to handle them yet. "I'll have an egg and bacon sandwich." He paid for both coffees and took the sandwich, stepping back so Tess could order. If he was fast, he could finish the sandwich before the coffees were ready.

Tess bit her lip, a slight furrow between her brows as she studied the options. She turned to him. "You said the Chiko Roll was good?"

He chuckled. "It's something everyone should experience at least once." He bit into his sandwich, careful not to let the runny egg yolk explode from the wrapping.

Her eyes widened, and she smirked. "Hm. Then I'll have a Chiko Roll and some chips."

Adventurous. He liked that, though he should have guessed it about her when she agreed to travel with him. The barista was almost finished with the coffees, so Ed stuffed a few more bites into his mouth to finish the first half of his sandwich. He wrapped the rest and grabbed his drink with a nod of thanks.

Back in the car, he took a long sip of the life-giving substance. His eyes rolled back. So good. Then he looked for somewhere to put the cup. No cup holders. Of course not.

Tess had spotted the problem as well. "Let me hold your drink." She had her chip cup between her knees and her Chiko Roll on her lap, while she held her own coffee cup.

"Thanks." After they were on the road again, it wouldn't be difficult to hold it. There was only one intersection between here and Geraldton. He fired up the engine, relieved when it started first go, and the heater coughed back into life. When he hit the highway, he reached for the coffee and savoured the strong flavour.

Tess picked up the Chiko Roll and examined it. "So what is it?"

He grinned. "Australia's version of the spring roll. Miscellaneous filling, but cabbage is definitely one ingredient."

She glanced at him, her doubt clear, and then shrugged and took a large bite. She chewed slowly, a frown on her face as if trying to figure out what she was eating. When she swallowed, Ed asked, "What's the verdict?"

"It's... interesting." She took another bite. "The outside's kind of crisp and the inside's mushy."

Ed sipped his coffee as she continued her exploration, taking a nibble of just the outside.

"It's not bad," she finally said. "Easy to eat as well."

The rest of his sandwich still sat in its wrapper on his lap. He'd get to it when he'd finished his coffee. "Next stop you'll have to try the Corn Jack."

"I don't understand why you're excited about all this fried food."

"It's kind of tradition," he said. "A road trip isn't complete without some kind of slightly dodgy, been-lying-on-the-bain-marie-all-day food that you regret buying."

She shook her head. "Australia is a strange country."

"Have you been here long?"

"Eighteen months, but this is my first road trip."

"Then I'll have to make sure it's memorable," Ed said. "Roadhouse food can be checked off the list."

"What else is on it?"

He thought about it. "First kangaroo—dead or alive, being stuck behind an oversized load, almost being blown off the road by a road train, and up this way, first termite mound."

The concern was back on her face, and he laughed. "Don't worry. I'm mostly joking."

"That's not reassuring," Tess muttered, but smiled at him.

"So what have you done in Perth?"

"Not much. University keeps me busy, and I work in a restaurant when I'm not at class."

A shame. What was the point of studying overseas if you didn't get to experience any of the culture? "I can give you a list of places to visit in Retribution Bay."

She hesitated, and then nodded. "That would be great."

"Were your friends picking you up from the airport?" They were out of phone range.

"Ah, no. They are flying in tomorrow." She glanced out the window and her hand shook as she sipped her coffee.

The heater was as high as it would go, so she couldn't be cold. Was she nervous? "We should be there by then." He tried to put her at ease. "Next time we stop, you should call them. I'm happy to speak to them if they want to know who you're driving with."

"I might."

There wasn't much else Ed could do to make her comfortable. It was a weird situation for both of them. He finished his coffee and handed the cup to Tess. The hire company had been kind enough to provide them with a plastic bag for a bin. "There's one more road trip requirement." He pulled his phone out of his pocket and handed it to Tess. "Music. You want to be DJ?"

Her smile was a little unsure. "OK. Let's see what you've got." She scrolled for a minute and then pressed play. AC/DC blared from the small speaker.

Ed grinned. She kept surprising him.

They were making good time, but after four hours of driving almost non-stop, Ed needed a break. Not long until they reached Geraldton, where they could get an early lunch and maybe Tess could drive for a stint. She'd kept up a good range of tunes as they drove, but spent most of the time staring out the window. She must have dropped off a few times, because occasionally she'd jerk and glance at Ed with fear in her eyes.

The third time it happened unease crept into Ed's stomach. What was she so fearful about? He understood it could be disorienting to wake in a strange car, but it wasn't confusion, but real terror in her eyes.

Had his initial suspicion been correct? Was she on the run? Now wasn't the time to ask, not when they were confined together in a small vehicle. Perhaps he could bring it up at lunch, then if she reacted badly, they would both have an out. Geraldton was large enough to have hire cars and probably a bus to Retribution Bay as well. He shifted in his seat. "We'll stop in Geraldton for lunch," he said. "Do you want to take a turn at driving afterwards?"

She glanced at the gearstick. "I don't know how to drive a manual."

Damn it. "That's all right. I'll be fine." He'd have a double dose of caffeine with his meal. They had another nine hours to drive. He pulled into one of the fast-food franchises along the main road through Geraldton and got out, stretching his muscles. The rain had stopped north of Gingin, and now the sun's rays beat down, erasing any memory of the downpour. He'd switched the heater to cool air about an hour ago, and now stripped off his jacket, throwing it into the back. Across the car Tess did the same, revealing a white buttoned shirt. Without the jacket, she looked like a waitress.

At the counter, Tess opened her backpack. It wasn't big, about the size of a school backpack, and there were no clothes inside. Tess shifted, blocking his view and retrieved some cash. She ordered the cheapest thing on the menu, and now, she carefully counted her change.

Her story didn't make sense. If she was meeting friends for a holiday, she'd at least have clothes.

They sat by the window to eat. Despite the air-conditioning, he felt the strength of the sun through the glass. Testing his theory, he said, "You might want to change before we leave. It's going to get hotter from here, and black pants will be uncomfortable." She looked startled, so he added, "There are rest rooms over there."

She glanced where he pointed and then said, "I'll be fine."

The niggly suspicion grew stronger. What reason could she have for not changing? His own jeans were still slightly damp, and he hadn't been as wet as her. Perhaps she wasn't comfortable baring her legs. "All right. I'll change after we eat." And keep a tight hold on the car keys.

"How much further is it?"

"We're about a third of the way."

Her eyes widened. "Only a third?"

He nodded. He didn't love the idea of driving at night in the dodgy van, but it couldn't be helped. Perhaps he could convince Tess to stay the night at the Ridge, and he could drive her the extra hour into town tomorrow morning. As they ate, Ed balanced his intake of sugary caffeine versus the distance between rest rooms on the rest of the trip. The idea of stopping on the side of the road to relieve himself with Tess in the car did not appeal.

He also debated the different options for why Tess was so nervy. He'd made an effort to be relaxed and charming, so she was comfortable.

If she was on the run, then it could be from an abusive partner, in which case he would help her any way he could.

But what if she had committed a crime? Would he be charged with aiding a felon?

"I hope the burger battles the Chiko Roll and wins," Tess said as she finished her drink. Her smile washed the worry from her expression, and Ed's shoulders relaxed.

He laughed. "I warned you."

"I couldn't refuse experiencing it myself."

Underneath her nerves was a woman with an adventurous heart. Perhaps he was being paranoid. How did one subtly ask if she was in trouble?

His phone rang and Sheridan's name came up on the screen. What now? "What's up, mate?"

Sheridan groaned. "Code red disaster. The update glitched last night so half the computers have the update and the other half have stopped working. It's a nightmare."

Ed winced. "That sucks. You're not calling me in, are you?"

"Nah. Just heard about the strike on the radio. Did you get out?"

"I'm driving up."

"What in? I've got your car."

"I hired a van and I'm carpooling with another stranded passenger."

"Tell me it's a beautiful woman with long legs and blue eyes."

Ed rolled his eyes. "You're half right." Tess was beautiful.

"Which half?" Sheridan demanded.

"I'll tell you when I get back. I need to hit the road again. Bye." He hung up to Sheridan's complaints.

Tess glanced at him. "Problem?"

"No, just my house mate checking in. It's fine." He hesitated. "Listen, Tess, are you all right? You've been a little anxious all morning."

Her eyes widened and she avoided his gaze. "I'm fine." She hugged her backpack to her chest. "It's, ah, not like me to get a lift with a stranger." Her smile was forced. "It's a bit awkward."

"Do you want me to talk to your friends? Or I can call Sheridan back and let him vouch for me?"

"No, it's fine. You've proven you're nice. I'm, ah, just, ah, an introvert. It takes me a while to open up."

He studied her a moment, but she seemed sincere. "OK, but tell me if something worries you. I'll just get changed and we'll go." He'd take her at her word, but he wouldn't drop his guard. The rest had eased some of his fatigue, and his confidence was back that he would be home tonight.

That confidence was shattered an hour later when he approached a large flashing sign and traffic cones blocking the road. He swore and stopped the car.

ROAD CLOSED. FLOODING.

They had to be kidding.

He'd seen the weather reports of the winter storm making its way down from the north, but he hadn't considered the implications outside of his flight being delayed.

"Can't we just go around?" Tess asked.

"Yeah, but going around in this part of the country adds several hundred kilometres," Ed said, getting out his phone to check the best way to go. This van wouldn't handle any of the dirt roads, so they would have to stick to the bitumen. He also wasn't confident enough about its reliability to take any road which got little traffic. If they broke down, they might be stuck out there for hours or days, and Ed didn't have that kind of time.

He sighed as he scrolled through options. They'd have to go back to Geraldton, then across to Mount Magnet and up the Great Northern Highway. He wasn't getting home tonight.

"Ed?"

He tucked his phone away. "We'll have to stop somewhere overnight," he told her. "The detour will add another eleven hours to the trip."

She gaped at him as he did a U-Turn. "Aren't there any other roads?"

"None that I'd risk this old thing on."

"But you've got a wedding to get to."

"Not until Saturday." He had an extra day up his sleeve, a day when he was supposed to be helping Amy set up everything. At least others in town would pull together for her, plus they had Brandon's teammates arriving. Ed frowned. He hadn't considered they might also need a way north. He'd have to ring Brandon's best friend, Sam, when they got back to Geraldton to tell him about the strike.

They arrived back in town, and Ed pulled in to fill the van with petrol.

"Didn't you just fill up?" Tess asked.

He nodded. "But there might not be another petrol station until Mount Magnet, so I'm not risking it." He smiled at her. "When you travel north in Australia you've got to be prepared." Speaking of which, he would head into the supermarket next door and pick up food and water. He wasn't as familiar with the other highway as he was with this one. Better they had too much food than not enough. He'd check the spare tyre too. And the oil and water.

Ed went through everything, putting more air in the nearly flat spare, hoping it was neglect and not a puncture that had made it deflate. Then he took Tess into the supermarket and headed down the snack aisle. "Anything you want?" Ed asked.

She shook her head.

Perhaps she didn't have a lot of money. "My shout," he said. "Add what you think looks good."

He found a ten-litre bottle of water and put it in the trolley. Perhaps he was overcompensating, but his father always taught him it was better to be over-prepared. He closed his eyes, wishing his father would be at the station to greet him. The house wasn't the same without his mother's eighties tunes playing on the stereo, the smell of something baking, and his father coming in at dusk, kicking off his dusty boots at the door and hanging his Akubra hat on the hook inside. Ed's throat closed over and his vision blurred.

"Ed? Is this all right?"

He swallowed hard and opened his eyes to find Tess holding up a packet of Tim Tams. He smiled over the pang of loss. "Great choice."

Thinking about his family reminded him of the phone calls he had to make.

Tess bit her lip. "I need to get a couple of things. I'll meet you at the checkout."

Good, she wouldn't hear his conversation. First, he called Amy to tell her about the road closure and to apologise that he wouldn't arrive until sometime tomorrow.

"Don't worry about it, Ed," she said. "Drive safely and keep us posted, all right?"

"Sure. Hey, do you know when Sam's flying in?"

"He arrived yesterday." Someone spoke to her in the background and Amy laughed. "He said to tell you he learnt not to trust the baggage handlers last time he was here."

Ed rolled his eyes. They'd both been caught up in the go-slow actions, but Sam was right. Ed should have monitored things. "Thanks." He hesitated. "Listen, I'm carpooling with someone. Her name's Tess and she's studying a Bachelor of Science in biochemistry and molecular biology at UWA. She's from Singapore."

"OK. Why are you telling me this?"

"She's been a bit nervy. It's probably because I'm a stranger, but you know, in case she turns out to be a serial killer, you'll have somewhere to start looking." He laughed.

"Ed, that's not funny. Can you send me a photo?"

He should have thought of that. "I'll try, but don't worry, I'm sure it's nothing. I'll see you when I get there."

Tess wasn't at the checkout when he arrived, so he paid for their snacks. By the time he was done, she was at a checkout a few down from him. Ed took a quick photo and sent it to Amy, joining Tess in time to see her stuffing a T-shirt and underwear into her backpack.

His unease returned. "Forget something?"

She flinched and stared at him a second.

"That will be forty-seven dollars fifty," the cashier said.

Tess paid, her hand trembling as she placed the cash into her purse. "The trip was a last-minute thing. My friends called me this morning to say another friend had cancelled and I could have her flight. So I threw a few items in my backpack and rushed to the airport. I figured I could buy anything I forgot in Retribution Bay." Her smile was a little forced.

Yeah, there was definitely something more going on with Tess, but at least his family knew about her now.

"All right. Let's go."

Not long after, they were back on the road, heading east. It would be over three hundred kilometres before he could turn north again, and the idea made him tense. What if something else went wrong? What if they got caught behind one of those wide loads which carried large machinery to the mine sites up this way? That could add hours. If he didn't make it in time, Amy and Brandon would have to get married without the rings.

He sighed and tried to shut out the pessimism. At least the sun was overhead now, and he wasn't driving directly into its rays.

He'd give thanks for small mercies.

Chapter 4

Tess had never seen so much emptiness. Perhaps that wasn't the right word. There were shrubs and small trees, the occasional wire fence, but nothing else. Open country with very few signs of human occupation.

Sure, she'd seen photos and documentaries on the Australian outback, but they didn't convey the scope of it. The land was endless and seemingly unchanging until suddenly she realised the trees were gone, and a different type of shrub bordered the roads. Every kilometre felt like they were getting nowhere, and if it weren't for the signs marking the distance to the next town every ten kilometres, she would have been overwhelmed.

At least there was little chance of Tan finding her here.

She'd switched her phone back on in Geraldton, ready to call the police, but she'd been inundated by missed call after missed call from Tan and just the sight of his name had her shaking and turning off her phone again.

She'd looked for a payphone, but hadn't seen one, and wasn't sure how to explain why she wanted to use it, and not her phone to Ed.

He was suspicious enough as it was. She hated lying to him, especially after he'd been so kind to her.

If she was braver, she would have left him in Geraldton and hired her own car, but to go where she didn't know. At least with Ed she had a plan—get to Retribution Bay.

Her earlier concerns about her safety with him were gone, but she was worried he might call her on her lies and leave her somewhere. And she wouldn't blame him in the least.

What a mess.

The more she thought about Tan, the more confused she became. He hadn't hesitated to shoot the woman, which told her he was dangerous, that he'd done it before. But her parents had insisted he was an important and upstanding citizen.

How did they know him?

The question circled around and around in her head and none of the potential answers were comforting.

"Can you check the road closures?" Ed asked as they drove into the small town of Mount Magnet.

"What?"

"The Main Roads website records which roads are closed. I'm planning to take the road through Karijini, but I want to make sure it's open."

She dragged her phone from her bag and turned it back on. No more messages from Tan. She heaved a sigh of relief. Finding the site, she showed the map to Ed. He pointed to a section. "Zoom in there."

She did as he asked, and he nodded. "It's open. Great." He finished his bottle of cola as they drove out of town.

His concentration was on the road as it had been all day. He had to be exhausted, but he hadn't suggested she drive again. She should have insisted on learning to drive a manual car, but her parents only had an automatic.

But Da wouldn't have let that stop her. Perhaps she could learn now. All she had to do was figure out the gears.

"Is it hard to drive a manual?" she asked.

He glanced at her. "Not really. All you have to do is work the clutch through the gears, and the engine noise tells you when to change."

She bit her lip. "Do you want to teach me?"

He hesitated, and then sighed. "Yeah, all right. It might help if you could drive for a couple of hours." He pulled into one of the rest stops on the side of the road. "Watch my feet and put your hand over mine," he said.

She hesitated before placing her hand over Ed's on the gearstick.

"Gears are written on the handle. Always press the clutch to the floor when changing gears." He shifted the stick. "First, second, third, fourth, fifth," he said as he moved through them.

It seemed easy enough.

He explained how to accelerate and when they reached the end of the rest stop, he did a U-turn and put the car into neutral and put the park brake on. "Your turn."

She swapped places with him and shifted the seat into position.

"Clutch in and keep it down while you move into first."

She did as he said.

"Now slowly take your foot off the clutch. There's a point where the car will start moving on its own. When you get to there, gently press the accelerator."

Her heart thumped as she did as he requested. The van crept forward, and she pressed the accelerator down, lifting her foot from the clutch.

The car jerked and stalled, and she shrieked.

"It's all right. Next time don't lift the clutch so

quickly, not until you've accelerated some more."

The second time she did better and managed to change to second gear before they reached the end of the rest stop, and she stalled when she braked.

"Clutch in whenever you're stationary and not in neutral," Ed said. "Try again."

He seemed unfazed by her poor driving, but when it took her ten minutes to reach the other side of the rest stop with her bunny-hopping and stalling all the way, he said, "How about we try again tomorrow? It'll be getting dark soon, and you don't want to drive when the 'roos are out."

She'd seen enough dead carcases on the side of the road and didn't want to be responsible for one.

"All right. Sorry."

"No problem. We're both tired. It's not the best state to learn."

They swapped seats and she stared out the window. He was so kind, but she felt useless. By the time Da was her age, she'd spent a year free diving for pearl shells. She hadn't let anything stop her, and Tess couldn't even drive a manual car.

She was reliant on Ed's good will, because she wasn't brave enough to go it alone. It wasn't good enough. She needed her own plan of what to do when they got to Retribution Bay, but to do that she needed to know more about the destination. Hoping to smoothly segue into questions about Retribution Bay, she started with, "Tell me about your family. Your brother's getting married, right?"

He nodded. "That's Brandon. He's the eldest and just moved back to Retribution Ridge. He was in the army for twelve years." The scowl on Ed's face intrigued her.

"You don't get on?"

Ed shrugged. "I don't know him that well. He left home when I was eleven and didn't keep in touch. I saw him once or twice a year when I moved to Perth."

"Is his fiancée happy to move to Retribution Bay?"

The frown disappeared, and he smiled. "Amy was working at the Ridge when they met. She's the best."

Tess knew nothing about sheep stations. "What does she do?"

"We've opened a campground. People come and stay with their tents or caravans, and Amy runs that aspect of the business."

Why would they want strangers camping on their land?

"Darcy is next oldest," Ed continued. "He runs the station with Brandon, but he never left. His daughter, Lara, is ten." He waved to a car passing in the opposite direction. "Darcy's engaged to Faith, who runs the pony club in town, and is a lawyer. I don't know her very well, but Lara loves her." He chuckled. "Mind you, Lara loves everyone. She's a hoot." Real affection filled his voice.

A hoot. Her mother would be horrified if anyone described her daughters as 'a hoot'. They weren't supposed to be amusing, they were supposed to be gracious and unassuming.

"Finally, there's Georgie, the baby of the family. She's a couple of years younger than me. She's just finished uni and moved back to the Bay, but she lives in town."

"Georgie's the one working on the tour boat?"

"Yeah. She loves the ocean. I call her Mermaid because she could live in the water." He smiled.

It all sounded like such an adventure. "What was it like growing up on a farm?"

"I didn't know any different," he said. "But I didn't love it as much as my siblings did. Georgie loved the horses, Charlie loved motorbikes, and Darce and Brandon loved everything."

"Charlie?"

"Another brother. He died when I was eleven."

So much tragedy in the family. She pressed a hand against her heart.

"I wasn't great at much on the farm aside from shooting. I could hit any bottle or can in front of me, but even that was pointless because I couldn't kill anything."

She flinched, seeing Tan's gun as if it was in front of her. He hadn't any qualms about pulling the trigger. She hugged herself.

"Are you OK?"

She shook her head. "Guns scare me."

"As long as you're careful, they're all right. We keep them locked in a gun safe when we're not using them."

She shuddered remembering the explosion of blood.

Ed changed the topic. "I was also pretty good at tracking. Charlie's best friend, Matt, taught me." He shifted his gaze to her. "What about you? What's your family like?"

Tess exhaled, trying to slow her heart rate. She could do this. If she freaked out, it would only make him more suspicious. Taking another breath in she said, "I have an older sister who married last year in a huge ceremony. She's already trying to get pregnant." Joy had always done the right thing in her parents' eyes. Find a nice man, marry, have children. Her whole family was so old-fashioned, they were ancient.

"What about your parents?"

"Dad works in customs on the docks. Mum entertains and takes care of the house." Though she remembered a time when she was younger when both her parents had worked long hours to make ends meet. She and Joy had freedom to do what they wanted, but all that changed when her father started in customs. They had more money, and were expected to act appropriately in their new social group.

"I always appreciated having Mum at home," Ed said. "Though she worked out on the station when we were at school. She made the best scones."

His wistfulness made her guilty. She should appreciate her family more.

It was getting dark as they approached a town called Meekatharra. Ed had switched on the headlights, but they barely highlighted the road. Suddenly, he slammed on the brakes and the seatbelt cut into Tess's chest. The tyres screeched, and in front of them a kangaroo bounded across the road, just missing the van.

Ed swore as he slowly accelerated again, but not up to the speed limit.

Tess's heart pounded. "Are you all right?"

"Yeah." He cleared his throat. "Let's stop in Meekatharra for dinner. I still want to get a few more kilometres under us before we stop for the night, but dusk is when the 'roos are most active. There's a roadhouse with a caravan park another couple of hours north if you don't mind sleeping in the back."

Tess glanced behind. There was room for both of them to sleep, and the van had come with a quilt and sheets. Ed had been nothing but kind to her since they'd started the journey, but she didn't love the idea of sleeping under the same bedding as him. Her face heated.

"We can stop at the store and pick up a sleeping bag, so I don't have to worry about you hogging the quilt," he added with a smile.

Someone had been looking after Tess when they'd put Ed in her path. Relief filled her. "That would be great."

"Can you check our food options?" He handed her his phone.

She searched for options, but there weren't many.

"What have you found?" Ed asked.

She looked up and realised they'd entered the town. Ed pulled over to the side of the road in a parking spot. She gave him his phone. "There are a couple of motels ahead and the tavern."

He scrolled through the options. "Have you got a preference?"

"How about the tavern?" The food looked cheap and she could offer to pay for them both. He was already paying for all the petrol.

"All right. But let's buy the sleeping bag first." They hurried inside a general store, which was about to close. At the back was a small camping section. She spotted the sleeping bags and her shoulders relaxed.

"I figured they'd have some," Ed said, grabbing one from the shelf. "A lot of campers come this way, and someone always needs supplies."

Ed paid for the sleeping bag and drove them to the pub, where she insisted on paying for dinner. She couldn't keep taking advantage of his generosity.

As they sat at the bar, Ed heaved a long sigh. Under the bright lights, he looked exhausted. She reached out to him. "Thank you for driving, Ed. I really appreciate it."

His smile was filled with fatigue. "I should thank you. It's nice to have company."

She pressed her lips together. "Maybe I can try to drive again," she said. "After we're out of town, we can switch in one of those rest stops."

"Maybe tomorrow," he said. "The headlights are rubbish and you're not used to the wildlife." He yawned. "I'll be right after some caffeine and decent food."

He had a point. She'd monitor him and find some vibrant tunes to play until they stopped for the night.

They shared a delicious pizza and then headed back to the van. Ed stretched before he got in.

"Are you sure you're all right to drive? We could stay here for the night." She wanted to insist, but he was the one with the wedding to get to.

"Yeah. I'll take it slow. It will mean we've only got

twelve hours to drive tomorrow."

Which meant they would arrive late on the eve of the wedding. No wonder he was pushing his limits.

They drove out of town and were shrouded in darkness. Ed switched on the high beams, which made little difference in the abyss. He drove twenty kilometres under the speed limit and stared ahead, his hands gripping the steering wheel.

Would music be too much of a distraction from watching for wildlife?

Tess turned her attention to the road. Any early warning of a kangaroo would be needed. They weren't ten kilometres out of town when eyes glowed on the side of the road. "There!" She pointed.

Ed slowed. The kangaroo blended so well with the surrounding bush, she wouldn't have spotted it during the day. It watched the car and when they had almost reached it, it hopped out in front of them. Ed slammed on the brakes and swore as the kangaroo bounded off into the bush on the other side of the road.

Tess gasped. "Why did it do that?"

"Who knows?" Ed increased his speed again. "That's why I slowed so much; they do stupid things."

Tess's heart pounded. Then the road in front of them got brighter and brighter. Ed winced. "Road train. Brace yourself."

Before she could ask what he meant, a truck overtook them, shaking the van, and Ed fought to keep it on the road. The truck had to be forty metres long or more. Enormous. Finally it passed, and they were left in the dark again.

She let out her breath.

Ed chuckled. "Another tick for your road trip checklist."

"I think I would have preferred to skip that one."

"We'd be right if we weren't going so slowly. They're

so big 'roos don't bother them."

Tess's skin prickled, and the sweat had nothing to do with the residual heat outside. She wanted to tell Ed to pull over, or turn around and head back to Meekatharra, but she was conscious he had to be home for his brother's wedding. He was doing her the favour by letting her tag along while she figured out what to do next. She kept her mouth shut and pointed out two more kangaroos, which kept still as they drove past. She gritted her teeth. Ed had said the roadhouse was two hours ahead, but at the speed they were going, would it be longer? Ed jacked on the brakes and this time it was a cow in the middle of the road. He pressed the horn, which was a pathetic high-pitched toot and the cow trundled into the bush.

"Why is there a cow in the middle of the road?"

"There are cattle stations in the area. Probably escaped when a fence was down."

He didn't seem perturbed, but every muscle in Tess's body was tense. She prayed they would stop soon.

Her prayers were answered five minutes later when a mob of kangaroos bounded across the road. One of them brushed the car as Ed braked and Tess shrieked.

Ed swore. "All right. That's enough. I'll pull over at the next rest stop if you can handle roughing it for a night."

Her concerns about sleeping near Ed were insignificant compared to her fear of the animals. She'd thought she only had to be worried about snakes and spiders killing her. "It's fine." She'd spent the previous night next to a dumpster, so anything would be better.

A few kilometres later, he pulled into a gravel rest stop. A yellow bin was centred on the side, but other than that it was empty. Thank goodness she'd used the bathroom before they'd left Meekatharra. Ed parked upwind of the bin and switched off the engine. Its quiet tick was the only sound, and as he flicked off the headlights they were plunged into darkness. Ed opened his door, but no light came on. He laughed. "That would figure." A moment later, his phone torch illuminated the area. "Let me check if the light in the back works."

Tess undid her seatbelt and stretched while Ed slid the door open. No light. At least she wouldn't have to worry about her modesty if she changed into a clean T-shirt.

"Can you hold my phone while I make the bed?" Ed handed it to her and transformed the back into a bed, spreading out the sleeping bag and quilt, and placing the pillows at opposite ends of the bed so they would lie head to toe. "That might be the best." His smile made her nerves disappear. Then he shut the privacy curtains around the windows.

She returned his phone, and he placed it on the centre of the bed as he dragged out the ten-litre bottle of water. He poured himself a cup and cleaned his teeth. Tess dug into her bag and pulled out the toothbrush she'd bought in Geraldton and her phone. It lit up with a bunch of notifications. She froze. She'd forgotten to turn it back off after Mount Magnet. Only one person would call her. Sure enough, message after message telling her she'd missed a call from Tan Lewis. With a shaky finger, she switched off the phone.

"Everything all right?" Ed asked, concern on his face.

"It's fine." She tucked the phone back into her bag. "Nothing urgent. I'll call them when I get to Retribution Bay." She finished cleaning her teeth and then splashed some water on her face. It was much cooler now, but she didn't want to sleep in the clothes she'd been wearing for over twenty-four hours. She retrieved the spare clothes she'd bought.

Another road train roared past, but the bushes between the rest stop and the road blocked some of its light.

Ed had no hang-ups as he stripped off his T-shirt and changed into another one. He was an attractive man. She blinked at the inappropriate thought. He was her rescuer. She wouldn't see him again after they reached their destination. She wouldn't drag him further into her mess.

Ed glanced at her, saw her clothes in her hands. "Tell me when you're done." He turned his back.

Such consideration. Her mother had warned her Australian men were unrefined, but she'd never met Ed. Tess changed. "I'm done." She closed her backpack and placed it on the passenger seat.

"Great. Sleeping bag or quilt?"

The idea of the sleeping bag made her feel claustrophobic. "Quilt."

He gestured. "After you."

As she climbed in, he closed the back door and circled the van as if to check everything was all right. Tess settled under the quilt, pulling it up to her chin as he got in.

Ed pulled the curtains shut on the remaining windows and then shuffled into his sleeping bag. "Night, Tess."

She smiled, as the quilt wrapped her in its arms. "Night, Ed."

She closed her eyes and sleep claimed her.

***

Tess woke with a start. Someone was moving next to her. Her heart pounded. Where was she? Had Tan broken into her room?

"It's just me—Ed."

Her heartbeat slowed at his gentle voice. They were in the van, somewhere in the middle of Western Australia, and it was still dark outside.

"I drank far too much caffeine today," he said as he slid open the door, the sound loud in the quiet.

There was no bathroom… oh. She prayed she didn't

need to go before they reached a roadhouse. "What time is it?"

"Just after one," he said. "Won't be long. Sorry for waking you." He closed the door.

Better he wake her now than when he returned. That would have really freaked her out. With her pulse returning to normal, she lay staring at the roof of the car. Lying here in the dark, it was easy to forget the world around her, and imagine she was in a bubble of her own. She peered outside the curtains. Above, the stars glittered like a carpet. They felt so close and yet so endless.

When they arrived in Retribution Bay, she'd go straight to the police station and report what she'd seen. She couldn't delay any longer. Then maybe the police could help her figure out what to do next.

A soft rumble grew louder as a car approached. Another road train? She'd hate to be a truck driver, out on the roads at this time of night, particularly with all the kangaroos around. The car came closer and slowed, then she heard the crunch of tyres on the gravel. It was stopping here.

Her heart jumped. Silly. Of course, there would be other people on the road who would use the rest stop. The lights behind the curtains disappeared, and the car crept closer. She froze. Why would a car turn off their lights before coming to a stop?

She lay still, her skin hot as the engine switched off, and the door opened.

Where was Ed?

Steps circled the van, and Tess sat up, clutching the quilt to her chest as she quietly shifted to the back. The steps stopped outside the sliding door. The urge to peer out from behind the curtains was strong, but any movement might alert whoever was out there that she was awake.

Could it be Tan? Had he found her?

No, it couldn't be. There was no way he could track her to the middle of nowhere.

There was a soft clunk as the door released, and then ever so slowly opened. She could only see the legs of a man, the privacy curtain hiding his face, but the legs were too thick to be Ed's. Her mind raced as she debated staying where she was and attacking him. He reached for something, and his hand lowered, holding a gun.

She froze, terror coursing through her.

"Tess, you've been a very bad girl."

Tess stifled a whimper. Salvatore had found her.

Chapter 5

Ed heard the car slow as he stood behind the only tree in the rest stop. He sighed. That would figure. The only time he needed to pee, and a car was stopping at the exact rest stop he was at. He tried to hurry, but it never worked. He closed his eyes to retain his night vision as the headlights illuminated the tree he stood behind. Hopefully, the tree blocked him from sight. Then the lights switched off, and the car pulled to a stop in front of the van.

Odd.

He finished his business and tucked himself away as the car door opened.

Ed shifted away from the tree and spotted a man walking towards the van. He frowned. Was he planning on apologising for arriving so late? Ed almost called out to him, but something in the way the man moved slowly, cautiously, made him hold his tongue.

The man reached for the van handle and Ed picked up the branch he'd tripped over earlier. It was heavy and might be enough to dissuade the man from doing whatever he planned. He moved forward as the man spoke.

"Tess, you've been a very bad girl."

This was no random act.

The man slowly raised a hand. He had a gun.

Fuck.

Ed's branch wasn't any match.

"Please, no. I didn't see anything," Tess cried. The terror in her voice tore through Ed. What was she involved in?

He moved behind the man, carefully placing his steps as Matt had taught him when he'd shown him how to track an animal. A leaf crackled under his foot, and the man turned. Ed reacted, taking several steps forward, and used the branch like a baseball bat to smack the guy across the head. The man stumbled with a roar of pain, the gun clattering to the ground, and Tess shrieked.

Ed's heart pounded as he dived for the gun, his fingers wrapping around the warm metal, and he pointed it at the man. "Don't move." He stood between the man and the van.

The man straightened, one hand on his head. "You won't shoot."

Every vein in Ed's body throbbed and his hand shook, but he channelled every bad guy he'd ever watched. "You want to bet?" He prayed the gun had more than one bullet and aimed for the man's back tyre, pulling the trigger. The shot blasted into the night, and he jumped, but so did the man. Maybe his time spent shooting cans hadn't been wasted.

"I don't know what the bitch told you, but she's wanted by the police for murder."

He'd known she was hiding something. Then he frowned. "Bullshit. If you were a cop, you would have identified yourself."

Tess sobbed inside the van, her gasps loud and jerky.

"Tess, the keys are in the side pocket at the back. Grab them, shut the side door and climb into the front."

The man growled. "You think you can kill me?"

Ed pointed the gun at the man's stomach. "Plenty of places to hide a body out here." He was proud of his even tone. Sam had told him part of any altercation was about the mental attack, making the opponent unsure. He urged Tess to hurry as the van door slid shut. She climbed into the driver's seat. She wouldn't leave without him, would she?

"Move away from the van," Ed ordered.

"And if I don't want to?"

Ed aimed for the man's feet, and the man shuffled back a few steps. "Keep going." Tess started the engine, and the van lurched forward. "Put it into neutral," Ed called.

The man laughed. "You don't know who you're dealing with. She won't get away."

"Give me your car keys."

"They're in the car."

The gears crunched as Tess put the van into first gear. Ed moved out of the way in case she turned on the lights and blinded him.

The passenger window slid open. "Ed, get in," Tess called.

At the rate Tess was going, the man would catch them before they left the rest stop. "Drive the van to the road," he said. "Press the clutch to put it into first gear, then let the clutch out slowly as you press the accelerator."

"I can't."

"You can. You did it before. When you get to the road, put it into neutral and keep the engine running." He needed her out of the way so he could backtrack to the man's car and get the keys.

He winced as she bunny-hopped towards the road but kept his gaze on the man in front of him. Ed had to prevent him from following. His car was some kind of souped-up sedan and Ed was tempted for a second to take it instead, but until he knew what Tess was involved in, he didn't want to risk being arrested for stealing a car. Plus he couldn't leave his hire van in the middle of nowhere, no matter how shit it was.

When Tess reached the road, Ed moved to the sedan and opened the door. The keys were in the ignition. He slid them out. The man moved towards him.

"Don't." Ed shifted away and fired a bullet into the front tyre before aiming at the man again. He shut the door and locked the car, just in case the man had more weapons inside.

He might have a spare set of keys, but he wouldn't have two spare tyres. As Ed backed closer to the van, he shot the other front tyre as well. He wasn't taking any chances.

A road train barrelled past, and Ed lowered the gun. As soon as they were gone, the man could go out to the road and flag someone down for a lift, which meant they had to keep moving. "Get to your knees."

As the man slowly did so, Ed kept backing away and the moment the man's knees touched the dirt, Ed took off, sprinting for the van. He glanced behind to see the man charging after him. He let off a shot, aiming for the ground, and the man yelled and stumbled, hitting the ground.

Ed kept running, praying he hadn't hit him. Tess had climbed into the passenger seat, so he jumped behind the wheel. "Hold this." He shoved the gun into Tess's lap, slammed the car into first gear, and took off.

The van crawled up to speed, and the privacy curtains blocked Ed's view behind him. Eventually he hit forty kilometres, then sixty, then eighty.

His hand trembled as he put his seatbelt on. Tess was quiet next to him, holding the gun as if it were a snake.

They were safe, for now.

"You want to tell me what the hell that was all about?"

Ed fought to keep the anger from his voice as his body shook.

She sobbed, her eyes wide in fear. Shit, he couldn't stop yet, and he couldn't take his eyes off the road. "Tess, talk to me." He reached out to touch her knee, and she cringed back.

Yeah, she was terrified. "How much trouble are you in?"

"I did nothing wrong."

He wanted to believe her. From their conversations today, she didn't seem like a criminal. She was too innocent. "Then why is a man with a gun after you?"

"It was Salvatore. I saw something I shouldn't. They killed a woman."

That Ed could believe and it explained why she was so nervous and had packed nothing. "Why didn't you go to the police?" His body was high on adrenaline right now, but kangaroos didn't care. He forced himself to slow a little, wishing he could see behind him.

"The police who come into the restaurant are friends with the owner. I didn't think they'd believe me. I was going to call in Geraldton, but I thought if you overheard me, you might leave me there."

Ed swore and glanced at her. "How long have you been on the run?"

"Since last night."

But they'd already tracked her here. "How did they find you?"

"I don't know."

"What have you got in your bag?"

"My laptop and my phone."

She hadn't used her laptop today. "It must be your phone. Get rid of it."

Tess nodded and wound down her window. For a moment she clutched her phone to her chest and then she threw it into the bush.

The next police station would be in Newman, but they might get phone reception at the roadhouse. "We need to call the police."

"I know," Tess said. "But I'm scared they won't believe me."

Sergeant Dot Campbell would, but she was the officer in charge in Retribution Bay, and he didn't have her direct number. "Tell me exactly what happened."

He listened as she explained what she had seen and how she had run. No wonder she'd been so desperate at the airport. He needed his phone, needed to know the second they got reception, but it was in the back and with the amount of 'roos they'd seen on the road he didn't want Tess climbing into the back to get it. Up ahead was a sign for another rest stop. He'd risk stopping for a second.

"What are you doing?" Tess shrieked as he pulled in.

"Getting my phone and opening the curtains." He shoved the door open. The road behind them was empty. Quickly, he opened the curtains, handed Tess his phone and took the gun from her. It was similar to one he'd used when his workplace had gone to a shooting range for their end-of-year Christmas party. He released the clip and cleared the bullet from the chamber before handing it back to her. "Put it in the glove box."

He hit the road again. "Tell me when we get a signal."

His entire body slumped as the last of the adrenaline left him. Exhaustion threatened to overwhelm him, but he didn't dare stop. Chances were high the next car along the highway would pick up Salvatore and give him a lift. People didn't leave anyone stranded out here. With that in mind, he made note of the odometer reading so he could tell the police where they'd camped.

There were fewer kangaroos on the road now, and aside from the glow from his phone and the headlights, there was no light and little sound. Tess didn't speak, and

Ed was too tired to make conversation. He'd got himself into this mess trying to do a good deed, but he couldn't abandon Tess now. It was over an hour before Tess said, "You've got signal."

They weren't far from the roadhouse where he'd been planning to stop. "Call the police and put it on speaker." He told her the number to call and when the person answered, he explained about Salvatore and leaving him stranded at the rest stop. There was a small chance they'd catch him there, but the car licence should give them an address at least. Maybe Ed should have left the man with a bottle of water as well.

"I'll need your contact details," the woman said.

"We're about to go out of range again," Ed said. If what Tess had said was true and the man who was after her had contacts in the police, he didn't want to bring more trouble down on his family.

"Sir, it's important."

"I'll call my cop friend when I get where I'm going," he said.

"Signal's cut out," Tess said. "Do you think they'll catch him?"

Ed shrugged. "Depends if anyone stops to pick him up." Damn, he was tired. He wound down the window to let the cool air in.

"Who's your friend?" She sounded worried.

"She's in charge of the police station at Retribution Bay," Ed said. "Brandon went to school with her." Dot would know what to do. "You should get some rest. It's another couple of hours before we'll reach Newman and I'll stop to get petrol there." And coffee, lots of coffee.

"What about the kangaroos?"

He grimaced. "I'll keep my eye out. Better you sleep now, because I'm going to need you to do some driving when it gets light. We've got another thousand kilometres to go." He'd had about four hours sleep, which would keep him going for now.

"You must be tired."

He forced a laugh. "I'm fine. I've spent more hours awake when I've done mammoth gaming sessions with my friends." He really wished he hadn't spent the night before his flight doing just that. "Trust me, Tess."

She was quiet for a moment. "All right."

Her quiet answer jolted him. There was honesty in it, and after all she had been through, it meant something. "Sleep well."

He smiled and focused on the never-ending road ahead.

Chapter 6

The sun was rising as Ed approached the mining town of Tom Price. He'd stopped in Newman to fill up with petrol and get coffee before continuing. The police station wasn't open, so he couldn't risk stopping yet. If Salvatore had hitch-hiked north, he would get dropped at Newman, and Ed didn't want to be there when he was. When Ed reached the turnoff which took him through Karijini National Park, he reduced the van's speed. For all his assurance to Tess that everything would be fine, he was shattered and didn't want an accident. But now he was off the main highway, his shoulders relaxed. Salvatore wouldn't expect them to be heading to Retribution Bay because no one took this route if they wanted the shortest distance. Even if the man hired or stole a car, he'd drive north looking for them.

Ed yawned and followed the signs into town to find an open service station. Tess woke as he parked.

"Where are we?" She blinked sleepily, her hair on one side mussed. Cute.

"Tom Price. It's the last town before Retribution Bay. If you want breakfast, it's best to get it here." His brothers would be awake by now. Perhaps he should warn them about what was going on. Might be good to get Dot's number from them too. He filled the van and Tess got out to stretch. When he paid, the man at the register said, "Early start?"

Ed nodded. "Heading to Perth." It wasn't likely Salvatore would trace them here, but he wasn't risking it. "Is there somewhere we can get breakfast?"

"Bakery should be open at the shopping centre."

"Thanks." He wandered back to the car, and they both got in. "You said you had your laptop, right?"

Tess nodded.

"You have any security tracking on it?" He drove into town.

"No."

He pursed his lips. "Any chance the guy after you could have put software on it?"

She paused. "I brought it from home, and it's password protected, but it's usually in my bag. I guess he could have taken it while I was working."

Damn. "Bring it with you. I'll check it."

It wasn't ideal. If the software was there, it would ping with their location, but better it says Tom Price than Retribution Bay.

The bright lights, smell of coffee, and freshly baked bread reinvigorated Ed as they walked into the bakery. Quite a few people were lined up, wearing high-visibility clothes, waiting for their coffee. On their way to work at the mine. He joined the line and after they ordered, they sat at one of the small tables by the window. Tess passed her laptop to him, and his fingers flew over the keyboard as he searched for the software. After ten minutes, he sat back with a sigh. "I can't find anything."

Depending on the guy's resources, it might be something more sophisticated, but Ed doubted it. He wouldn't have thought he needed to track Tess down. He sipped his coffee.

"That's great," Tess said. She'd been quiet while he worked. "Maybe you should leave me here."

He glanced at her, surprised. "Why?"

"I don't want to cause you more trouble," she said. "This looks like a big enough town. I can figure out what to do from here."

He hesitated. It wasn't the right thing to do to desert her, and his mother had always taught him to do the right thing. "No. You'll be safe in Retribution Bay. My family's sheep station is in the middle of nowhere. They won't find you there and Dot will help you."

"It's a lot to ask, Ed. You've already been threatened."

The sensible part of him agreed. His family had had more than their share of trouble lately. This would only add to it. But he couldn't turn his back on Tess either. "So you could say I'm invested now." The coffee and breakfast pie had energised him. Before they left, he'd call his brothers, and it would give the kangaroos more time to get to their beds.

"This is serious, Ed," she said.

"I know, which is why I'm not letting you face this on your own."

Gratitude and surprise filled her expression. He reached over and squeezed her hand. "We help each other out in the country."

Her eyes glistened. "Thank you." Her soft voice and heartfelt gratitude twisted around him.

"Any time." He stood. "Stay here and finish your meal. I need to call home, tell them what time we'll be arriving." He exited the bakery into the cool morning air and strolled over the grass, which glistened with dew. His brothers should already be out on the station by now, and Amy wouldn't give him as much grief about the situation.

Darcy answered.

Damn it. "It's Ed—"

"Ed, what's wrong? You're never up this early."

He winced, hating the fear in his brother's voice. "I'm fine, but I've got a situation here. I need Dot's number."

Darcy swore and a moment later Brandon asked, "What's going on?" He must be on speaker.

"Long story. Tess, the girl I'm carpooling with, is on the run. She witnessed a murder, and they were tracking her phone. A guy with a gun came after her, but we escaped."

"Where are you?" Darcy asked.

"Tom Price. We stopped at a rest stop north of Meekatharra to sleep, and that's where they caught up with us. I've been driving all night."

"I'll come and get you," Brandon said.

Surprise filled him. Brandon had never gone out of his way for Ed before. "Don't be stupid. It's five hundred kilometres and your wedding is tomorrow."

"Then I'll come," Darcy said.

A warmth filled Ed at his immediate support. "It's not necessary. Tess is going to drive. She's from Singapore, and I didn't want her driving at night with the 'roos." Tess sat watching him from inside the bakery. "We should be there just after midday." He sighed. "I called the police when we had reception, but haven't explained the whole story, and I'd rather tell Dot than a stranger."

"Yeah, I get that," Darcy said. "I'll text you her number."

"What do you know about Tess?" Brandon asked.

"She's an international uni student. The guy she's staying with is a friend of her parents, and he killed a woman in the back of his restaurant. She'd gone back for her phone and witnessed it, and has been on the run ever since."

"Doesn't sound great. Could she be involved in something illegal too?"

He hesitated. "My gut tells me she's not." But could

he really trust it?

"Amy showed me her photo," Brandon said. "You're not being swayed by her pretty looks?"

Annoyance filled him. "Give me some credit, Bran." His older brother had no idea who he was.

Brandon grunted, and Ed's phone beeped with Darcy's text. "I'll call Dot," he said. "I'll see you when we get there. Have we got a room for Tess to stay?"

"We'll sort something," Darcy said.

"Great. Is Georgie out there yet?"

"Coming out this morning," Brandon answered.

"Ask her to bring an extra dress in case Tess is there for the wedding." He didn't want her to feel out of place.

"You sure you're seeing things clearly?" Brandon asked.

Brandon was questioning his integrity. He was the one who had abandoned their family. Ed shook his head, trying to keep the irritation from his voice. "I'm going."

"Watch out for the 'roos," Darcy said.

"Will do." He hung up, feeling better that his brothers were aware of what was happening. He took a deep breath and dialled the police sergeant.

"Sergeant Dot Campbell." Her voice was cheerful despite the early hour.

"Hey, Dot, it's Ed Stokes."

"What's happened?" Alert now and not impressed.

He chuckled. "It's a bad thing when you associate my name with trouble."

"After the past couple of months, I'm expecting it. Spill."

He'd always liked Dot, remembered her coming out to the station when she dated Brandon. He'd thought her beautiful and so cool. "I picked up a woman at the airport who it turns out witnessed a murder and is on the run."

She swore and his eyebrows raised at the colourful

language.

"They tracked her via her phone, and they attacked us at a rest stop last night," he continued.

"You still have the phone?"

"No, she threw it away after we left. When I called the police, we lost reception before I could explain everything." It was a lot to explain. "Long story short, I got his gun, stole his car keys, and left him stranded at the rest stop. I imagine he hitch-hiked, but the car might still be there. It's about fifty kilometres north of Meekatharra."

"You told dispatch that?"

"Yeah."

"I'll follow it up. Where are you now?"

"Tom Price. Hope to get home around midday."

"I'm heading out there this afternoon to help set up. I'll get all the details then, but what can you tell me about the murder?"

"Not a lot."

"Can I speak to the girl?"

Tess had finished her meal, so he waved at her to come outside. "Yeah, give me a second." He held out the phone to Tess. "Dot wants to speak with you."

She shook her head.

"She can't help you without details, and the sooner they can get to the murder site, the more chance they have of finding evidence." He wasn't sure of that last bit, but it sounded right.

Tess took the phone. "Hello?"

There were enough cars around to add noise to the morning, and Tess kept her voice low. He listened while Tess told Dot who she was and why she was in Australia. "I work for Tan Lewis, who owns a Singaporean restaurant in Balga."

Ed froze. Impossible. It couldn't be the same person who had been harassing his family for the past six months. "Say that name again," he demanded.

She glanced at him. "Tan Lewis."

He grabbed the phone. "Dot—"

"I know. I'll check into it."

Good. He gave the phone back to Tess, his mind racing. If Tess witnessed Tan Lewis shooting someone, or ordering it, then he would go to gaol and stop coming after Ed's family. Though Stonefish Enterprises was a large company, and probably had a lot of people they could throw at them, it would feel like a win against them finally.

"How do you know Tan?" Tess asked.

He waved towards the phone. "I'll explain later. Finish talking to Dot."

It took a while for Tess to tell her story and answer the myriad questions Dot had and then finally, Tess handed the phone to him.

"All good?" he asked Dot.

"Not even close. I thought you were the one Stokes I didn't have to worry about." She sighed. "I'll see you at the Ridge."

"Yeah, thanks Dot, I owe you one."

"No, you owe me a dozen," she said. "Drive safely."

He smiled and hung up. Dot was all bark. "You ready to go?" he asked Tess.

"How do you know Tan?" she demanded again. The concern on her face was impossible to ignore.

Ed sighed and walked back to the van. "It might not be the same man," he said. "But there's a guy by that name who has been harassing my family to sell the station. Works for a company called Stonefish Enterprises." It took him a second to realise she'd stopped walking and was staring at him. "What's wrong?"

"I've seen invoices with that name on it at the restaurant."

Excitement simmered. Perhaps she could help him put Tan away. "That's great. When you get to the Ridge, you can tell Dot everything and hopefully she'll have enough to arrest him."

She shook her head. "No. I can't go with you." She glanced around, as if looking for other options. "If he finds me, he'll kill me, and he might hurt your family too."

Ed grasped one hand she was waving about. "He's been hurting my family already," he said. "Or at least sending his goons to do the work. They've sabotaged the station, set fire to our feed and kidnapped my niece to force us to sell. We haven't been able to trace anything back to him, but *you* can. You can help us send him to gaol."

She bit her lip.

"We need you, Tess."

"But he might find me at your station."

Was it wrong of him to put her in danger because he wanted the guy caught? "Brandon is ex-military and half his team is at the Ridge for the wedding. They'll be able to protect you."

She swallowed and then nodded. "All right." At the van, she asked, "Do you want me to drive?"

The sun was above the horizon, but the wildlife might still be active. "I'll take us out of town." His energy had spiked after eating and speaking to his family, and the thought they might finally stop Stonefish. "Let's go."

He was almost home.

Chapter 7

Tess stared out the window at the flat, dry land with only the occasional shrub taller than her. Barely any trees, but earth so richly red she almost couldn't believe it was real. After a day of travel, they were still in the middle of nowhere. How was it possible? It gave her some hope Salvatore wouldn't find them, but if Tan had been after Ed's family's station, would he come north himself? Was she playing right into his hands? Her worry was slightly allayed by the thought of a bunch of military men willing to protect her. And together they could put Tan away, so he couldn't hurt anyone again.

But what would she do after that?

She couldn't go back to Tan's place to live, and the second semester of university started in a couple of weeks. She no longer had a job, and her parents might order her home when they found out about everything.

If she had her phone, she'd start looking at work and accommodation possibilities. It was probably too late to get a room at one of the colleges and her classmates had complained about the expense of housing around the university.

But maybe one of them would have a room they

could rent her.

She sighed. First she needed to stop Tan, otherwise none of the rest would be possible. "Do you want me to drive?" The past few times she'd offered, Ed had said he was fine.

"No, we've got less than an hour now."

They'd stopped at a roadhouse for more fuel and food a couple of hours ago. Tess didn't know how Ed was still functioning. She'd had far more sleep than he had, and she felt disgusting. She hadn't showered in over forty-eight hours, her brain was sluggish from the lack of sleep, and her whole body was stiff. All she wanted was a safe place to shower and then rest. Fatigue sat heavily on her eyelids and the air-conditioning blasted them with cool air. "Are you sure you're OK?"

"Yeah," he answered, flashing her a grin. "I'm excited to get home."

His smile wiped away some of her fatigue. "How often do you visit?"

"At least twice a year," he said. "It's a great place for star-gazing."

She frowned. "I thought you worked in IT."

"Astronomy is a hobby," he said. "Wish I'd studied it at uni instead of computing."

"Why don't you go back?"

He shrugged. "More IT jobs than astronomy jobs," he said. "I volunteer at the observatory instead."

She understood. She would have much preferred to study history instead of science. She checked the time. "Will I be in the way when we get there? The wedding's tomorrow, right?"

"Yeah. I'm not sure what will still need to be done, but there'll be plenty of people to help." Ed tapped his fingers on the wheel.

"How many people are invited to the wedding?" she asked, wanting to understand what she was in for. The day before her sister's wedding had been chaos and stress.

"I don't know exactly, maybe forty."

She blinked. That was tiny.

"Georgie and Faith are Amy's bridesmaids," Ed continued. "Lara's the flower girl, and Darcy and Sam are groomsmen."

"You're not a groomsman?" Weren't all siblings meant to be part of the wedding party?

"No."

"Does that upset you?"

He shrugged. "I was only eleven when Brandon left. We're not super close."

Still, it had to hurt to be the only family member not involved.

"You could call me the ring bearer since I have them in my backpack." His chuckle sounded forced.

That wasn't the same thing, but it wasn't her place to judge. She didn't know these people. Maybe he was like her, the odd one out in the family. "What about Amy's family?"

"She doesn't have a great relationship with her father and brother," he said. "But it turns out her brother is one of Brandon's army mates, so he should be there." Ed pointed to the left. "This is the start of the station here."

Tess looked, but the only difference in the land was a fence running perpendicular to the road. She scanned the road ahead for a driveway but saw nothing. "Where's the entrance?"

He laughed. "Not for another fifteen kilometres," he said. "We've got quarter of a million acres."

Her mouth dropped open. She couldn't have heard that properly. "How much?"

"Two hundred and fifty thousand acres," he said.

"That's bigger than Singapore!"

He nodded. "A lot of land in Australia."

She shut her mouth, not quite believing him. She reached for her phone and stopped. No. It was on the side of the road somewhere. Which was a good thing, except the loss of it made her feel more vulnerable. She had no way to communicate with the world. Her skin tensed as a thought occurred to her. She only had Ed's word that Tan was an adversary and not a friend. What if he was lying to her?

She gripped the armrest and glanced at him. Don't panic. Would he really be pushing so hard to get home if he was a colleague of Tan's? It would make more sense to leave her in Tom Price for Salvatore to collect.

Tess exhaled. Her first task when she got to Retribution Bay was to buy another phone.

Soon afterwards, Ed slowed the car and a gravel driveway appeared. The sign at the entrance had a large angry-looking ram on it and declared *Welcome to Retribution Ridge*.

"Home," Ed said.

He slowed to a crawl as the van bumped over the gravel. They rounded a corner and buildings came into view. A few trees and a small garden surrounded a rambling house, the greenery at odds with the dry land around them. Across from it was another building with a bunch of doors in it, kind of like a dormitory, and behind it were sheds and pens. A dozen different caravans and tents were set up in another area not far from the second building with children playing outside, and a couple of stray sheep grazed over a small patch of grass. It was a small community in the desert, a haven. Tess instantly relaxed.

"I mentioned we have camp guests during the season," Ed said. "It's a new thing since the beginning of the year. The building with all the doors in it is the shearers' quarters."

A white ute pulled up outside the house with a dog in

the tray, and two men got out, both wearing brown cowboy-style hats like she'd seen in souvenir shops, but with far more wear to them. Brothers perhaps, both with dark hair and similar builds, but they looked nothing like Ed.

Ed stopped the van next to the ute and sighed. "Made it." He unstrapped. "Come on, I'll introduce you."

Tess was conscious of her cheap white T-shirt and black shorts, and she probably smelled. Not the best first impression. As she hopped out clutching her backpack to her chest, Ed hugged the two men, and did that back slap thing men did. She hovered at the bonnet of the van, and the dog trotted up to her, tail wagging. She stroked his soft, dusty fur, getting comfort from the animal. The slightly shorter, more solid man gazed at her with suspicion, but the lankier man grinned, and held out his hand. "You must be Tess. I'm Darcy, this is Brandon."

His firm handshake jolted her, and she stuttered. "Nice to meet you."

"You both look exhausted," he said. "Come inside and have some lunch."

The back door of the house slammed open, and a dark-haired girl appeared. "Ed!" She flew down the stairs and threw herself into Ed's arms. He picked her up and spun her around. "Hey, La La."

She laughed as he put her onto the ground. "You smell. Didn't you shower this morning?"

Tess cringed. If he smelled, she would be far worse.

"Nope. I'm hoping you saved me some hot water." He gestured to Tess. "This is my friend, Tess."

Lara waved at her. "Hi!" Then she lowered her voice. "You never said you had a girlfriend."

"I don't," Ed said, casting an apologetic look at Tess. "Your dad mentioned something about lunch."

"Yep, Amy's put the kettle on, and lunch is on the table. We've been waiting for you to arrive."

Ed gestured for Tess to follow, and she slid past the two brothers, feeling their eyes on her. They probably didn't appreciate the trouble she'd brought to Ed.

The door they entered took them straight into the kitchen. Four women and a man sat at the long wooden table, which had plenty of room for more people. Though the cupboards were all dated, there was a real homely feeling to the room, whether it was from the fresh scent of baked goodness, the fruit bowl on the table, or the magnets with papers and drawings on it stuck to the fridge. The people at the table rose when they saw Ed, and Tess hung back as they greeted him with hugs. She clasped her hands, shifting over to the corner so she wasn't in the way. One woman with short black hair in a pixie cut strode straight across to her. "Tess?"

She nodded.

"I'm Sergeant Dot Campbell."

Tess tensed and stepped back, hitting the kitchen counter.

"You'll be safe here," she whispered. "But I need to get your statement." She glanced over her shoulder. "Lara knows nothing about what happened to you and Ed, so we'll talk in private."

The young girl didn't need to be told about such ugliness.

Ed held out his hand to Tess. "Let me introduce you." He pulled her forward, glaring at Dot. "My sister, Georgie." He pointed to a woman with blue hair, but the same brown eyes as Ed. "Amy, our bride-to-be." A curvy woman with frizzy blonde hair. "Faith is Darcy's fiancée." She was slim with short, styled brown hair, a casual elegance about her. "And Matt is our station hand." The dark-skinned man waved at her.

"Are you hungry?" Amy asked.

Ed answered. "We could both use a shower before

we eat."

"Go for it."

Ed led Tess down a corridor lined with family photographs to a bathroom. "Have you got a change of clothes?"

She nodded.

"I'll grab you a fresh towel." He reached into a nearby cupboard and handed her a soft, blue towel. It felt like luxury. "Take your time, use whatever soaps are in there, and then go back to the kitchen when you're done. The others will get you food and drink."

The bathroom called to her like a siren, but she stopped Ed before he could walk away. "Thank you."

He smiled. "Any time."

She shut the door to the bathroom with a sigh. It was a small room, but a bath was squeezed in next to the shower and basin. The beige tiles appeared old, but it was clean. She locked the door and placed her backpack on the ground. Ed's family's greeting gave her hope she might be safe here, but she had to be mindful not to get in their way. She retrieved her only other T-shirt and turned the shower on, waiting until the temperature was right before she undressed. The warm water flooded over her, and she tilted her head back to wash her face. Glorious. It felt as if a month's grime was washing from her. She slicked her hair back and rubbed her skin before examining the soap and shampoo bottles on the ground. Frangipani body wash. She sniffed it and then slathered it liberally over her body, needing to scrub away the dirt and sweat of several days. She washed her hair next and sighed with pleasure as the soap ran down her. For the moment, all she wanted to think of was getting clean.

When she was dressed and ready to rejoin the family, she hesitated at the door. Had Ed finished showering yet? The image of a naked Ed popped into her head and she blushed. Eager to wipe the inappropriate thought from her mind, she opened the door and stepped into the hallway. The voices came from the left. She followed the sound, moving slowly, nerves tickling her skin. As she turned at the main corridor, she stopped to examine the photos on the wall. Ed's graduation photo caught her eye and next to it was his sister, Georgie's photo. As she continued, the photos included all the children; high school graduation, first day of school—Ed with tear-stained cheeks—and baby photos. So sweet to have them all on display like this.

She hesitated in the kitchen doorway. Ed wasn't back yet, but the others sat at the table drinking tea and passing around food. Three more large men had joined the family—perhaps they were Brandon's army team. The young girl, Lara, noticed her and waved her in. "Come, sit by me, Tess."

Suddenly she was centre of attention as everyone faced her. She cringed but forced herself to move forward and sit next to Lara. Amy handed her a bowl of salad. "Help yourself. I wasn't sure what you would like."

"This is fine. Thank you." She dished up salad and took some fresh bread from a plate.

"Ed never said he was bringing anyone to the wedding," Lara said. "Do you work with him?"

Tess glanced at the policewoman. Was she supposed to lie? "No, I'm still at university."

Lara opened her mouth to ask another question, but Darcy was faster. "What are you studying?"

"A bachelor of science majoring in biochemistry and molecular biology with an additional unit of Australian history."

"Why Australian history?" Amy asked, interest on her face.

"I discovered one of my ancestors was a pearl diver in WA and wanted to know more."

Lara grinned. "Has Ed told you the story of the

Retribution?"

Matt groaned. "Don't get her started."

Lara stuck her tongue out at him.

Tess smiled. "Yes, he has. It sounds fascinating."

"I'll take you out to see the plaque and the island while you're here," Lara said. "Do you ride?"

"A bicycle?" Seemed an odd place to cycle.

Lara laughed. "No, a horse… or motorbike."

"No." But both sounded exciting though a little scary.

"We could teach you while you're here," Ed said, coming into the room, his light hair still damp. He motioned Georgie to make room and sat across from Tess. "Faith's a horse-riding instructor."

"She's great," Lara assured Tess. "You'll be riding in no time."

Warmth filled Tess at the conviction and encouragement. Her mother would be horrified at the idea of Tess riding a horse.

Ed grabbed two slices of bread and made himself a sandwich. "Where are we at with wedding prep?"

The conversation moved to the wedding, and Tess ate her food, taking it all in. Amy was remarkably calm as she went through her lists of what was left to do. Brandon lost his military stiffness as she spoke, his gaze softening and a smile playing at his mouth as he watched her. Darcy reached for Faith's hand and squeezed it when Lara remarked they would have to do something similar for her father's wedding. Georgie kept glancing at Matt, who seemed unaware of her attentions. Next to him was Dot—who stared at Tess, interest and speculation on her face. Tess forced a smile. They had a lot to discuss. Had Tan's restaurant been searched?

After lunch, the men were tasked with setting up seating and shade for the ceremony, while Amy, Lara and Faith were putting together the flower arrangements. "Do you want to help, Tess?" Lara asked.

Tess glanced at Ed.

"I was going to get her to help me," he said.

"All right." Lara followed the others out of the kitchen, which left only Georgie and Dot with them.

"There's an empty room in the shearers' quarters where you can chat to Dot," Georgie said.

Ed nodded and held his hand out to Tess. "Come on."

She slipped her hand into his, grateful for his support. They walked across hard-packed red dirt, the sun beating down and a brief gust of wind blowing dust into her nose. She sneezed.

"Bless you," Dot said.

She smiled, but before she could go any further, a movement caught her eye. A small kangaroo hopped towards them. She gasped.

"That's Maggie," Ed said. "Dad rescued her when her mum was killed by a car."

The kangaroo stopped next to them and watched them steadily. After a night full of fear of kangaroos, it was so different seeing Maggie up close. She was much smaller than the kangaroos that had bounded across the road last night.

"Come on," Dot said and led them up the steps and into one of the rooms. Inside were a couple of chairs, a desk, and an unmade single bed. Ed pulled out a chair for her.

"Did the police find his car?" Ed asked.

Dot nodded. "But no guy." She held the door open. "Ed, you have to leave while I get Tess's statement."

Tess's heart leapt. Why? She felt safer with Ed around.

"You going to be all right?" Ed asked, his brown eyes gazing with concern into hers.

He trusted Dot and Tess trusted him. She could be brave. "Yes, but you should interview Ed first. He's barely slept in two days."

Dot's gaze softened. "I can wait for Ed's statement. Go, sleep for a couple of hours," she ordered him. "No wedding stuff."

Ed chuckled. "Yes, ma'am." He gave a half salute and strolled back to the house.

Tess clasped her hands and waited for the sergeant to ask her first question.

It would be a while before she got any sleep.

Chapter 8

Tess spent over an hour giving her statement to Dot. She'd half expected the woman to go through the motions, not caring about what Tess said, but the sergeant was meticulous, making her explain every step of that night, and then every moment since then. When she was satisfied, she asked questions about Tan himself.

"How did you come to work for him?" Dot asked.

"He's a friend of my parents," Tess said. "They didn't want me coming to Australia to study until Tan agreed I could stay with him and work in his restaurant."

"And how do your parents know him?"

She shrugged. "I don't know. I'd never heard of him before they said I would live with him." Which was a bit strange now she thought about it. She'd been forced to help with the guest list for her sister's wedding and her mother had explained every single relationship of the hundreds who were invited. She didn't recall Tan's name being mentioned.

Dot pursed her lips. "What do your parents do?"

"My father works in customs and my mother doesn't work."

A flash of interest on Dot's face before she made

another note. "When was the last time you contacted your parents?"

"I call them every Sunday." Which meant she had another two days before they would expect a call from her. She still hadn't figured out what to say to them.

"You didn't call them after you witnessed the murder?"

Tess shook her head. "They couldn't help me. My plan was to fly somewhere safe and then call them. I wanted to go home, but Tan has my passport."

"Then it was lucky you bumped into Ed." Something about the way she delivered the offhand comment made Tess stiffen.

She nodded slowly. "Very lucky. I was frantic when I couldn't hire a car."

"It was brave to go with a complete stranger."

"I was desperate." Tess glanced at the door. She didn't like where the questioning was going. It was as if she was under suspicion. "Ed seemed kind, and he was heading north immediately. I figured it was my best chance."

"Strange Tan didn't track you to the airport."

"I turned off my phone after he almost caught me at the shopping centre," she said. "Then briefly switched it on again when we stopped in Geraldton, but all the missed calls from him freaked me out. I didn't turn it on again until we reached Mount Magnet. Ed wanted me to check for road closures."

"You didn't consider Tan might track you?"

She shook her head. "He searched the area I was hiding, so I turned my phone off when he rang." But now she thought about it, Tan had insisted she install an app on her phone which allowed it to be found if it was lost. At the time she'd thought it kind, though it had also felt a little controlling. It had been the first indication that she might not get the freedom she'd craved by coming to Australia.

The sergeant pulled out a blank notebook and a pencil. "I need you to describe the woman you saw."

"You're going to draw it?"

Dot nodded. "I've taken sketch artist courses. Out here you have to do as many jobs as possible."

It made sense. Tess closed her eyes and flinched as the image of the woman's dead eyes flashed into her mind. She clenched her hands together. Without Tess, the woman's family might never know what had happened to her. She could do this. Swallowing hard, she began to describe the victim.

***

"Astro Boy, it's time to wake up."

Ed groaned at Georgie's sing-song tone and pulled the sheet over his head, turning his back to her.

"Come on, Ed, you've been sleeping for almost four hours. Isn't that enough?"

He blinked and struggled to remember why four hours was a bad thing. Through the sheet, daylight streamed in. Why was he sleeping in the middle of the day?

"Dot wants to speak to you now," Georgie continued.

He sat upright and rubbed the sleep from his eyes as the memories came flooding back. "Has Tess finished? Is she all right?"

"Seems a little uncertain, but is otherwise unharmed by the masses," his sister joked.

Yeah, the Stokes family might be something she's not used to. He threw the sheets back and got up.

Georgie stepped away and averted her eyes. "Ew, Ed, I don't need to see you in your underwear."

Ed chuckled. "It's not like you haven't seen me in them before." He pulled on shorts and a T-shirt. "Where's Tess?"

"Helping to make dinner."

He jolted. "What time is it?"

"Almost five. Everything is ready for tomorrow except we need the rings."

Disappointment filled him. He'd wanted to help but hadn't set an alarm because he'd figured Tess would have only been with Dot for an hour. Stupid. He dumped his backpack on the bed and unzipped the pouch he'd put the ring boxes in.

"Are you all right?" Georgie asked. "Bran and Darcy wouldn't give me details about what happened because Lara was around."

He nodded. "All that shooting practice paid off."

Her eyes widened. "You shot someone!"

He hushed her. His room was next to Lara's. "No, I shot out some tyres and threatened to shoot a guy." The gun was still in the glove box, unless Tess had given it to Dot.

"Ed, what the hell happened?"

"I'll explain later. I'd better go talk to Dot."

Georgie stood in front of the door, arms crossed. "No. You'll give me the short version now."

She had that stubborn tilt to her jaw. He sighed and filled her in. When he was done, she threw her arms around him and squeezed him.

"You must have been shit scared. I'm so glad you got the gun."

He smiled, drawing comfort from his younger sister. "I managed all right."

"Are you sure Tess is innocent?"

The question made him pause, but he nodded. "She was terrified. I trust her, Georgie."

"What if she's working with Tan and making it all up?"

Not something he'd considered. Unease crept its way onto his shoulders, and he frowned as he reviewed the events. Stonefish had no way of knowing he would offer Tess a lift, even if they had known about the baggage handler strike, and about his flight that morning. It was a long shot. "I don't think she is."

"I'll keep an eye on her," Georgie told him. "Keep her close."

Ed bit his tongue to stop from protesting. Georgie would do what she wanted, regardless of what he said. "Fine." He followed her into the kitchen, where everyone gathered. There were two guys he didn't recognise chatting with Sam, and Ed assumed they were Brandon's army buddies. Which one was Amy's brother? Neither looked like her. Tess chopped carrots at the table, not taking part in the conversation, her eyes heavy with fatigue. Had the others not ensured she got some sleep? "Amy, I've got the rings." He handed them to her, and she opened both boxes, grinning.

"Thanks, Ed." She hugged him. "I really appreciate it."

It was nothing. They'd ordered the rings a month ago, and they'd only arrived on Monday. It was a small thing for him to drive over to the jewellers and pick them up. "No problem."

He caught Dot's eye, and she nodded towards the door outside. As he crossed the room, Lara called, "Did you have a good sleep, Ed?"

He smiled. "Yeah, thanks La La."

"Do you want something to eat?"

How could he get outside without her noticing? "Not right now. I need to get something out of the van." Dot had already left the kitchen, and he followed her out. Behind him, Lara asked, "Where's Dot?" He winced as her voice rose. "What's going on? Did something happen? Is Ed talking to Dot about something?"

Ed kept walking. Darcy could sort it out. Though Lara was only ten, she'd been involved with Stonefish, and she deserved to know the truth. Like Georgie, she was stubborn enough to get it too. He entered the shearer's room and closed the door behind him.

Dot sighed. "Lara's been through a lot. I wish she didn't have to hear about this."

"Yeah, but Darcy will help her through it."

"So will Faith."

Ed nodded. He didn't know Faith well. One week she was Lara's pony club instructor, and practically the next week, she was Darcy's fiancée. Darcy looked happier than he had in a while though, so Ed figured she was good for him. "What do you want to know?"

"Tell me your story from the moment you met Tess."

He frowned. "Why from there? Isn't the guy with the gun the important part?"

She raised her eyebrows. "Don't argue with me."

He was just about to, when he noticed the dark rings under her eyes, and the weary slump of her shoulders. Dealing with Stonefish had to be difficult for her as well. "All right." He explained that Sheridan had almost run over Tess and he'd later seen her looking distressed at the hire car counter.

"She didn't ask for a lift?"

"No, she was hesitant to accept, and wouldn't say where she wanted to go."

"You didn't think that odd?"

"She seemed a little nervous, but if a strange man asked Georgie where she was headed, I hope she wouldn't tell him." He grinned. "Even if he was as handsome as me."

Dot chuckled. "You saw no one suspicious at the airport? No one who could have been watching you?"

"Dot, the airport was packed full of pissed off people. Even if someone had been watching me, I wouldn't have noticed. My focus was getting a hire car before they ran out and getting home." But her questions mirrored those

Georgie had asked. "You think Tess is a plant?"

She pressed her lips together. "It's a possibility I'm not willing to rule out yet."

"She was terrified, Dot."

"But was it because she'd witnessed a murder, or because Stonefish were forcing her to do something she didn't want to do?"

Crap. She had a point. Stonefish had forced others to do their bidding. "What about the dead body?"

"It hasn't been found, and there are no missing person reports which match Tess's description."

He ran a hand through his hair. "Right. I'll be careful about what I say around her." He didn't believe Tess was lying, but he'd be stupid not to be cautious.

"Now, tell me about the attack last night."

Ed gave as much detail as he could. Dot pulled out a photograph. "This him?"

"Yeah, where did you get that?"

"Looked up his driver's licence." She showed him a second, hand-drawn picture of an older woman. "Do you recognise her?"

He shook his head. "Did you draw it?"

She nodded.

"That's amazing, Dot. You're even better than I remember." Once when she visited Brandon she had brought out a sketch pad and Ed had sat next to her as she'd drawn the view from the sand dunes near the house. He'd been so excited to hear his dad praise her skills, and it had given him hope he wouldn't have to be a farmer if he could find something else he was good at.

Dot rolled her eyes. "It's adequate."

"Is she the woman who Tess saw killed?"

"Yeah." She stood. "Now you can give me the gun. I've dusted the door handle for fingerprints. Did he touch anywhere else?"

Ed considered the question. "No, but I've got his car

keys too."

They went out into the dusky evening. The warmth was pleasant after a winter in the city. Dot got supplies out of her car and bagged the gun and keys, writing details on the bags with a confident hand. "I'm going to run these into town now," she said.

"The 'roos will be out."

She laughed. "I can handle them. I need to secure these and update my contact in Perth. Tell Amy I'll be out early in the morning to help with set up."

Ed hugged her. "Thanks, Dot. I don't know what the family would do without you."

She stepped back, a furrow on her brow. "It's fine, Ed. It's my job." She drove away.

The sun sat on the horizon as he returned to the kitchen. Darcy drained a steaming bowl of pasta in the sink, and Amy placed a bowl of bolognaise on the table. Ed inhaled, and the scent of garlic butter hit his nose as Matt took three loaves of bread from the oven.

"Just in time," Brandon said. "Where's Dot?"

"She had to go back to town. She said to tell you she'll be out early tomorrow to help."

Amy frowned. "I'll call her later. Everything's set up, so she just needs to arrive for the ceremony at nine."

Lara ran up and hugged him. "Dad told me what happened. I'm glad you weren't shot."

He laughed, hugging his niece back. "Me too, La La." When she let him go, Ed moved further into the room, but before he could reach Tess, Brandon interceded.

"A word." He nodded towards the hallway.

What now? Ed followed Brandon into the lounge room. "What's wrong?"

Brandon raised his eyebrows. "You bring a potential Stonefish spy to my wedding and you ask me what's wrong?"

Ed stiffened. "We don't know she's working for

them."

"We don't know she's not," he countered. "What are you going to do to make sure she doesn't cause trouble?"

The inferiority he'd always felt around Brandon at the Ridge came back with a vengeance, so he went on the defence. "I did what any decent person would do for a woman in trouble. I helped her, and I'll continue to help her. Until Dot can prove Tess is lying, I'll treat Tess as if she's telling the truth, because I believe she is."

"Don't be naïve, Ed. This is Stonefish's MO."

All of Ed's insecurities rose up in the face of his brother's disdain. He'd never been good enough, had never done the right thing. "Don't question my judgement, Bran. You don't know me." He strode out of the room, his heart racing and all his fears battering to get out. He entered the kitchen and went over to the sink to pour a glass of water and give himself a moment to calm down.

He met Tess's gaze, saw the worry in them. Was she really a plant? Taking another breath, he sat next to her. "You OK?"

She nodded. "Your family is very kind."

"They're the best." Mostly. He ignored Brandon when he came in. He reached for the jug of water in the centre of the table. "Do you want some water?"

"Please."

Around them people helped themselves to the food, and then Brandon tapped his fork on his beer bottle to get everyone's attention. "I wanted to thank you all for your help today. Amy's put together this wedding in record time, and we appreciate you could all make it."

"We appreciate you getting us a few days' leave before we ship out," one of his army buddies said.

"Hey, that was all me," the other guy, shorter and with large ears, said.

Brandon grinned. "Thank you, Dobby." He raised his

beer bottle. "The last couple of months have been hard—" He cleared his throat. "Tomorrow I get to marry the woman I love," he kissed Amy's hand, "on the land I love, and I never dreamed any of this would be possible."

Ed pressed his lips together as resentment settled in his gut. His parents hadn't been here to see Brandon come home. Everyone had welcomed Brandon back without questioning why he hadn't returned sooner, why he'd abandoned all of them. And he'd inherited the station, rather than Darcy, who had never left. But Darcy didn't seem to care. No one did.

"To Brandon and Amy," Darcy called.

Ed echoed the words and clinked his glass against Tess's, who looked a little uncomfortable. The dishes were passed around and Ed caught the soldiers' attention who sat across from him. He smiled. "We haven't met yet. I'm Ed and this is Tess."

The shorter guy grinned. "Damien, but they call me Dobby on account of my ears."

"And because he's our slave," the other guy joked. "I'm Heath."

So where was Amy's brother, Arthur? He glanced at her, but she was chatting to Sam.

"You drove from Perth in that wreck of a van out front?" Dobby asked.

"Yeah. It was an adventure."

"So I hear," Heath said.

Brandon must have told them about it. Ed passed Tess the bowl of pasta and sat back, content to listen to the talk around him. The Ridge kitchen was built for this—lots of people, good conversation, family and friends. He remembered too well those days after Charlie had died and Brandon had left, when the table had felt empty and full of sorrow. At eleven, he'd had no idea how to fix things, to bring Brandon back and make the family smile again. His one attempt—the letter he'd written Brandon—had never been answered.

He clenched his teeth against the wave of betrayal. He should be over it by now. A couple of years later, when Darcy got Sofia pregnant and she'd moved in with them, life had looked better. Ed had latched onto Sofia, helping her however he could with her pregnancy, hoping she and the baby would turn around his family. Except she'd deserted him too. It was Lara who had brought colour, light, and noise back into the house.

And now Amy and Faith had added to the joy.

If only his parents were here to witness it.

Ed focused on his meal. Next to him Lara was telling Tess all about the Retribution. "The sailors mutinied," she said, her eyes wide. "But there was no reason for them to, unless there was treasure involved." She lowered her voice. "I reckon they had gold on board and were taking it north. The convicts were going to steal it and use it to buy a boat and sail to freedom."

"But why mutiny when they had no ship to get away?" Tess asked.

"Well…" Lara took a deep breath, and Ed grinned. He'd heard Lara's theories before, but Tess seemed genuinely interested in the story, so he didn't interrupt.

After dinner, Ed caught Tess yawning. He took Amy aside. "Have we got somewhere for Tess to sleep?"

"Kind of," she said. "We're playing musical beds tonight. Brandon and Darcy are sleeping in the shearers' quarters with Matt and Brandon's army mates. I thought Tess could sleep in Lara's room and Lara can sleep with Georgie."

Which left him without a bed. He normally shared a room with Georgie. "Aren't there extra rooms in the shearers' quarters?"

She winced. "I hired them out to some backpackers before we set the date of the wedding."

And the station needed every cent they could bring in.

"Would you mind sleeping in the swag, or in the van?" Amy asked, eyes beseeching.

"Yeah, it's fine." He'd been the one to bring an extra guest, so it was his own fault. "Where's Arthur?"

Her eyes narrowed, and a mix of anger and disappointment filled her face. "Got called out on an urgent mission which was far more important than my wedding."

Ed winced. That didn't help their strained relationship. Amy and her brother had spoken a couple of times since they'd become reacquainted, but the wedding was supposed to be their time to reconnect. Sounded like Arthur was a real douche. "I'm sorry."

She shrugged. "Don't be. I've still got all of you."

After the dishes were done, Sam hustled Brandon and the rest of the guys outside, carrying a bottle of bourbon. "Time to drink to celebrate the end of your single days." The other guys cheered.

"I'll be right with you," Darcy said. "Story time?" he asked Lara. She nodded, and Darcy and Faith took her down the hall.

Ed felt a pinch that Sam hadn't invited him to go with them, but he had Tess to take care of. He wandered over to her. "Are you tired?"

She glanced up at him and nodded.

"No one will mind if you go to bed. Do you want me to show you to your room?"

The gratitude on her face told him he should have asked her earlier. "Please."

He took her to Lara's room, where the bed was full of stuffed toy animals. He cleared them off. "The toilet's down the corridor, and help yourself to anything in the kitchen." Did he need to worry about leaving her in the house unsupervised? If she was working for Tan, she could do anything while the others were distracted with wedding celebrations. Though she did look dead on her feet.

"Where will you be?"

"Outside. I'll set up a swag behind the house." That way, the lights around the buildings shouldn't interfere too much with his view of the stars.

"I don't want to take your bed," she said.

"It's fine. I like sleeping under the stars. Do you need anything before I go?"

She shook her head.

"Night." He ran into Faith and Darcy in the corridor, coming out of his bedroom. "Story time over?"

Darcy smiled. "Yeah, though I'm not sure she'll get any sleep tonight. She's so excited about being a flower girl."

Of course she was. Lara had sent him photos of her dress and she'd look like a princess. They entered the kitchen, where Georgie was making margaritas. The women were having their own celebration.

Darcy kissed Faith. "Have fun."

"We will."

His brother stopped at the door and looked back. "You coming, Ed?"

He rubbed his chest. "Yeah, I just need a word to Georgie, and to set up my swag."

"See you there." Darcy headed outside, and Georgie stopped mixing to ask, "What do you need?"

"Did you bring something for Tess to wear tomorrow?"

Georgie frowned. "I brought a couple of options, but they might be too big."

"Dot's about her size," Amy said. "Maybe she'll have something."

Ed hated to ask Dot for more, but he also didn't want Tess to feel uncomfortable. "I'll call her."

A short conversation later, and Dot had promised to bring out some options in the morning. Georgie and his soon-to-be sisters-in-law had their margaritas in front of them when he hung up.

"It was nice of you to think of Tess," Faith said. "I'm sure she'll appreciate it."

"Ed is the most considerate of my brothers," Georgie said. "He takes after Mum."

The comparison made him equally embarrassed and pleased. "Is the swag still in the shed?" he asked Amy.

"Yeah, do you need a hand?"

He shook his head. "I've got it. Enjoy your night."

He headed outside. Across the campgrounds, a camp fire burned, and he recognised Brandon's face in the firelight. They were over near where Darcy had started to build a house for Sofia and Lara.

Ed continued to the shed, flicking on a light. His gaze fell on the two farm bikes parked next to each other, and he cringed, absently rubbing his forearm. Give him a horse any day.

Avoiding the motorbikes, he moved to the back wall, where the camping gear was shelved next to the telescope his father had bought after Ed had become fascinated with the stars. He closed his eyes. Though Ed hadn't wanted to be a farmer, his father had encouraged his other pursuits. They had so many nights together, staring at the night sky and chatting about life.

The tightness in his chest made it difficult to breathe, and he took a moment to let it pass before grabbing the swag. After switching off the light, the night was darker than before, so he used his phone torch to find a spot behind the house and set up his swag.

Across by the fire, voices murmured, punctuated by the occasional burst of masculine laughter. Ed hesitated. Was there any point in going over there? He had little in common with his brothers and couldn't imagine what he could talk about with Brandon's army mates. Maybe that was unfair. He and Sam had got along well when he'd come to the station for the funerals. It would be so much easier if he was a manly man, active, working with his hands, liking beer and all that stuff. Instead he sat on his arse all day, using his fingers and brains to work magic, and loved an array of wines.

Some country boy he was.

He gazed up at the sky, the Milky Way clearly visible, and he found the Southern Cross and Orion. His world was up there, amongst the stars, or in front of his laptop.

With a sigh, he pried off his shoes and climbed into the swag.

The stars were plenty of company for tonight.

Chapter 9

The unusually comfortable bed was Tess's first clue she wasn't in her granny flat when she woke the next morning. The next was the giant teddy bear staring at her from across the room. She sat, heart racing, as her gaze darted to the pile of stuffed toys on the floor, the posters of horses on the wall and the small cubed shelving full of books. Lara's bedroom. She let out her breath. Light filtered through the gap in the blinds, and she reached for her phone to check the time.

The bedside table was empty. Her phone lay in the dirt somewhere north of Meekatharra. There was, however, a clock across the room which told her it was six-thirty. Somewhere in the house, a shower ran, which meant others were up. The wedding was this morning. Would Ed already be in the kitchen?

Though everyone had been kind, Tess noticed Georgie watching her. She couldn't blame her. She'd be suspicious of anyone who'd led her sibling into danger. Footsteps padded down the hall outside her door and Lara said, "Can I get into my dress now?"

Tess smiled. If Lara was up, she was happy to go into the kitchen. The young girl made her feel so welcome, and after she'd discovered Tess was interested in the Retribution shipwreck, she'd told her all about it. Tess made the bed and then looked in her backpack. She had bought only two T-shirts and a pair of shorts. Nothing appropriate for a wedding, though Ed assured her she would be welcomed. Perhaps tomorrow Ed could take her into town so she could buy more clothes, and a phone. By then the police might have captured Salvatore and arrested Tan.

Her laptop caught her eye. Her parents only expected her to call on Sundays, so she could delay it another day. Before she did, she wanted to ask Ed about what Tan had done to the Ridge so she could get an idea of what else he was involved in. What her parents could be involved in. She'd heard Tan mention a business up north, and she'd figured it was another restaurant, but maybe it wasn't.

She'd wait for the right time to speak with Ed, maybe tomorrow. She didn't want to bring up what could be an unwelcome topic during the wedding.

Today, she wanted to fade into the background as much as possible. The wedding was a family affair, and she didn't want her issues to interfere.

She ambled down the corridor, nerves tickling her skin. Everything would be fine. The Stokes were kind people. Inside the kitchen, Lara, Faith, and Amy were having breakfast. Lara waved. "Morning, Tess. Would you like cereal?"

The nerves dissipated. "Yes, please." A box and several clean bowls sat in the centre of the table.

"Did you sleep well?" Amy asked.

Tess nodded. "Thank you for lending me your bed, Lara."

"It's cool. I got to sleep with Georgie, and she was so funny when she came in, bumping into things."

Faith chuckled. "She had too many of her margaritas.

We won't see her until it's time to get ready."

"I wonder how the guys fared," Amy said. "The farmers are usually awake by now."

"Will you see Brandon before the ceremony?" Tess asked.

"Yeah, I'm not superstitious." Amy held up a jug. "Coffee?"

"Please." She'd slept solidly all night, and now she needed something to clear the remaining fatigue from her system. "Is there anything I can do to help?"

"We got everything ready yesterday," Amy said. "We just need the celebrant to arrive, and Lindsay's bringing the cakes in from town."

"How far away is the town?"

"About an hour's drive," Faith answered.

That wasn't close. There'd be no popping in to get food if anything was forgotten. Her mother had been a nervous wreck the morning of Joy's wedding, sending people out to get last-minute things she'd decided were essential. Amy was the picture of calm.

Heavy footsteps stomped on the porch outside, and Sam staggered in. "Coffee, I need coffee." He sank into a chair, placed his head in his hands, keeping his sunglasses firmly on his face. Tess smiled.

"Overindulged last night, did we?" Faith asked.

Sam groaned. "It's not every day my best friend gets married."

Tess hunched over her bowl, trying to make herself inconspicuous as Darcy, Brandon, and the other guys wandered in. Six large Australian males dominating the room. None of the other women seemed the least bit concerned. A huge grin covered Brandon's face as he pulled Amy into his arms and kissed her. "Morning."

Tess's shoulders relaxed, though Ed was missing. How had he fared last night?

The kitchen was soon full of excited chatter and the

scent of bacon, toasting bread, and coffee, lots of coffee.

Georgie came in and plonked down next to Tess with a groan. Tess poured her a coffee and placed it in front of her.

"You're an angel." Georgie closed her eyes and sipped the hot drink.

"Who wants bacon?" Brandon asked.

Georgie raised her hand. "And eggs, and whatever fried food you can give me."

"Always with the appetite," Matt teased, and Georgie scowled without responding.

Tess was content to watch as Dobby and Sam told Lara stories of Brandon's exploits in the army. It was so far from the drama, tears, and stress of her sister's wedding. Heath plonked himself beside her. "Feeling better, this morning?" He was at least ten years older than her, and his dark colouring spoke of a middle Eastern background.

She nodded, surprised he was talking to her.

"It's got to be tough being dropped in the middle of all this. If you need any help, or someone to talk to at the wedding, you can hang with me."

It was sweet of him to offer. "Thank you."

Half an hour later, Ed still hadn't arrived. People were taking turns in the showers, the guys were about to leave the house to get ready and still no Ed. No one seemed to have noticed.

Tess leaned over to Georgie. "Is Ed still asleep?"

Georgie frowned and glanced around the kitchen. "Anyone seen Ed this morning?"

A chorus of nos and shakes of the head.

"How much did he drink last night?" Georgie asked.

Darcy and Brandon exchanged a glance. "He wasn't with us. I figured he stayed with you."

Tess stiffened. Had something happened to him? Had Tan and Salvatore taken him? She stood without realising it, and everybody turned to her. Heat rushed to her cheeks. "Where was he sleeping?"

"In a swag around the back," Darcy answered.

She hesitated. Traipsing outside by herself sounded like a bad idea. She clutched her hands together. "Should I go and wake him?"

"Good idea," Darcy said. "I'll show you where he is."

She followed him out of the house and around the side to where a swag was set up on the ground.

Before she could walk over, Darcy touched her arm. "Are you OK this morning?"

Another kindness. "Yes, thank you."

Darcy studied her for a moment and then smiled. "Good luck with Ed," he said. "He's not a morning person." With that warning, he headed back inside.

Tess glanced over at the swag. Ed had set it up away from the house, and small shrubs, grasses really, surrounded him. Darcy hadn't warned her about snakes, so perhaps it wasn't something she needed to worry about. Ed wouldn't set up his bed where he might be attacked. Taking a deep breath, she strode over, her eyes scanning the ground for any movement. The top of Ed's swag was flung back and only a fly screen covered him. Inside, he slept curled on his side, hair spiked in different directions. Calm and at peace. Her guardian angel. She smiled.

"Ed," she called. "Time to get up."

He didn't stir.

Louder, she repeated, "Ed, wake up. Everyone's getting ready for the wedding."

This time she got a grumble, and he turned away from her.

Her smile widened. Darcy had been right. Which made Ed's sacrifice the morning before even more heroic. He'd put his sleep aside for her. Her hand hovered over the zip. Was unzipping the swag the equivalent of walking into his bedroom unannounced? Her only other option was yelling at him, and she didn't want to wake him so abruptly. She slid the zip open, but even that noise didn't stir him. The fly screen brushed Ed's face, and he swatted it away. Cautiously, she placed a hand on his arm. "Ed, time to get up."

His eyelids flickered and he turned back over, his bleary eyes meeting hers. "Tess?" He blinked, and then smiled. "Morning."

It was impossible to resist his sleepy smile. She smiled back, her heart beating faster. "Morning. The others have already had breakfast and are getting ready."

He shifted to sit and checked his phone in the swag next to him. "Right. I thought the cockatoos would wake me."

A flock of cockatoos sat in a tree on the other side of the house, but their screeches were loud even here. She wasn't surprised they hadn't woken him. He'd slept little in the past couple of days.

As he stood, she shifted back to give him room. He slipped his feet into a pair of shoes and examined the swag. He sighed. "I should pack this up so it doesn't get in the way of any photos." He bent over and pulled out a couple of poles and pegs and rolled it up. He tucked it under his arm. "Have you eaten?"

"Yes. Lara arranged it for me."

"Sorry I wasn't there. I know it's difficult for you not knowing anyone."

They were all so considerate. "It's fine. The others were welcoming."

Across the yard in the shearers' quarters, the men sat on its porch chatting. As Tess and Ed reached the house, Dot drove up and waved.

"Any news?" Ed asked.

Dot shook her head. "Salvatore's gone to ground," she said. "I'll tell you as I hear more." She grabbed her bag out of the back seat. "Tess, I brought a couple of dresses so you could choose."

Tess frowned. "Dresses?"

"For the wedding," Ed said. "I figured you wouldn't have anything to wear."

How incredibly kind. She squirmed. "I don't want to intrude. I can stay inside and read."

"You're not intruding," Ed said. "The more, the merrier."

They headed inside where Georgie had spread makeup and hair products on the kitchen table. "Hey, Dot. Just in time." Faith, Amy, and Lara wore summer dresses, and their hair was tied back in ponytails.

"Tess, you can get ready with us," Amy invited.

She glanced at Ed, unsure.

"I need a corner of the table for breakfast," Ed said.

"Well, hurry," Georgie said. "This should be a girls only area."

Tess caught Ed's flinch before he replied, "Too much oestrogen here for me, anyway."

Amy pulled him into a hug. "You're always welcome."

He squeezed her back. "Thanks, Ames." He gestured for Tess to sit next to Lara and made himself a coffee and toast. Next to Tess, Lara bounced in her seat. "No more sleeps, no more sleeps."

Tess chuckled at her enthusiasm. "How long have you been waiting?"

"*Months,*" she said. "Amy and Brandon got engaged in May."

It was July. That wasn't a lot of time to organise a wedding. Dot and Faith hovered around Amy, doing her makeup while Georgie poured glasses of champagne. Where were all the extended family, aunts, and cousins?

It wasn't her place to ask, but she was curious. "Do you have cousins coming?" she asked Ed, as Georgie handed Tess a glass of champagne.

"No, this is us."

Such a small family. At her sister's wedding she'd met cousins and second cousins for the first time. Of the two hundred people attending, she was related to two-thirds of them.

"Granny and Grandfather died," Lara added, her voice trembling.

Georgie hugged her. "But they're here in spirit." Her eyes glistened, and Tess wished she hadn't asked.

She sipped the bubbly champagne, and the lightness settled in her belly.

She sat back and watched while the friends prepared the bride, far more relaxed than she'd been at her own sister's wedding.

***

Ed didn't really fit anywhere. He shouldn't have thought today of all days would be any different than normal. After he'd showered and dressed in his best suit, he stopped at the gallery of family photos, which covered the hallway wall. Every child as a newborn with their parents and siblings, and then on the first day of school, and graduation. His parents looked so young in the photo of a newborn Brandon, but they were probably about his age. He closed his eyes at the ache in his chest. God, it hurt so much to look at them, to know his mother wouldn't be fussing around the kitchen making sure everyone had something to eat, or his father wasn't hurrying back from seeing to something on the station before getting ready for the wedding. They should be here to see Brandon return home, find love and now marry.

He swallowed hard and examined the photo of the other missing person. Charlie.

How he'd worshipped, envied, and at times actively disliked his older brother. Charlie had been full of confidence and bravery and spoke of travelling the world when he was old enough. He'd always tried to drag Ed into one of his capers, but getting into trouble had never interested Ed. Sure, he liked to ride, but he preferred horses to motorbikes, and at a far slower pace than Charlie's open throttle. Particularly after one accident. He closed his eyes as he remembered the wind whisking away his shouts to slow down, his fingers aching from where they gripped underneath the seat and Charlie's laugh, *Don't be a wimp.* They'd hit something—a rock, a hollow, a rare wet patch—and Charlie had lost control. Ed vividly remembered the terror as he flew through the air and then landed with a crack on the hard ground. He'd broken an arm and had hated motorbikes ever since.

Charlie had stood over him while Ed had held his arm. *It's your fault. You should have held on tighter.* Ed had believed him, had thought he wasn't tough enough, though now he realised it was just Charlie's way of assuaging his guilt. Charlie had never stopped for long enough to consider how his words or actions might hurt.

Ed exhaled, rubbing his tired eyes.

That last day they'd had such a fight. Charlie had stuck chewing gum under Ed's favourite book, and the cover ripped as Ed picked it up. The words were imprinted on his memory like they'd happened yesterday. *I hate you. You're such a stupid head.*

Charlie was never one to offer an immediate apology. *Well, you shouldn't read so much. You're boring.*

Brothers always knew which buttons to push. Ed always felt he was different with his love of reading and cooking, and Charlie had been touchy about his poor grades at school. *Better to be boring than stupid.*

Charlie had shoved Ed onto the bed, and stormed out of their bedroom with a *Loser* thrown back at him.

Ed's stomach clenched at his parting words. *I wish*

you'd go away.

And Charlie had. Somewhere no one could follow. Ed had spent years wishing he could take back those words, and feeling as if he was responsible for Charlie's death. It wasn't until he was at university that he'd realised how foolish that was. As if his one wish had the power to change the world.

He sighed. If Charlie had been alive, would he have flown back from wherever in the world he was for the wedding? Probably. He might have even hung around after his parents' funeral to catch up with his family, because Ed had no doubt that if Charlie had lived, he would be living whatever dream life he wanted. Charlie hadn't taken no for an answer.

"Hey, why are you lurking in the corridor?" Georgie asked, walking towards him, a brush in her hand, already wearing her pale blue bridesmaid dress.

Ed shrugged. "Just looking at the photos."

She slipped a hand around his waist and looked with him. "It doesn't seem real they're not here. I keep pretending they've retired and are on an extended vacation somewhere, and any day they'll drive in and tell us stories of their adventures."

"I like that thought." He squeezed his sister. "How've you been coping, really?" They spoke regularly on the phone, but Georgie liked to pretend she was fine.

She pressed her lips together, eyes shining. "Not today. We can talk later, OK?"

"OK." He kissed her forehead and let her go.

"Are you ready?" she asked.

"Yeah, was just going to see if Amy needs anything."

"Thanks. The guests should arrive in about half an hour, so direct them to the garden and stop any of them from coming into the house."

Ed smiled. "You think I'll be able to stop Jenifer?"

Georgie laughed at the mention of their mother's best

friend. "Maybe don't get in her way." She kissed his cheek. "Love you, Astro Boy."

"Love you, Mermaid." The two of them had banded together to face the world back when Charlie had died. He'd taken on the role of looking after his younger sister.

Georgie headed further into the house to get whatever it was she needed, and Ed continued into the kitchen. Faith was pinning the final flower into Amy's hair. She'd done something to tame the normal frizz so that Amy's curls were tight ringlets which fell in layers past her shoulders. Amy grinned at him with no signs of fatigue, her makeup a light dusting and she positively glowed. Ed grinned back at her. "Looking gorgeous, Ames."

"Thanks, Ed." Amy touched her hair and Faith brushed her hands away.

"None of that, you'll mess it up." She clasped a silver necklace around her neck and then fiddled with the cowl neckline of her bridesmaid dress to make sure it sat right.

"Ed, look at this." Lara twirled around, and the skirt of her blue dress flew out like an umbrella.

"Cool," Ed said.

Dot's bright red dress caught his attention next as she poured herself a glass of water. Ed blinked. He couldn't remember the last time he'd seen Dot in a dress. She caught him staring. "What's the matter?"

"The red suits you, Dot. You should get them to change the police uniform colour."

She grinned. "I don't think they'll go for that."

His gaze finally fell on Tess, and he almost didn't recognise her. Wow. Her long black hair was tied back in some kind of bun, and the makeup applied to her eyes made them appear larger, warmer. The dress neckline was modest, but hinted at her smooth skin underneath, and the vibrant emerald green suited her. Her hands were clenched.

"You look stunning, Tess," he said. The bright colour was amazing on her, and she appeared older than her twenty-one years. She was beautiful.

"Thank you," she replied.

Someone knocked on the kitchen door. Lee, who had stayed at the station on and off since the campgrounds opened, had offered to take photos of the wedding. He stood there, camera in hand, a big smile on his face. "Can I take some photos of you getting ready?" Tall and lean, with his black hair always neatly parted down the side, Ed had never seen him look anything but totally put together.

"Come in, Lee," Amy called. "I'm not sure there's much for you to see."

The man walked in. "I've been checking wedding photographer websites, and they always have photos of the bride and groom getting ready," he said. "I've taken photos of Brandon."

Next to Ed, Tess drew in a sharp breath and she stared at Lee, a frown on her face.

Ed shifted, so he was between Lee and Tess, and murmured, "Something wrong?"

Lee's attention was already on Amy, taking photos of her, Faith and Dot.

Tess shook her head slowly. "He looks familiar."

Not good. "Come outside with me." He hustled her outside. More than once, he and his siblings had wondered whether Lee could be involved with Stonefish Enterprises. He'd been at the station on both occasions when Stonefish struck, but each time, other people had been involved. People his family had trusted.

The air held a hint of the warmth the day would bring. Ed led Tess around the side of the verandah onto the lawn where chairs were set up in neat rows, ready for the ceremony.

"Where do you know Lee from?" Ed asked.

"I don't know." She worried at her bottom lip.

"From the restaurant?" he prompted. "Did he visit Tan?"

"I'm really not sure. He could be someone I met at university… where's he from—Singapore?"

"I've never asked. He's got an Aussie accent, so I assumed he was from here." But what should they do if he was working for Stonefish? They couldn't let him see Tess.

"Something wrong out here?" Dot asked, joining them in the garden, her gaze shrewd.

Relief filled him. Dot would know what to do. "Tess recognised Lee."

Dot immediately stiffened. "Where from?"

Tess shrugged. "I'm not sure. He looks familiar. He might be someone who has eaten at Tan's restaurant, or I might have seen him around the university campus."

Ed turned to Dot. "Have you checked him out?"

She hesitated for a split second before giving a curt nod. "Of course. I can't trace him to Stonefish."

But it didn't mean he wasn't connected. None of the others had been easily traceable to them, either. The company was hard to pin down.

"Maybe I shouldn't go to the wedding," Tess said. "I could hide inside."

Dot shook her head. "Lee's staying for a couple of weeks. You won't be able to avoid him for that long."

"So we find somewhere in town," Ed said. "Georgie will let us stay at her place."

"Ed, you've done enough," Tess said. "If I can get a lift into town after the wedding, I'll figure out something." She hugged herself.

"No," he responded, taking one of her hands in his. "You're not dealing with this alone." The offer was instant, but then he remembered Dot's warning. Maybe he should be more careful.

Relief and doubt fought across her face.

"I agree with Ed," Dot said. "We can monitor you easier out here. Brandon and Sam both have experience in protection."

"How long's Sam staying?" Ed asked.

"A few more days."

Ed hoped it wouldn't take longer than that to clear up this mess.

"In the meantime, avoid Lee, and if you remember where you've seen him before, tell me immediately," Dot said.

Tess nodded.

The first guest drove up to the house.

"Take Tess with you to greet the guests," Dot said. "We'll keep Lee busy inside."

"All right." Ed slipped his hand into Tess's and squeezed. "Come on. We'll keep you safe."

He wasn't letting Stonefish hurt another innocent person.

Chapter 10

Tess felt like a meerkat sentinel, constantly scanning the surroundings. Why couldn't she remember where she'd seen Lee before? The only reason she didn't bolt for the shed and hide was Ed by her side. His presence calmed her. When he wasn't hugging and greeting guests, he was by her side, a beacon of safety to relax her nerves. She smiled at people, but names slipped away from her as her attention was on the house, waiting for Lee to reappear.

When it came time for the ceremony, Dot approached her. "We can get a seat at the back," she said. "Lee will have his attention on the couple."

Ed nodded. "There are three seats there."

Was he kidding? "No. You're not sitting with me. You should be at the front with your family."

"You're my guest."

Tess shook her head. "I won't let you miss out." She straightened his galaxy patterned tie, full of purples and blues and thousands of stars. "Go."

Dot added, "Lara will need someone to sit next to."

"All right." His smile charmed Tess. "If you insist."

She took a moment to watch him walk away. His grey suit pants fit nicely, and though he wore a white shirt, it was rolled up to the elbows like the groomsmen's.

Sophisticated and sexy.

There was no denying it. He was handsome.

A soft piano instrumental of a popular love song played from a speaker set up at the front where the celebrant, groomsmen and groom waited. The entire crowd turned to watch Lara walk down the aisle, sprinkling red blossoms as she went, her grin so wide there nearly wasn't enough room on her face. Tess shifted, glad she was on the far corner of the seating where no one was looking at her.

Faith followed Lara, her gaze shifting from the girl in front of her, to Darcy who stood waiting next to Brandon. Georgie was next and she scanned the crowd as if looking for someone, and then finally the bride appeared.

Amy looked gorgeous. She had been sitting in a dressing gown when Tess left the kitchen, but now she wore a long, canary yellow dress with a cowl neckline which hugged her curvy figure and then fell in lines to her feet. Last night Amy had explained she'd bought the dress on a whim from an op shop in Byron Bay because she'd adored it so much, but had never worn it. It suited her and this more casual wedding style.

Across the garden, at the end of the aisle, Brandon only had eyes for Amy. His intensity and the warmth of his gaze created a longing in Tess. Would anyone look at her that way? She blinked. Where had that come from? She'd been so focused on her study and getting away from Singapore that she hadn't paid men much attention.

Until Ed. She glanced at him as Lara sat next to him and whispered something. He slid his arm around his niece and she leaned into him. Then the ceremony began. The small, strappy celebrant smiled as she spoke. "When I first met Brandon, he was wailing, and from the smell of him, he'd just soiled his nappy."

The guests laughed, and Dot murmured to Tess, "Lindsay owns the supermarket in town."

As the couple exchanged vows, Lee took photos, constantly moving to get a better angle, but never too close to be in the way. Whoever he was, he was good at this. He shifted his camera towards the guests and Tess ducked down, her heart racing.

A minute later, Dot murmured, "You can look now."

Tess raised her head as Brandon and Amy kissed, Lee's attention on the couple. She appreciated Dot's awareness of the surroundings.

The guests cheered, and the couple came down the aisle together, both beaming. Behind them trailed Georgie and Sam, and Faith and Darcy, with Lara following, her hand in Ed's. A sweet picture.

On the verandah, the couple formed a casual receiving line to greet all the guests, and Brandon's army mates moved the chairs to form a perimeter around the garden.

Ed appeared by her side. "I'm going to check the caterers," he said. "Do you want to come?"

"Please." Lee was taking photos of the guests as they congratulated the couple. "Thank you, Dot."

Dot smiled. "No worries."

Tess followed Ed away from the garden and across the red dirt to the building where Brandon's army friends were staying. Around the side was another room where a kitchen and sitting area were located. "Is this someone's house?"

"No, it's all part of the shearers' quarters," Ed explained. "At shearing time, we get a dozen people in to help. They stay in the rooms, and there's this kitchen and lounge where they can relax at the end of the day. Mum cooks for them all..." Sadness crossed his face. "Ah, I guess Amy or Faith will cook for them this season."

She squeezed his hand. "I'm sorry. Are you OK?"

He shrugged, and the silence stretched before he said, "I'm thrilled for Amy and Bran, but I keep thinking Mum and Dad should be here."

They should be. "I'm sure they're watching from somewhere."

"Still not the same." He strode over to speak with the caterer who was plating up various hors d'oeuvres.

Tess hovered at the door. Ed spoke confidently as he ensured the caterer had everything she needed and arranged for the servers to circulate with drinks and food. It was mid morning, so the food was light, and the drinks were plentiful. When Ed was satisfied everything was under control, they crossed back to the garden. People were mingling now, and the bridal party was having a few photos together.

Something had been bothering Tess since she'd seen Lee. "Why do you think Lee might be involved with Tan?"

Ed frowned and moved further away from the guests. "I hope he's not," he said. "But Stonefish have been a step ahead of us for the past couple of months."

"What have they done?" She needed to know the scope of Tan's business so she could figure out whether she could continue to stay in Australia when this was all over.

He sighed. "It started at the beginning of the year. Tan wanted to buy the station but my father refused to sell."

"Why did he want it?"

"We can't figure it out. Our neighbours are willing to sell, but Tan's not interested in her place, just the Ridge."

Odd.

"Then Mum and Dad had their car accident, and it turns out someone we trusted was asked to cut the brake line of their car."

Tess touched his arm, wishing she could take away

the pain on his face. "Tan asked them to?"

"Yeah, or someone working for Stonefish."

So Tan was responsible for more than just the woman's death.

"There's been a bunch of sabotage around the property and Stonefish ordered another person we trusted to kidnap Lara last month, so that Bran would sign the station over to them, but we got Lara back before he did."

"Why would your friends do that?" Tess asked.

"Because they owed Stonefish money, or Stonefish were threatening their loved ones. Some of them were asked to come to the station to make trouble."

No wonder Dot had seemed suspicious of her. "What could they want?"

"I wish we knew."

She had to figure out how she knew Lee. If he worked for Tan, she would have to leave immediately so she didn't bring any more trouble to the Stokes family.

"Come on. Let's enjoy the wedding." Ed swiped two glasses of champagne from a server and took Tess over to where Matt was chatting with an older couple. "Tess, these are Matt's parents, Helen and Cecil."

Tess smiled. "Nice to meet you."

"Are you Ed's girl?" Helen asked.

Her face heated. "We're friends."

The woman grinned, and her eyes sparkled. "Has he shown you the sky yet?"

What was she talking about?

"Not yet, Helen," Ed answered. "We only got in yesterday. It was a long drive."

"Make sure you get him to show you the emu," she continued. "He knows all the proper constellations."

Ed turned to her. "I spent a few nights with Helen and Cecil, and they explained how they view the stars. The positions tell them when different seasons are starting."

How interesting. She'd attended a couple of talks by Aboriginal elders while she'd been at university. "I'd love to learn more."

Helen smiled. "Get Ed to bring you over while you're here."

Excitement shimmered. "Thank you."

She chatted with the group while Ed excused himself to talk with Georgie. It appeared as if he was making sure everything ran as it was supposed to.

"He always has to know what's going on," Matt said, as his parents moved away to chat with others.

She blinked and found Matt grinning at her. She blushed and sipped her champagne. "Maybe that's because his family leave him out of everything."

Matt frowned. "The Stokes include everyone. It's their way."

She raised her eyebrows. "So why was Ed the only family member not involved in the bridal party?"

He scanned the crowd as if checking she was telling the truth. "I don't know."

"He wasn't involved in the drinking last night either," she said. "Was he invited?"

"I'm sure Darcy invited him."

Annoyance simmered. "And no one noticed he was missing until I pointed it out."

Matt held up his hands. "All right. I see your point. It's nice he's got someone to look out for him."

She nodded, though she wasn't certain why she was so annoyed all of a sudden. "Excuse me." With a quick check to ensure Lee was still taking photos, she hurried inside to the bathroom.

When she was done, the house was quiet, but outside voices murmured and people laughed. As she walked down the hallway, Lee entered from the other end. She froze, her heart leaping to her throat. Before she could duck into the nearest bedroom, the man waved. "Hi. Lovely wedding, isn't it?"

She nodded. Lara's bedroom was to her left, but it didn't have a lock on the door.

"This is going to sound weird, but you look familiar," Lee continued. "Are you from Perth?"

She shook her head, hoping to throw him off. "Singapore."

He smiled. "Were you at the Lim-Yang wedding?"

She gasped. "Yes. It was my sister's wedding."

He snapped his fingers. "That's where I know you from. I met so many people, and I'm hopeless with names. I'm Lee." He moved closer and held out his hand.

Could she trust him? Tess cautiously shook it, and his grip was firm. "What was your connection to the wedding?"

"Cousin of the groom," he said. "It was a great excuse for a holiday. Singapore is lovely. I took some fabulous photos while I was there."

"It is lovely," she agreed.

"We'll have to chat later," Lee said. "I haven't heard from the happy couple recently." He slipped past her and into the bathroom, closing the door behind him.

Tess slumped against the wall, her breath leaving her in a huff. Lee wasn't working for Tan. She was safe here a little longer. The relief made her light-headed, and she stayed where she was until the toilet flushed. Then she raced down the corridor and out of the house, before Lee could see her and think she'd been waiting for him.

Back in the garden, she found Ed talking with Dot. "Are you all right?" he asked.

"Yes. I just ran into Lee." At his concerned expression, she hurried to explain. "He was a guest at my sister's wedding. A cousin of my brother-in-law."

He grinned. "That's great."

"Might be worth calling your sister and confirming,"

Dot said.

Her spirits fell. "You think he's lying?"

"I think Stonefish has a way of knowing a lot about the people they deal with," Dot answered. "We shouldn't trust anything on face value." She paused. "Have you called your family yet?"

Tess shook her head.

"When you do, don't tell them where you are. Just tell them you're safe."

Unease swirled in her belly. "Why?"

"Just being cautious."

Ed slipped an arm around her waist. "Why don't you call them now?"

Dot nodded. "If you video call, don't do it outside. Make sure there's nothing in the background that will identify where you are."

Tess wanted to be sick. Could her parents really be involved with Tan? But even if they were, surely they would never put her in danger. Though they would probably believe Tan's word over hers, if he'd already contacted them. In their eyes she was still a child with an active imagination, and Tan was a respectable member of society. "I don't have my phone."

"You can use mine. Let's go into the lounge room," Ed said. "It's private."

She nodded. Lee was chatting with Darcy, a drink in his hand. She followed Ed inside and waited while he downloaded the app she used to call her family. Her mother would be horrified to hear what had happened, and Tess wasn't certain if her father was working this morning, so she called her sister instead. Joy answered almost immediately. "Tess! Where are you?" Joy's makeup was flawless, and she was at a restaurant somewhere by the harbour.

Tess smiled. "In Australia."

Joy made a face. "You know what I mean. Mum called

to say Tan said you'd run off with a man!"

So that was the story he was going with. She supposed it was kind of true. "That's not the whole story," she said. "Can I ask you something first?"

"No. Dad is upset. He said I must call the second I hear from you."

"Joy, please. Focus. Is Dylan with you?"

Her sister nodded and shifted the phone to show her husband.

"Do you have a cousin, Lee? Tall, lean, black hair?" It wasn't much of a description to go on.

"Yes. He lives in Australia. Did you meet him at the wedding?"

"Yeah." She hesitated. "Saw him again at the restaurant, and he looked familiar. He had a camera with him."

Dylan grinned. "Sounds like him. He's a photographer and has a camera stuck to his hand."

"Why ask about him?" Joy asked, turning the camera back to her. "Is he the one you ran off with?"

"No! It's been bugging me, that's all."

"So where are you? Mum's frantic."

"Somewhere safe." How much should she tell her sister? She didn't want Joy involved. "Tell Mum not to worry, and I'll call her later." She hung up before her sister could say anything else.

Ed shifted from where he stood by the door, watching the hall. "That corroborates Lee's story."

She wasn't looking forward to calling her parents, particularly not if Tan had lied to them first. Her mother did get hysterical over the slightest thing, and Tess running off with a man would be a big thing. She sighed.

"What's up? It's good Lee isn't a suspect anymore."

"Yeah, but I have to call my parents, and it won't be pleasant." And what if they confirmed they were somehow involved with this Stonefish company? Would that mean they were criminals? Would they ask her to do something to the Stokes family?

Ed's smile was sympathetic. Outside, people called for speeches. What was she doing, dragging Ed into her mess? "Go outside and enjoy the speeches," she said. "I'll be out after I've made my call."

He glanced down the corridor. "You're sure?"

She nodded. "Mum's going to freak out. You don't need to witness it."

He smiled. "Come and get me if you need me," he said. "I'm here for you." Ed waited until she nodded and then left the room.

She placed a hand on her chest.

How did she get so lucky to find this white knight?

There was no way she would let Tan hurt him further.

Chapter 11

Ed wandered outside and around the verandah to rejoin the wedding. Tess had asked a lot of questions about Stonefish, and now didn't want him there as she talked to her family. Could she be working for Tan, and calling him now? He hesitated, glancing back towards the house. Should he go back, eavesdrop?

He crashed into Sam, who stepped onto the verandah. "Sorry."

Sam grinned. "You want to do the speech instead?"

Everyone was gathered, waiting. Ed cringed and shook his head, joining Georgie on the lawn. He couldn't go back inside now and he definitely didn't know enough about his brother to do a best man's speech.

Sam waited for silence. "Unlike Lindsay, I can't claim to have seen Brandon in a nappy, but I could probably top her with stories about other unfortunate circumstances I've found him in."

While the crowd chuckled, Ed wondered whether he could say the same. What stories did he have of Brandon? Brandon and Darcy had spent most of their time together, roaming the station after school. Charlie would go with them when he could, but Ed preferred to stay at home with his mum and Georgie. He had memories of them all together as a family, but few he could single out as just him and Brandon.

"We went through basic training together and from that moment, I knew he had my back, and I had his. Brandon would do anything for his teammates."

And yet he'd left his family without a backward glance. Over the years, Ed had tried not to let it bother him. Brandon had helped him settle into university in Perth, and they'd occasionally caught up for dinner, but now Brandon was back at the station as if he'd never left. Darcy accepted him, and Lara thought he was wonderful. Ed was back to being the only black sheep, the only one who couldn't handle the country. He shoved the unwelcome jealousy aside.

Perhaps he was still tired if he was feeling sorry for himself. Ed had lived for his visits home, his mum's cooking and mothering, catching up with Darcy, Georgie and Lara. When he'd got his dad hooked on astronomy, it had been something they could share. Heading back to Perth had become more difficult each time he left. Now though, everything was different.

Amy and Faith lived in the house, his parents weren't there to greet him, and he literally didn't have a bed to lie in anymore. Ed rubbed his chest. He didn't begrudge Amy and Faith's presence. He liked them both and loved how happy his brothers were. It would simply take some time to adjust.

People laughed at something Sam said, and Brandon shoved him playfully. Ed blinked, bringing his attention back to the speech, but it was too late. Sam stepped off the verandah and Georgie took his place as maid of honour. He studied his sister, her blue hair freshly dyed, and a cheeky grin on her face. No one would know she was struggling with the loss of their parents, but he knew the signs—her ragged nails from biting them, and he'd caught her twisting her hair into knots. He'd have to spend some time with her before he flew home.

With the speeches done, the cakes came out, little cupcakes with bright yellow icing. Amy and Brandon cut one in half and fed each other, and they passed the rest around to the guests. Tess hadn't returned. If her mother freaked as much as Tess expected, it would take some time to explain the situation, but maybe he could check how she was, and try to overhear some of the conversation. As he moved towards the house, Dot intercepted him.

"Lee is related to Tess's brother-in-law," Ed told her.

She nodded, as if satisfied. "And her parents?"

"She's still talking to them."

"Let me know how she goes."

Before she could walk away, Ed touched her hand. "Thanks, Dot. I appreciate everything you've done for my family."

She smiled and patted his arm. "Just doing my job." She strode away.

Someone turned on music, and the country tunes got people dancing. Amy and Brandon danced arm in arm, though the beat was fast.

Now was his chance to check on Tess. Ed headed inside. He found her sitting on the couch, staring at his phone. "Everything OK?"

She looked up. "Ah, yeah. All good." She glanced away.

Why wouldn't she look at him? He sat next to her, drawn by the uncertainty on her face. "What's wrong?"

Tess hesitated. She glanced at the door and then back at him. "Nothing. We should get back to the wedding." Tess handed his phone back to him. "I've logged out in case it can be traced."

Unease filled him. He deleted the app and then tucked the phone into his pocket.

They could hear the music from here, but Ed didn't have a great desire to return. Not now that suspicion had entered his mind. If Tess was working for Tan, the less she saw, the better. "There's no rush."

"Are you sure? I don't want you missing your brother's wedding."

"Brandon and I aren't close."

Tess hugged him. "Thank you, Ed. I feel safer with you here."

Surprised, he hugged her back. Warm and soft, she fit so perfectly against him, and he closed his eyes trying to keep hold of his neutrality. Could this all be an act to make him trust her? Tan might have identified him as the weakest link of the Stokes family.

He stepped away, the thought leaving him cold.

Outside, the music level rose to blaring and then cut off.

Tess jolted, and they both turned towards the silence.

Someone tapped on a glass. "It's time for us to go," Brandon called. "Check-in's at two."

A couple of whistled cat calls and Amy laughed.

"Amy and I want to thank you all for coming," Brandon continued. "We'll see you in a couple of days."

Ed turned his attention back to Tess, trying to see her as a potential spy rather than a beautiful, uncertain woman. She bit her lip, her cheeks flushed. "I'm sorry you missed the rest of the wedding."

Damn, it was difficult. She was sweet. "Let's go into the kitchen and put on the kettle. Everyone will want a cup of tea and a chat when they come inside." She slipped her hand into his, and it felt right holding her hand and walking with her through the house.

He needed to be certain she wasn't working for Tan, but he had no idea how to prove it. He should have checked who she had called before he'd deleted the app from his phone.

Tess sat at the table while Ed filled the kettle and took a jar of biscuits out of the cupboard. He doubted people would be hungry after all the food at the wedding, but it was a habit.

Matt and Dot were the first to wander in as the kettle boiled. Matt filled the coffee plunger and the tea pot Ed had readied and placed both on the table. So easy, so familiar.

Faith and Lara were next. "That was the best wedding, *ever*," Lara declared.

Ed chuckled. "It's the only one you've been to, La La."

She stuck her tongue out at him. "Still counts. I've got so many ideas for Dad's and Faith's wedding." She faced her soon-to-be stepmother. "It's going to be epic."

Faith grinned. "Don't get too carried away. It's not the wedding that matters, it's the vows we make to each other."

Lara nodded, her expression serious. "I'm going to help Dad with his, because he doesn't have a clue." She turned to Ed. "He wasn't even going to propose properly!"

Ed had heard the story several times already. "I'm sure you'll sort him out."

"Another man down," Heath announced as he strode into the kitchen.

"No rescue mission will succeed," Dobby said.

Sam laughed. "Brandon doesn't want to be rescued. He's exactly where he wants to be." He held the door open for Georgie and Darcy.

Georgie poured herself a mug of coffee. "One down, one to go," she declared, raising her glass to Faith and Darcy.

"Have you set a date yet?" Ed asked.

Faith shook her head. "Sometime later in the year," she said. "I want to set up my businesses and move all my stuff from Perth, sell my apartment…" She sighed. "Too much to do without worrying about organising a wedding."

"Besides, it's just a day," Darcy said, slipping his arm around his fiancée. "Faith's here with us and that's what matters."

Did anyone feel that way about him? Tess drew Ed's gaze. Stupid. She was still a potential threat.

Georgie stretched, as if preparing for some exercise. "Right, I have a rare afternoon free. Who wants to go to the beach?"

Ed shook his head. "Don't you get sick of the ocean?"

"She's got gills," Matt said. "I'm sure of it."

Georgie rolled her eyes. "These guys aren't up here for long. We need to show them how amazing Retribution Bay is."

"You're taking them out on the boat tomorrow, aren't you?" he retorted.

"Actually, they're going out with my dad." Faith glanced at Sam.

"Yeah, I wanted to talk to him about the business," Sam said. "I'm thinking of buying it."

Ed's eyes widened. "You going to move up here?"

"Maybe."

Tess shifted beside him and he explained. "Faith's father is selling his whale shark tour business and retiring. Georgie works on a different boat."

"I can ask Dad if there's room for more tomorrow," Faith said. "If you want to come."

"What about the other sharks?" Tess asked.

"Don't see many of them," Georgie said. "Plus they're not interested in us. They get plenty of food on the reef."

Tess glanced at Ed, and he nodded. "It's pretty safe."

She hunched her shoulders. "I can't swim."

"They've got life vests and pool noodles," Faith said.

"They'll take care of you."

She probably didn't have the money for it, but Ed did. "They go snorkelling on the reef as well," he said. "It'll be fun."

She flushed. "I don't have bathers."

"I've got plenty of pairs," Georgie said. "You can borrow some, or head into town with Ed and buy some."

"It's an experience not to be missed," Ed added. If she was Tan's victim, he wanted her to have some fun while she was here, and if she was working for him, the less time spent at the Ridge the better.

"All right. If they have room."

Faith called her father and not long after had arranged for them all to join the tour the next day.

Dot stood. "I have to get back to town and chase up a few things."

Ed nodded. "I need to exchange the hire van." Normally he didn't bother with a hire car when he was in town, because he could borrow one at the Ridge, but he wanted to have something available in case Tess needed it. He'd get an automatic. "We could get you some bathers," he said to Tess.

"All right."

The others decided to go swimming, so it wasn't long before they went their separate ways. Ed and Tess changed into more casual clothing and followed Dot's blue sedan most of the way to town. Ed stopped at the airport to swap cars, and on their journey into town, Tess asked, "How much is the tour?"

He shrugged. "Don't worry about it. I'll pay."

She shook her head. "You've already done so much for me, Ed. I want to pay. I have money saved."

"It's about two hundred dollars," he lied, halving the price.

She swallowed. "That's a lot."

"Faith's dad might give everyone a discount. I'll ask."

And if he wasn't, maybe he'd tell her he was, and pay most of her fare.

"All right."

He parked at the small shopping centre in the middle of town and took Tess into the shop which catered to tourists with swimming gear ranging from bathers to surfboards and diving gear. Ed gave her space to browse, not sure if she would appreciate him hanging so close by while she looked. Instead he chatted to the guy behind the counter, someone Georgie had gone to school with.

"Ed?" At some stage Tess had gone into the change room. She now wore a brightly coloured bathing suit, which, while modest, gave him a great view of her trim body.

He moved closer. "The colour looks good on you." An understatement. She was gorgeous, and her shyness made him want to protect her even more.

"It's not too bright?"

"It's perfect," he said. "Are you comfortable in it?" She nodded.

"Then go for it."

A few minutes later, Tess paid cash for the bathers and a towel, and then Ed took her to get a new mobile phone. When they were done, he led her across the mall to the bakery. "You can't come to Retribution Bay and not try something from here."

Tess examined the items in the display cabinets and pursed her lips. "There's a lot of choice."

"I can recommend the custard tarts." He ordered a coffee and a tart, and Tess ordered a cream-filled doughnut, and then they sat outside at a table.

A loud bang made Ed jump.

Tess stiffened with a yelp, and scanned the surroundings, her eyes wide and fearful.

Across the way, someone picked up the box they'd dropped.

"Everything OK?"

She shook her head, her hand shaking. "Tan's out there somewhere. We should be careful."

She was right. He'd been so caught up with his concerns she might be a spy that he'd forgotten the potential danger. "Let's take the food to go. Head back to the Ridge."

"OK."

Ed headed inside and requested the drinks to go. All the way back to the car, Tess scanned the surroundings, her steps fast.

Afraid.

He hated to see it, but it gave him hope she was telling the truth.

"Which way's the beach?" Tess asked as they drove away from the shopping centre. She hunched down, hiding her face.

"This way." Ed detoured to the town beach. The turquoise ocean spread out before them, and Tess relaxed as he pulled into the near empty car park. She smiled. "It's beautiful. I never get to the ocean when I'm in the city."

"Where were you living?"

"Balga," she said.

"Well, you can go to the beach as much as you like while you're here."

How long would that be? Dot hadn't updated them at the wedding, so he had no idea how things were progressing. In two weeks he had to be back at work.

"Ed, I don't know what to do." The soft admission made him put the car into park and turn to her.

"The police are involved now," he said. "You're not in this alone."

"I'm sure you didn't realise what a mess you were getting into when you offered me a lift." Her wry smile warmed his heart.

"I haven't had much adventure lately." Work was a daily grind. The only fun he had was playing on the computer or volunteering at the observatory. He was already tired of answering the same questions repeatedly on the help desk. He hated to admit he might have made a mistake with his choice of career. But computers had always been his escape from the Ridge, a way to explore the world.

He'd enjoyed learning to code and creating programs, but finding a job doing what he loved had been difficult.

"I'm sure it was more adventure than you bargained for," Tess said. "Thank you."

He shrugged. He wasn't a hero.

A black car with dark tinted windows pulled in next to them. The kind of car mobsters always drove in movies. Ed's heart pounded. "Duck."

Tess gasped and buried her head in her lap as Ed put the car in reverse, and hit the accelerator. As soon as he'd backed out, the car's doors opened and two young kids leapt out, carrying towels.

False alarm. He exhaled, as the parents got out calling for the kids to wait.

It was definitely time to head back to the Ridge. As he drove out of town, Tess said, "There aren't many places in Singapore this quiet. I'm so used to people everywhere."

He wanted to know more about her. "When was the last time you were home?"

"At the beginning of the year."

"Do you miss your family?"

She shrugged. "We're not close. I thought studying in Perth would give me a chance to see some of the world and have independence." She sighed. "But my parents insisted I stay with Tan, and work at his restaurant. I went from my strict family to him."

He understood her frustration. "When they arrest

Tan, I'll show you around this area." He pointed to the ranges in the distance. "That's the Cape Range National Park," he said. "The view from up there is gorgeous. Then we can go around the point to Ningaloo Reef and go snorkelling."

"How close to the shore do the whale sharks come?" Tess asked.

"Depends. The tours leave from the other side of the peninsula." He finished his coffee. "And can go quite far from shore."

She hugged herself. "It sounds scary."

"You'll be fine. I won't let you out of my reach."

"But you might miss seeing the shark."

"I've seen one before." He smiled.

Tess hesitated for a second and then smiled. "Thanks, Ed." Her smile warmed him, wrapping around him like a hug.

He prayed she was telling the truth. Because right now, he didn't regret for a moment giving her a lift.

Chapter 12

Tess's stomach swirled with nerves and nausea the next morning as she sat at the breakfast table. Outside it was still dark, but the kitchen was warm and bright with everyone chatting about the day to come. The farmers got ready for work, and Brandon's teammates were excited about the whale shark tour.

"Reckon we'll see any manta rays?" Dobby asked.

"I hope we see some tiger sharks," Sam said with a wink at Tess.

She stiffened. No. That definitely wasn't what she wanted to see. She wasn't used to boats and the ocean. Had no idea what to expect from swimming with the biggest fish in the sea. Fear sparked, and she pushed away the rest of her barely eaten toast.

"Cut it out, Sam," Ed said. "Tess is nervous enough as it is."

Heath punched Sam playfully on the arm. "You forgot about your needle phobia?" he asked. "I can remind you if you like."

Sam shook his head and held his hands up in surrender. "Sorry, Tess. I was just kidding. We'll all take care of you."

Some of the nerves leached away. She forced a smile, knowing they weren't trying to be mean. She wasn't used to being teased, and if she wasn't so nervous, she might have enjoyed it.

As it was, she'd been a mess since yesterday. She'd lied to Ed.

She hadn't called her parents, hadn't told them she was safe, or what Tan had done. As she'd sat on the couch, she'd kept thinking about them sending her to live with Tan, about Ed telling her other people had been forced to do what Tan wanted them to do by threatening loved ones, and she couldn't bring herself to call them.

What if they were involved and asked her to hurt Ed or his family in some way?

She couldn't do it. Not after they'd been so kind.

So she'd lied and avoided talking about her family as much as she could.

"Let's go," Sam called.

They piled into the four-wheel drive Ed had hired from the airport. Ed ensured Tess had the front passenger seat while he drove. She felt kind of guilty about the three large men squashed in the backseat, but they didn't seem to care.

The red dirt and dull green leaves on the shrubs were familiar to her now. She smiled as the ocean appeared on the right side of the car, so out of place when it felt as if they were in the middle of a desert. As they drove around the tip of the peninsula towards the harbour on the Indian Ocean side, they passed enormous towers touching the ground at a point and were kept balanced and in place by long metal cables. "What are they?"

"They're submarine communication towers," Ed said. "They send signals underwater."

Interesting. She'd never considered how to transmit underwater before.

Finally, they arrived at the boat harbour where buses

and cars with boat trailers filled the car park. She spotted Georgie over by a bus talking to a group of people who were going on her tour. Another group stood by a different bus, and there was no one standing alone, keeping watch for a Singaporean student on the run.

But she scanned again, just to make sure, looking in cars to make sure no one was inside.

No matter how many times she told herself Tan couldn't know she was here, she couldn't shake the fear.

Ed pointed to a boat with a bright blue and green logo of a whale shark on the side. "We're going on that one." He led them over to a tanned woman with short blonde hair peeking out beneath her baseball cap. She wore a polo shirt with the same logo as the boat, and denim shorts which only just covered her butt, exposing her long legs. Fit and gorgeous, perhaps in her early thirties, like Brandon's teammates. Next to Tess, Heath nudged Sam and said something under his breath that she didn't catch, but his grin spoke volumes.

"Hey, Gretchen," Ed said.

"Ed. I didn't realise you were coming today."

"Couldn't miss it. This is Tess, and Brandon's military mates, Sam, Heath and Dobby."

"Welcome," she smiled. "I'll take you out now before the bus with the other guests arrives."

Good. When she was on the boat, she would be safe. Ed had promised to stay next to her, so no one could hurt her.

Tess's steps slowed as she walked along the jetty to where an inflatable boat was tied. It was a decent size, and the ocean was smooth, but the tour boat was a distance from the shore. A different fear gripped her. Was it really safe for her to go?

Ed glanced back and stopped, waiting for her to catch up. He took her hand. "Nervous?"

She nodded as her pulse raced for an alternative

reason, but the butterflies in her stomach settled.

"Gretchen can get you a life jacket."

She didn't want to be the odd one out, the one too frightened to go on a boat which must be safe. They did this every day. She would not be a wimp. Da Lim would take it all in her stride. "I'll be fine. You'll sit next to me?"

"Sure."

So easy going. She closed her eyes. Could she forget about being on the run today? Swimming with a shark was a huge adventure, one she should enjoy. Her mother would be horrified if she knew about it. Tess smiled. For the first time, she was doing something she had hoped to do—experiencing Australia.

She climbed onto the inflatable and sat between Sam and Ed, with the other two men balancing the opposite side. Once on board, she was given a long-armed, long-legged suit to wear, which was kind of like a wetsuit, but with a thinner Lycra fabric. "We haven't had any sightings of Irukandji recently, but better to be safe," Gretchen explained.

"Irukandji?" Tess asked.

"Jellyfish," Gretchen replied.

Tess stiffened. Was that something else she needed to be terrified of?

Ed murmured, "Don't worry, they're rare at this time of year."

Was there any animal in Australia which wasn't deadly?

After the rest of the dozen passengers joined the boat, the crew was introduced, and Gretchen took them through a safety briefing. Then they were given the equipment they needed; mask and snorkel, as well as flippers. Tess looked at Ed for guidance.

"The core thing is making sure the mask fits properly, so it doesn't leak," Ed said. He helped her put it on and demonstrated how to tighten it and how to breathe through the snorkel. It didn't seem too complicated.

After taking off the mask, she inhaled deeply, smelling the salty air, and gazed at the crystal clear ocean. The boat barely rocked as it cut its way through the still water. Dark patches in the water were the coral reef, and she spotted fish moving under the water. Sam chatted to the captain, Faith's father, an older man about retirement age.

Then the boat slowed and people donned masks. Gretchen gave her a life jacket and checked she did it up correctly and also handed her a pool noodle. "For extra flotation."

Other crew were helping the guests, and there was a woman with a large waterproof camera who would take photos for them.

Dobby and Heath were the first to get in, sliding off the marlin board into the water and hovering by some nearby coral. Tess waited where she was until most of the guests were in the water, and then she and Ed went down to the board.

Heath gave her a thumbs up and she realised he and Dobby were waiting for her like they promised. "I'm fine," she called. "You go."

They swam off and her heart thumped as she slipped on the flippers and adjusted the mask. She looked at Ed.

"Ready?" he asked.

"Yes." She stuck the snorkel in her mouth and pushed off the back of the board and into the surprisingly warm water. She half expected to sink to the bottom, but with her life jacket she floated, bobbing on top of the water.

"Lie on your stomach, and put your head under the water," Ed said.

She flopped forward and the sandy bottom appeared with clarity only a couple of metres below her. A fish darted along the bottom, and she kicked, trying to follow it. The movement propelled her faster than she expected and she stopped, awkwardly looking up to find Ed swimming next to her, close enough to touch. He took the snorkel from his mouth. "You're doing well. Want to kick over to the coral?" He pointed ahead of them to where most of the group had gathered.

She could do this. She nodded and got into the rhythm, kicking slowly through the water. The life jacket kept her afloat, and with the sand not far away, Tess felt confident she wouldn't drown. Ed tapped her arm and pointed to a stingray gliding along the bottom. She gasped, her heart racing, uncertain if it was in fear or excitement. Then they reached the coral, and she forgot about being scared.

Colour and life. More fish than she'd ever seen in her life swam around the brightly coloured corals. It seemed almost like a competition what would be the most vibrant, the coral or the fish. Tiny fluorescent blue fish darted around coral which looked like branches, and bigger rainbow fish swam around orange coral which reminded her of a brain.

So much was happening, Tess didn't know where to look first. Then she spotted a turtle lazily floating nearby, and she stopped breathing. Seeing things like this on TV didn't come close to experiencing it firsthand. It was all so visceral and real. She grabbed Ed and pointed frantically. He nodded, and he smiled at her, the motion awkward with the snorkel in his mouth. But their eyes met, and the connection was instant; understanding, but also a deeper attraction. She longed to slip her hand into his, and swim side-by-side together, but perhaps she was reading him incorrectly. Instead she circled the coral with him until Gretchen directed them back to the boat.

"What did you think?" Ed asked as he towelled himself dry.

"Incredible," she breathed. "I never expected such beauty."

"It's pretty special," he agreed. "Do you want to go up to the top deck? You can sometimes see turtles or manta rays from there."

She nodded and followed him up the steps to an open viewing platform. Dobby and Heath were already there with Sam, talking to one of the crew. Sam was asking about their schedule.

"I think Sam might be serious about buying the business," Ed said, steering her over to the railing where they could listen.

"Isn't he in the army?"

"He's getting out next month," Ed said. "He was going to head over east to help his pregnant sister, but she doesn't want his help, so he needs to find something else to do with his time."

Running a tour boat was a far cry from the army, but maybe that was the point. The boat was heading away from the shore into darker, deeper water. She shivered.

Ed wrapped an arm around her shoulders. "Cold? We can go down out of the wind."

"No, I'm fine." She liked his arm around her. "Do you do this often?"

He shook his head. "No, I went out with Georgie once, but most of the time I stay around the Ridge or snorkel off the beach."

"It looks like it's getting deep." She couldn't hide the nerves in her tone.

"Yeah, the continental shelf drops away not far off shore. But don't worry, you'll be fine. You did really well snorkelling."

His confidence in her was reassuring.

"We've found a shark," the crew was saying. "Heading there now."

Tess frowned, and Ed explained. "They have planes in the air looking for them. The pilots feed the coordinates to the boats."

Gretchen called them all together to explain what would happen when they arrived at the whale shark. "We're splitting you into two groups. One group will swim with the shark and the other will be dropped ahead of it." She smiled. "Then the boat will loop around to pick up the first group and drop them ahead of the second group."

Tess's hands clenched. They would be left in the middle of the ocean, alone, with a nine metre long creature. This was a bad idea.

Gretchen called out names for each group. Tess was separated from the others.

"Gretchen, I'll stick with Tess," Ed called.

She nodded and made an adjustment to her notes.

"I'll be right by your side," Ed murmured. "I won't let anything happen to you." He rubbed her back, and she realised she was panting. Not so subtle in her fear.

"Maybe you should go without me. I don't want to slow you down."

"Trust me, Tess. You don't want to miss this. It's incredible."

She'd trusted him enough to get in a car with him and drive over a thousand kilometres. "OK."

They suited back up, grabbing goggles and flippers, with Tess adding her life jacket, and readying themselves on the marlin board. Then the call came, "Go, go, go," and Tess didn't have time to be scared. She slid into the water and kicked furiously in the direction the guide swam, keeping in line with her as they'd been instructed. The clear, dark blue water seemed endless. She couldn't see anything except tiny spores of something, maybe plankton, floating in the water. Ed squeezed her arm and pointed. Out of the blue a massive mouth appeared, followed slowly by a body.

Tess stared, unable to comprehend something so big was only metres from her. It swam past, the white markings on its back contrasting with the blue surrounding it. Then Ed nudged her and she swam alongside it, floundering a bit as she tried to keep up. One slow stroke of its tail propelled it far faster than she could kick, and her breath came in gasps.

Then the guide called a halt, and it was their turn to wait for the boat to pick them up. When she was safely sitting on the marlin board, she pulled her snorkel out of her mouth. "That was amazing!"

Ed's grin warmed her even further. "Told you."

"Thank you. I can't believe how big and gentle it was."

"Ready for your next go?"

She glanced at him. "We go again?"

"Yeah. We can swim a few times if the shark doesn't dive."

She laughed. "I can't wait." She hugged him.

***

Ed's heart thumped harder as Tess grinned at him, the joy on her face making all the tension of the past few days disappear. Her eyes positively sparkled, and he fought the urge to kiss her. He shifted forward so his legs dangled into the water as the order to prepare came again. "Ready?"

She nodded and was the first into the water when the guide called them to go. Ed grinned, following her. Her fear had vanished as she kicked harder to reach the rendezvous point with the shark. He understood how she felt. That first moment, as the shark materialised out of the deep blue, always took his breath away. But now he enjoyed it on two levels, watching Tess's reaction at the same time. He was glad he'd convinced her to do this.

All too quickly, they had used their allocated time with the whale shark and were back on board.

"I can't believe I just did that," Tess gasped as she

stripped off her flippers and mask and placed them in the container.

"It was pretty epic," Ed agreed as he helped her up the steps onto the main area. Lunch was being served, and he handed her a plate so she could help herself to the selection of salads and meats.

Heath said something to her, and she high fived him, grinning.

"She's thrilled," Sam commented, coming to stand by Ed.

"Yeah," he agreed, unable to take his eyes off her as she chatted to the woman next to her. He hadn't seen this bubbly, babbling side of her, and he liked it.

"Dot's still not sure about her," Sam added.

His words sank in, and Ed looked at him, his mood deflating as he remembered his suspicions. "You think that's an act?"

Sam shrugged. "I hope not, but it's worth remembering before you get too attached."

Sam saw things far too clearly. "Yeah. Thanks." Ed scowled. "So, are you going to buy the boat?"

Sam pursed his lips. "I'm seriously considering it. Giving people experiences like that, making them as happy as Tess, would be a nice change from what I was doing."

Ed hadn't asked Brandon about his time in the army, but knew they'd been to several hot spots over the years. "Lots of hours, and few days off."

Sam shrugged. "I'm used to it. Plus, this area is beautiful. I don't much like the cold."

Brandon would enjoy having his best friend near as well. "Good luck with it."

Tess wandered over, balancing a plate full of food. Ed made room for her so she could sit down. "Worked up an appetite?"

Her blush spread over her cheeks. "Yeah. You should

get something before it runs out."

"Little chance of that happening." The catering was plentiful. He helped himself and then sat next to her while she chatted with Sam and Heath.

Her shyness had disappeared amongst her enthusiasm.

"What are you studying at uni?" Sam asked.

"Science and Australian history. My ancestor was a pearl diver at Cossack in the 1870s."

"Where's that?" Heath asked.

"Between here and Broome."

"That's pretty cool," Heath said.

She nodded. "She's the only rebel in my family. Didn't want to marry and have a family, wanted to make her own way in the world, make her fortune."

Ed knew the feeling. "So, did she make her fortune?"

Tess grinned, and she leaned forward like Lara did when she got excited. "It's not clear. Her journal hints at a windfall, but all the references are vague, as if she didn't want to put the exact details on paper."

No matter what Sam thought, Tess's passion was genuine. Ed wanted to show her the information they had on the Retribution. He loved this fearless, enthusiastic side.

"We've found some manta rays," Gretchen announced. "If you want, we can stop so you can swim with them."

Tess's eyes widened, and she called, "Yes, please."

Ed chuckled as she thrust her empty plate on the counter and turned to take his. She frowned when she noticed he wasn't finished. "Get ready, and I'll be right behind you," he said, shovelling the rest of the food into his mouth. He'd probably regret eating so fast once they were in the water, but he didn't care.

They swam a short distance to where an entire group of manta rays were circling, almost in a dance. Tess's gaze was affixed to the animals as they looped. Ed wished he had a camera to capture her expression.

They took turns with the rays until it was time to get back on the boat and head to their final snorkeling spot. When Tess had dumped her gear in the containers, she turned to him and flung her arms around his neck. "Thank you."

He stepped back, surprised by her affection, but couldn't resist hugging her back. "You're most welcome."

She turned her head and their gazes locked. Her eyes widened, and she glanced at his lips and then back at him. With a smile, she kissed him, no hesitation, full of joy and excitement.

Ed jolted, surprised, but his arms slid around her, tasting her cool, salty lips. This was what he wanted. She was what he wanted.

Heath hollered, "Go Tess!" and she broke the kiss, cheeks red.

She tucked her hair behind her ear and cleared her throat. "I appreciate it." She turned and playfully shoved Heath, who was still grinning at them.

Sam raised his eyebrows at Ed.

Yeah, he knew. He was supposed to be careful.

But damn it, he didn't want to be.

Chapter 13

As they tied up at the boat mooring that afternoon, Ed's phone rang. Dot. He shifted away from where everyone was gathered, ready to get on the inflatable boat and be transferred to the shore. "Hey, Dot."

"Ed, are you back in town yet?"

"Just arrived at the mooring."

"Can you and Tess swing past the station before you head to the Ridge?"

Ed's gut clenched. "Yeah, but I've got Sam and the guys with me."

"Tell them to get a drink at the pub. I'll see you when you get here." She hung up before he could ask what it was about.

Sam turned to him. "What happened?"

The man was always alert. "Need you to drop Tess and me at the station while you get a beer."

He frowned, but nodded.

Tess chatted happily with one of the other passengers, a girl about her age, and he didn't want to burst her bubble yet. When they got to town, he drove to the police station and gave Sam the keys.

Tess straightened from where she'd been dozing

against the window. "What are we doing here?"

"Dot asked us to stop by before we went home."

She stiffened and clenched her hands, all relaxation gone. "What about?"

"She didn't say." He turned to Sam. "I'll call you when we're done."

"Take your time."

On the pavement, he slipped his hand into Tess's. "It'll be fine." They pushed into the air-conditioned station, and Ed greeted Matt's sister, Senior Constable, Nhiari Roe. "We're here to see Dot."

Nhiari buzzed them in, and flicked back her long braid which had fallen over her shoulder. "She's been waiting for you." They followed her through to Dot's office.

Dot stood. "Thanks for coming in. Take a seat." She glanced at Nhiari. "I'll take it from here."

Tess's hand trembled, and he rubbed his thumb over the back of it before releasing it and sitting in the hard plastic chair.

Dot placed a photo in front of Tess. "Do you recognise this woman?"

Tess jolted away from the table and gasped. "Yes, that's the woman who was shot!"

The sergeant nodded, as if she had guessed it already.

"Who is she?" Ed asked.

"Charmaine Lansdell. Married to Roger, the man who tried to get Brandon to sign the contract selling the Ridge."

Ed's mouth dropped open. It was all connected. Last month, Stonefish Enterprises had kidnapped Lara, and Roger had presented the contract to Brandon to sign. Turned out he'd been little more than a minion, asked to do it because he owed someone money. "Why kill her?"

"Because Roger told us what he knew," Dot said. "It might not have been much, but I gather the murder was to show what happens to people who cross Stonefish." She sighed. "She was reported missing this morning, and fit Tess's description. When I saw the name, I had a hunch."

"You haven't found her body?" Tess asked.

"Not yet."

"So what now?" Ed asked.

"We'll continue searching for Salvatore, and for Charmaine's body."

"What do I do in the meantime?" Tess asked.

Dot pursed her lips. "When do you go back to university?"

"Not for two weeks."

"I can arrange for a new passport," Dot said. "You could return home—if you think you'll be safer there."

Tess hesitated and bit her lip.

Ed didn't want her to go, but he was surprised she wasn't more keen on the idea. Sam's warning buzzed in his head.

The thought Tess might be playing him made him feel ill, but he still couldn't leave her to fend for herself. "You're welcome to stay at the Ridge," he said. "I've got another ten days here, and hopefully by then, this will all be resolved."

"It's a lot to ask," Tess said.

"We're both fighting the same person. It makes sense to team up." He would keep a close eye on her, make sure she had no opportunity to sabotage anything.

"We've put the photo of Salvatore on social media, so hopefully someone will spot him," Dot said. "You should be safe at the Ridge as long as Tan doesn't decide to visit again."

"He'd be stupid if he did," Ed said. "Darcy and Bran are likely to run him off with the rifle."

Dot placed her hands over her ears. "I did not hear that."

Ed grinned and waited for Tess to decide. She stared out the window, and finally, she nodded. "All right. I'll stay, if you're sure there's room."

"Plenty. Georgie's gone home, so there's a spare bed in the house, and a couple in the shearers' quarters."

"I'll keep you posted." Dot stood and held out her hand for Tess to shake.

Once outside, Ed called Sam and discovered they'd gone to the brewery for a drink. It wasn't far so they could walk.

Tess was silent beside him.

"How are you feeling?"

"Tired," she said. "Relieved the woman has a name, and the police know who she is. I kept thinking her family may never discover what happened to her."

"They will now, thanks to you," Ed said.

The shadows fell long over the street as the sun sank towards the horizon. It was finally cooling down, but the heat hadn't been noticeable out on the boat.

"Ed, I feel awful bringing your family into this." The concern on her face touched his heart.

"We were already involved," he said. "We've been fighting Stonefish for months. But we still can't figure out why they want the Ridge."

"Tan never discussed business with me, but I heard him talking about a business in the north. Maybe it has something to do with that."

Ed frowned. "I'll mention it to Dot later. Maybe she can find out what it is."

A car slowed as it drove past, and Tess gripped his arm, but relaxed as Gretchen wound down her window. "Sam didn't abandon you in town, did he?"

Ed grinned. "No, just showing Tess around. We're meeting him at the brewery."

"Thanks for today," Tess called. "It was wonderful."

Gretchen smiled. "Glad you liked it. I've got to go

pick up my boy, but do you want a lift?"

Ed turned to Tess, who hesitated. "Is it far?"

"Just around the corner," he replied.

Tess scanned the street ahead. "We'll walk, but thank you for the offer."

"All right. Have fun." With a wave, Gretchen drove away.

"People are so friendly here," Tess said.

"Mostly," Ed replied. "We're so isolated, it pays to be on good terms with people." He picked up his pace. Tess was right to be wary. They still didn't know where Salvatore was.

"I never considered living in a small town before," she said. "Did you ever get lonely living on the station?"

All the time. He bit back the words. Was that fair? After Charlie died, he had Georgie, and then Lara had been born, but still he felt like the odd one out. "Sometimes. Georgie was into the ocean and horses, and Mum was often busy taking care of Lara when Darcy was working. I had my computer."

She nodded. "I had my books. I always wanted more adventure than my sister, and Mum insisted I had to get a sensible, well-paying job."

"Hence majoring in biochemistry, not history," Ed said.

"Yeah."

Perhaps they were more alike than he'd realised. "Well, you're getting your adventure now."

She rolled her eyes and chuckled. "More than I want."

"When we get home, I'll show you those trunks. You might find something interesting in them."

She squeezed his hand. "Thanks, Ed."

Sam's warning whispered in his ear, and he pushed it aside. He wouldn't believe Tess was playing him.

It would hurt too much.

***

Tan Lewis slammed the phone onto the table, anger pulsing through his veins. How hard was it to find one stupid girl? He'd never expected Tess to have the guts to run, didn't know why that night had been the one time she'd chosen to come back.

He'd told Salvatore not to bring Charmaine to the restaurant. The last thing he needed was for her to be associated with his place of business, but Salvatore had ignored his wishes again.

Tan was surprised Salvatore hadn't run for it, considering he'd fucked up twice, but Salvatore assured Tan he would find Tess and clean up the mess.

He'd better. Tan had few other options. It was like looking for a needle in a desert.

If his boss found out about this latest cock-up, Tan was screwed.

The anger still coursed, and he stood and strode across his living room. None of this was his fault. He'd been following orders, like he always did. He couldn't be blamed if his boss kept changing his mind.

Buy the land, he'd been told. Through any means necessary.

Retribution Ridge was strategically important to their northern operations, so he'd done what was requested, sending people to monitor the situation when Bill Stokes had refused to sell. He'd set up the fake company to extort their remaining hard-earned cash, something which should have tipped them right into bankruptcy. But somehow Bill had discovered it, said he was going to the police, so of course he had to go. The last thing Tan needed was police interest.

He'd underestimated the Stokes family, particularly Brandon Stokes. He hadn't factored him in at all, being the estranged son. That had been his only mistake.

The investigative spotlight had brushed by him, but he'd hidden his tracks so they hadn't seen him. Then the botched kidnapping, and Roger's confession had put him smack bang in the middle of the spotlight, almost blinding him.

People had to know what happened if they crossed him, hence the need to make an example of Charmaine.

Salvatore had been too eager to please. Tan should have left it to one of his more experienced men, but Salvatore had wanted to prove himself.

Now he was in Newman, lying low, because his picture was all over the police social media. Tan had ordered him to stay hidden for a few days and then head to Retribution Bay and contact their guy on the ground there. He might as well do something useful while he was in the area.

Tan had other men looking for Tess, but she could be anywhere.

Tan's phone rang again and when he saw the caller ID, the anger vanished, replaced with icy fear. His boss rarely called him.

He debated whether to pick up for a millisecond, but making his boss wait wasn't wise. "Boss."

Silence before the clipped tones. "Why did I hear about this latest mistake from someone else?"

Tan swallowed. "I hoped to find the girl before calling you."

"You've contacted her parents?"

He didn't know how his boss got his information, but he always knew the details of every interaction. "Yes. They haven't heard from her, but they've been told what to say when she calls."

"You still have her passport?"

"Yes. In my safe."

His boss made a sound of approval. "Australia is a very big country."

"She has to turn up sometime."

"Unless the police are hiding her."

"I have people working on it." His police contacts were still digging to find the name of the guy who'd reported Salvatore's attack on Tess, and the police officer who had taken Tess's statement. With the information he could track them down, but his police contact said all the information was being monitored, and didn't want to give himself away.

That cop should be more scared of Tan. Perhaps Tan should send him a reminder.

"Get them to work faster. How much closer are you to getting me the land?"

Tan wanted to lie, but he could almost guarantee his boss already knew the answer. "The money for the cattle was refunded last month."

Silence.

"We didn't want the authorities looking closer."

"And yet you failed spectacularly."

Tan's hand shook, and he moved out of the living room, away from the windows.

"Find the girl, silence her, and get me that land."

The only way to get the land would be to kill all the Stokes children and their partners, and while he didn't flinch away from that, it would bring more trouble than his boss wanted. "What about the station next to theirs? I've heard they want to sell."

"No. It must be the Ridge. Don't fail me, Tan." He hung up.

Tan went into the bathroom and vomited into the toilet. Then he wiped his mouth and opened his safe, checking his fake passport, identification and cash were all in order. He checked his grab bag to ensure everything was there. If he failed to resolve the situation, he would be dead. No more chances.

He rang his police contact at the station down the

road. "I need answers."

Chapter 14

Tess followed Ed over the brewery yard strewn with blue metal, the crunch of the stones announcing their arrival. Heath, Sam and Dobby sat nursing beers around a table made from a large wooden cable spool and the other tables held families or groups of friends. Heath raised a hand in welcome. "How'd it go?"

Ed lowered his voice. "They identified the woman who was shot." He explained where she fit in the story.

Tess couldn't quite believe everything was connected. It should scare her and prompt her to get as far away from the Ridge as possible, but being with Ed made her feel safe. It also helped that these army men had welcomed her, and it was as if she had three older brothers watching over her.

"We were going to order pizza if you aren't in a rush to get home," Dobby said. "It looks amazing and we're starving."

Ed checked with her, and she double-checked the tables for anyone suspicious. Nearby someone carried a pizza to their table, the scent of melted cheese and toppings making her stomach rumble. "Sounds good." Her skin was still covered in salt, her hair was a mess, and she wore shorts and thongs in a brewery, but no one seemed to care. In fact, it appeared as if it was normal. For once in her life, she fit in.

The brewery itself was a large metal shed, and most of the seating was outside under shade cloth sails. There were two counters where people could order food and drinks, and a pool table in the corner. The pair playing pool had just finished and were hanging up their sticks.

"Let's play," Heath said, getting to his feet and holding his hand out to her.

She stepped back. "I don't know how to."

"Then we'll have to teach you." Dobby grinned.

Their enthusiasm was difficult to ignore. "All right." She glanced at Ed. "Are you coming?"

"I'll order us some drinks and food. What do you want?"

"Anything." She didn't care. She didn't drink much alcohol, so whatever he chose would be new and interesting.

While Dobby set the balls on the table, Heath explained the rules, and then handed her a stick. "This is the cue. You hit the ball with the smaller end." He showed her how to hold it, and then sent the white ball hurtling towards the balls, cracking them apart. "Now decide if you're going for solid or striped balls," Heath said. "And use the white ball to hit the ball you choose into the pocket."

Did that mean she should go for the easiest shot? It was kind of awkward to get the stick sitting right, but with a bit of effort she managed it. Her strike barely budged the white ball, and it didn't hit anything.

Heath chuckled and reset the ball. "Try again."

Ed brought over her beer and set it on a nearby table. "I'm going to keep Sam company." He kissed her cheek, and she watched him go, a smile on her face. She couldn't believe she'd kissed him on the boat. She'd just been so full of joy that she'd thrown caution to the wind and channelled her inner Da Lim to take the chance. And he'd returned the kiss, rather than rejecting her. She hadn't imagined their mutual attraction. Her smile grew wider.

"Come on, lovebird. Pay attention," Heath said.

She screwed her nose up at him, and both men laughed. Tess focused on Heath's instructions, and it wasn't long before she sunk her first ball. When Dobby took his turn, she sipped her beer, the taste pleasant and cool. Over by their table, Sam studied her as Ed spoke to him.

She stiffened. There wasn't animosity in his gaze, just alertness. As if he was watching her, waiting for her to do something. Why?

"Your turn." Heath handed her the cue, and she caught Dobby glancing at Sam and shaking his head.

Goosebumps leapt on her skin. "What's going on?"

Heath frowned. "Dobby's had his shot, it's your turn."

She shook her head. "No. Why is Sam watching me?"

"Habit," Dobby said. "Hard to shift after years in the military."

Tess glanced at Heath. She didn't buy it. "But why me? Why not others in the brewery?" Something was going on. "Why are you being so nice to me?" Was it some kind of game to them?

Heath tried to shift the cue away from her, but she gripped it tighter. He held up his hands. "I don't know about the others, but you've been through a shit situation and you remind me of my little sister. She's living in the UK, and I hope if she was in a similar situation, people over there would help her."

The honesty on his face broke through her paranoia, and she squeezed his hand. "I'm sorry. I'm a little on edge."

"Understandable," Dobby said, "But we've got your back." He smiled.

"Yeah. I dub thee our honorary sister," Heath said, touching her shoulders and then her head. "Under our protection."

She smiled, warmed by the gesture. Her gaze went to Sam and Ed.

"And Sam's a suspicious git by nature," Heath whispered. "Now, are you going to play, or what?"

His banter released the remaining tension. She couldn't blame Sam for being suspicious. She'd brought trouble to his best friend's family.

On the journey back to the Ridge, fatigue hit her. Her head nodded several times, and each time she jerked awake. Next to her, Ed chuckled. "Rest against my shoulder."

She needed no further prompting, glad Sam had wanted to drive home. Ed smelled of saltwater, and his shoulder was the perfect height for a headrest. Her hand brushed his knee, and he covered it with his own. The movement and his warmth vanquished some of her fatigue, making her skin tingle in awareness.

It was about seven-thirty when they arrived at the homestead. She followed Ed into the kitchen, where he went straight to the kettle and switched it on.

"We're going to hit the showers," Sam called, and the guys headed to their quarters.

Darcy entered the room. "Did Dot get a hold of you?"

Ed scowled. "We had a great day, thanks for asking."

"Sorry." Darcy smiled at Tess. "Did you enjoy it?"

"It was the best thing I've ever done," she told him. "And yes, we stopped at the police station on our way back."

"What did she have to say?"

Tess let Ed explain as she got out the mugs and tea for the drinks.

Darcy sighed. "It's good they've got a name now." He turned to her. "You can stay here for as long as you need to. Stonefish have to be stopped, and you can help us."

She appreciated his support. She hadn't felt alone since she'd bumped into Ed at the airport.

"Is Lara sleeping in her room?" Ed asked.

"Yeah, she's just gone to bed."

Where would she sleep then?

"There's a room in the shearers' quarters, as well as your usual room," Darcy told Ed.

"We'll sort it out." Ed poured two mugs of tea. "Want one, Darce?"

He shook his head. "Faith and I have drinks in the lounge. You're welcome to join us."

"Maybe in a minute," Ed said. He set a mug on the table in front of Tess.

When Darcy was gone, she thanked him.

"You can sleep in the house," Ed said. "I'll take one of the rooms outside."

He'd already done so much for her, and she didn't want to kick him out of his own home. But she also wasn't thrilled about the idea of sleeping in the shearers' quarters, even though she'd be surrounded by military men. She hesitated. "The room has two beds, doesn't it?"

He nodded.

Her cheeks heated. "I don't mind sharing. It's your room, after all."

He studied her. "It wouldn't make you uncomfortable?"

"I feel safer with you around," she admitted.

He smiled. "Then I'll share."

So simple. She sipped her tea and settled into the chair.

"It's a clear night," Ed said. "I was thinking of getting

out the telescope. Do you want to come with me?"

"Where?"

"There's a spot behind the house where some sand dunes hide the light. It's a great place to star gaze."

She frowned. "Don't snakes come out at night?"

"Some do, but they'll steer clear." He grinned. "The stars are so bright here."

She couldn't believe he wasn't exhausted after their day on the boat, but his enthusiasm wrapped around her. "All right."

"Why don't you shower and change?" he suggested. "I'll get the equipment ready."

Tess stood. "I won't be long."

"No rush," he said.

He was wrong. There was a rush, because she didn't want to miss a minute of her time with him. She hurried to get ready for her next adventure.

***

Tess left the kitchen and Ed blew out a breath. He was getting far too attached. He found himself wanting to agree with whatever Tess wanted to make her happy. Watching her learn to play pool, that intense focus on her face, and the way she bit her lip as she concentrated, had made him smile.

Then, on the trip home, he'd covered her hand with his, but he wanted more. He wouldn't believe she was a spy for Tan. Her reactions were too authentic. But he'd have to ask her about her call with her parents to remove that niggling doubt.

His urge to protect her, to show her as many new experiences as he could while she was with him, was too strong to ignore. He ran a hand through his salty hair and grimaced. He'd have to shower before they went out as well. Quickly, he washed the mugs and headed across the yard to the machinery shed. His father's telescope was next to the camping gear.

Ed's gaze caught on the door into the storeroom where they kept their old history. Tomorrow, he'd take Tess inside. Maybe he'd take her to the gulf and show her the plaque dedicated to the passengers on the Retribution as well.

"What are you doing in here?"

Ed spun at the voice, heart thumping. "Give me a heart attack, why don't you?" he grumbled to Matt.

"Wanted to check who was here before I announced my presence."

Good point. They'd had people sabotaging the station over the past few months. "I'm getting the telescope," Ed told him. "Going to show Tess the stars."

Matt smirked. "Is that what they call it these days? Talking yourself up, aren't you?"

Ed chuckled. "Lay off. She's never done it before."

Matt continued to grin, and Ed ignored him while he got the equipment out. "You going to invite Sam and the guys to star gaze too?"

Damn it. Matt knew he didn't want to. "Don't think they'll be interested."

"I'm sure they would be. Didn't Sam tell them all about it?"

He was as bad a tease as Charlie had been. They'd probably honed their skills on each other. "Why don't you go ask them while I get the stuff ready?"

"You need a hand?"

"Nah, I'm good." For all his teasing, Matt was like a brother to him. He'd been just as lost as Ed when Charlie had died and had continued to hang around the station often.

Matt left the shed, and Ed carried the telescope over to the ute. He could carry it all the way over to the sand dunes, but it was heavy, and he wasn't feeling that energetic. Then he threw in a rug in case it got cold.

By the time he had everything ready, the guys were sitting out on the shearers' quarters porch having another beer. Ed was going to have to run the gauntlet.

He sauntered over, hoping they would be kind to him. "I'm going to set up a telescope to look at the stars," he said. "Do you guys want to join us?"

"Us?" Sam asked.

"Me and Tess."

All four men smirked at the same time.

Dobby stretched. "I haven't done any stargazing since we were on that op in the Middle East—it might be fun."

"Yeah," Heath agreed. "Think you can point out Uranus?"

There was always one who thought that was funny. Ed rolled his eyes. "If you're going to be childish, I'll retract my invitation."

Sam waved him away. "I think we're all content to sit here and bullshit. Next time."

Relief swept through him. "Great. See you later." He strode over to the house before they could change their minds, and their laughter rang out behind him.

It seemed he'd picked up three new brothers this year.

Tess wasn't in the kitchen, so he continued through to the bedroom where she was dressed and drying her hair with a towel. "The equipment's ready," he said. "I'll just have a shower. It might get a little cold out there, so help yourself to my jumpers in the drawer." He always kept spare clothes at the Ridge, because inevitably he'd forget to pack something.

She nodded, and he grabbed a change of clothes and dashed into the bathroom. When he returned, she was sitting on the bed, wearing his favourite galaxy jumper. His heart tugged painfully as she smiled at him. "Ready?"

No. There was something he needed to clarify first. He shut the door and she straightened, a look of alarm on her face.

"Tess, I need to ask you about something." He moved to the opposite bed, to give her space.

"About what?"

"What did your parents say when you told them about Tan?"

She flinched and glanced down at her hands, playing with her fingers.

"Tess?" He kept his tone gentle although his gut tightened.

Finally she looked at him. "I didn't call them."

"Why not?"

Fear filled her eyes. "Because I'm scared. What if Dot is right? What if they're involved with Tan in some way? I'd never heard of him before I came to Australia, and he's controlling and scary." She hugged herself. "I didn't want to talk to them and risk them asking me to do something awful to you or your family." She sighed. "I'm sorry for lying. But I promise you, Ed, if they are involved, I know nothing about it."

God help him if Brandon was right, and he was being sucked in by her good looks and sweet personality. He shifted to sit next to her and wrapped his arm around her. "I believe you." She leaned into him. "We can call Dot tomorrow and ask her the best way to go about it."

"I don't want my parents to be in trouble."

He needed to remember this wasn't just about his family, her family could be victimised too. "I know. We'll sort something out." He kissed her forehead. "Let's go look at the stars. We can work out a plan of action tomorrow."

"All right."

The stars shone brilliantly as they stepped outside. They drove the short distance to the base of the sand dunes not far behind the house. When he switched off the headlights, they were plunged into darkness.

Tess gasped. "It's so dark."

"It's perfect," Ed assured her. He flicked on a torch and handed it to her. "You can be my light." He took the telescope out of the back, setting it up on a wooden board he'd put out there specifically to give him a flat surface.

Tess was silent while he calibrated the equipment, choosing the best star to show her first. When he was satisfied, he said, "Take a look."

She stepped next to him and bent to look into the eye piece. He caught a whiff of the frangipani body wash she'd used in the shower. "What is it?" Her voice was soft, as if not wanting to disturb the peace.

"Alpha Centauri," he said. "It's one of the pointer stars for the Southern Cross and actually part of the Centaurus constellation. The Southern Cross can be used to find the south pole."

"You know a lot about it," she commented.

"It fascinates me," he admitted. "When Sheridan invited me to go on a tour of the Perth Observatory with him, I was hooked. There's so much *space* out there, so much we don't know."

She shifted closer. "You don't find the immensity of it overwhelming?"

"No, it's exhilarating." He turned to her. "The possibilities of what's there are almost limitless."

"It's a beautiful way to look at it." Her voice carried with it a longing. "It would be lovely to have those kinds of possibilities."

He understood what it was like to feel confined by expectations. He slipped his arm around her waist to comfort himself, as well as her. She leaned into him, warm and right.

"Thank you for showing me this." She gazed up at him. Though it was dark, her warm breath was so close to him.

Almost without conscious thought, he lowered his

head and brushed his lips against hers. She gasped and pressed her lips more firmly to his, kissing him, and all his doubts fled as he drew her closer. Her eager kisses shot straight through him, and he slowed them before they drove him insane, slipping his tongue into her mouth to tease her. Her quiet moan of delight was enough to make him rock hard, and he shifted so she couldn't feel him pressing against her.

He slid his hand across her back, lower to caress her backside, and she sighed against his mouth. Hell. He wanted to drag her down to the sand right here.

Cursing his sense of chivalry, he eased away. She followed him, and he bit back a curse and placed a hand between them. "Tess." He kissed her again before stepping back. "Maybe we should take this inside." Except, damn it, their room was next to Lara's. The shearers' quarters weren't any better because the walls were thin.

"Oh. I, ah, don't know…" She sighed. "I'm not… experienced." She stepped closer, running her hand up his chest. "But I want to touch you and kiss you."

He swallowed a curse and pulled her back into his arms. "I'm resisting the urge to drag you down to the sand." He kissed both cheeks and then her mouth.

"Wasn't there a rug in the back of the ute?"

Yes, there was. But he didn't think she was suggesting what he wished she was suggesting. Still, he retrieved the rug and spread it out over the fine sand. Tess lay down on it, and Ed's blood pulsed in his veins. He lay next to her, and hoping to cool the heat in his skin, he pointed out the emu in the sky, its shape outlined by the dark areas between the stars.

Tess shifted closer, so her arm brushed his.

He twisted to lie side on and slipped his hand over her stomach. She sighed, and the sound shot straight to his groin.

Unable to resist, he slid his hand under her top and she arched towards him, her lips meeting his.

Ed hadn't felt this much throbbing desire since he was a teenager. He couldn't stop his hand from sliding higher under her top to her breast.

"Ed." She pressed into him.

He pulled her against him and unclasped her bra. She flinched, a tiny movement, but enough to make Ed stop. Inwardly he cursed, but he kept his voice calm as he asked, "Too much?"

She hesitated. "No." She didn't sound convinced.

He pulled away. "How about you do it back up?" Unhooking was easy.

Again, she hesitated. "Will you keep going?"

"Only if you want me to," he said.

"You'll stop if I say so?"

"Of course." He brushed a kiss on her cheek. "I want you to enjoy yourself."

"Please touch me."

He felt a hundred feet tall at her trust, and he kept his movements slow as he inched his fingers across her stomach and up her ribcage. Such soft skin, warm. His thumb brushed the underside of her breast and stopped at her sharp intake of breath.

She squirmed below him, pressing into his hand.

Ed fought to keep his movements slow while his body ached with desire. He circled her breast, slow movements with his fingertips, and brushed her nipple.

Her moan was loud in the silence.

Unable to stop himself, he captured her mouth with his and kissed her, trying to keep it light, but she ignited under him, kissing him with an urgency, as his thumb circled her breast.

She broke away from his lips. "More."

He didn't need any further urging. He shifted, pushing her T-shirt up, and his mouth covered her breast. She bucked under him. "Yes, Ed."

She tasted so sweet. He licked and kissed, and her body grew tighter. Gently, he sucked her nipple, and she cried out as her body shuddered in release.

Well, damn.

Heady satisfaction filled him as her body relaxed. He moved to kiss her lips, slowly, with passion, and her sigh squeezed his heart. Though his whole body throbbed with need, he shifted her T-shirt back down so it covered her and pulled her into his arms. "OK?"

Her chuckle was shaky. "Better than OK." She paused. "Ed…" Her hand drifted down his side as if unsure.

While he desperately wanted his own release, he wanted it only when she was ready, and in the dark he couldn't make out her expression. He kissed her. "I should pack away the telescope."

With more strength than he knew he had, he got up and left her.

Chapter 15

Tess woke, hearing people moving in the corridor outside. For a second she couldn't figure out where she was, and her heart raced as she tried to make sense of the dark shapes around her. Then Lara called good morning to Faith, and her body relaxed.

A dim glow came from the window frame, and she checked the time on her new mobile. Only six-thirty. Ed had mentioned the night before that Darcy would be out on the farm at first light, and Faith was taking Lara to school before she went to work in town. They'd be gone by seven-thirty.

Which would leave her and Ed alone in the house.

Her cheeks warmed as she remembered last night. Ed was right to stop when they did. She had desperately wanted to continue exploring the heavy neediness inside her, but after he'd stood, and the rug had shifted, she'd realised they would have got sand in unmentionable places.

Plus they had no contraception.

She glanced over at him sleeping in the bed next to hers. When they'd arrived back, she'd wanted to keep exploring those amazing feelings, but his family slept in the next room. They had taken her in, and she didn't want to do anything they might not approve of. Her mother's voice whispered in her ear that it wasn't appropriate. She still believed a woman had to be a virgin when she married. But if sex made Tess feel as good as Ed had last night, she didn't want to wait.

But thoughts of her mother reminded her she hadn't called them yesterday like she normally would. She stared at the ceiling. The moment she called them it would shatter this peace she'd found at the Ridge with Ed. Yesterday had been a dream and she didn't want it to end.

Was it wrong of her to want to hang on to it?

What would Da Lim do?

She wouldn't give in to her parents' expectations, but Tess had discovered the letters Da had written to them regularly to reassure them she was safe.

So she really had to call her parents.

She closed her eyes.

One more day. She'd give herself today in case Dot contacted them with news, and then she'd call. Joy would have told them she was safe, so there was no rush.

The decision sat a little uneasy on her, but this was the first time she had done something for herself since she arrived in Australia. She deserved it.

The light outside grew brighter, and a car started, and then the engine faded as it drove away. Ed's fringe hung over his face, obscuring part of it, and she longed to brush it out of the way.

How would he react if she did that? If she climbed into his bed with him?

No. He could hardly consent to it if he was asleep.

So she contented herself with studying the scattering of freckles across his nose, only faintly visible as the sun rose higher in the sky outside. How much longer would he sleep?

More voices carried down the corridor, and she recognised Dobby's booming tone. Damn. She'd forgotten about them.

She shifted, her bladder telling her it was time to get up. In the bathroom, she tidied her hair and then stopped back in the bedroom to check if Ed was awake.

He didn't stir.

She smiled. Darcy had said he wasn't a morning person.

Letting him sleep, she moved down the corridor, only slightly nervous about walking into a kitchen full of men.

Sam, Dobby and Heath sat at one end of the table, each nursing a mug of coffee, but all eyes focused on her the moment she stepped into view. Alert.

Instead of making her uncomfortable, it made her feel safe. No one would sneak up with them around.

"Morning," she said.

"Morning," they chorused.

"You and Ed have fun stargazing?" Heath asked, and the others smirked.

Her cheeks heated, and she hurried over to the bench to put the kettle on. "Yes, thank you." They couldn't possibly know what she and Ed had done. "What are you planning to do today?"

"Darcy's putting us to work," Sam said. "They're tagging the new lambs." He shrugged. "I guess we're doing grunt work."

"Lambs?" She hadn't seen lambs before.

"Yeah. Matt and Darcy are rounding them up now."

Would Ed be required to help? Darcy clomped up the steps of the verandah and called through the door. "You guys ready yet?" He spotted Tess and smiled. "Want to come look at the lambs?"

She glanced back at the bedroom.

"Ed'll sleep until ten," Darcy said. "Leave him a note."

The other men got to their feet.

"Let me grab some shoes."

She hurried back to the bedroom. Ed didn't stir, even when she made a little more noise. She sent him a text, and the ding of his phone also didn't wake him. Tess grinned and returned to the kitchen, grabbing an apple from the bowl on the table before joining the men outside where they waited for her.

They crossed the yard to the pens where sheep and baby lambs were gathered.

The low bleating was the only sound in the cool morning air, and the small lambs leapt over imaginary objects, their gait a little unsteady. So cute! Matt was over by a gate, and Tess stayed outside the yard while the rest of the guys and the farm dog, Bennet moved inside, following Darcy's instructions to herd the animals towards Matt. As the sheep reached the gate, Matt shifted it, letting the ewes go into one pen and the lambs into another. Separating mother from child.

Tess's heart ached as the bleating became cries of anguish, and she moved around the yards to the lambs' pen. Darcy joined her. "They'll be reunited soon enough," he said. "We have to tag and vaccinate them."

He climbed into the yard and gestured her in. "You can keep them company if you want." He scratched a lamb's head.

Without as much grace as Ed's older brother, she climbed over the fence, and the lambs trotted around her. She knelt down, patting their soft wool, and grinned as they butted each other out of the way to get her attention. Here were some animals she wasn't scared of. She wanted to take them all home.

"No naming them," Darcy warned, and strode away.

Tess barely noticed, so utterly charmed by the young animals. She had a million questions to ask, but all the men were busy, so she crouched to give the lambs her complete attention.

"Named any of them yet?" Ed's call pushed through Tess's rapture. He stood leaning on the metal fence, watching her.

How long had he been there? "Darcy said I wasn't allowed to." She smiled and shifted to her feet, wandering over to him. It felt right to lean over and kiss him, so she did.

He grinned at her. "That's because any lambs that get named can't go to the slaughter house. Just don't tell Lara." He pointed to a couple of sheep which roamed around the camping area. "That's Flotsam and Jetsam."

She focused back on the cute babies she'd been playing with. They were all going to end up on someone's dinner plate. It almost made her convert to vegetarianism.

"Don't do it," Ed warned. He brushed her arm, and tingles spread through her, distracting her.

"Did you sleep well?"

"Yeah," he said. "You should have woken me."

"I wanted to let you sleep."

"I would have rather spent the time with you."

A glow filled her. She'd always felt the odd one out, first at home where she didn't meet expectations, and then at university when she always had to leave to go to work. But now she felt as if she belonged and had someone who wanted to be with her.

"If you're done with the lambs, I thought we could go to the gulf. You might be interested in the place the Retribution sank."

She perked up. She had been wanting to explore his family's history. "That would be great." She glanced over her shoulder. "You don't have to help?"

A frown flittered across Ed's face. "Nah. There's enough people." He raised a hand and called to Darcy,

"We're going to the gulf."

Darcy nodded. "Yeah, but you've got dinner tonight. Take a radio."

Ed gave him a thumbs up as Tess climbed over the fence, and they walked hand in hand back to the house.

"Have you had breakfast?" Ed asked.

"An apple."

"I'll make us a picnic, but do you want toast or cereal before we go?"

"Toast is fine." She washed her hands in the laundry, and by the time she'd returned, Ed had the toaster on and condiments on the table.

He was so good in the kitchen. She'd never seen her father do anything except eat in the kitchen. She shifted across to him, and he handed her a mug of coffee. "Thanks." She kissed him, but it wasn't enough. As if he felt the same way, Ed pulled her against him, and this time the kiss was longer, deeper.

She felt it all the way down to her toes. They broke apart, and she placed a hand over her pounding heart. His unhurried, amiable smile didn't help slow it.

The toaster popped, making Tess jump. She handed Ed a slice, frantically thinking of a topic to discuss. "Is the gulf where the ship sank?"

"Yeah. The island offshore is surrounded by a reef, and they were blown onto it by a cyclone."

Tess could imagine the terror. Rough seas, the ship lurching all over the place, feeling completely helpless in the face of Mother Nature. "Do you have any journals from the passengers?"

"I don't think so, but we can go through the trunks afterwards."

She beamed. "That would be great." If she could find references to other people who were in Western Australia at the same time as her great aunt, it might give her a path to search. "Thank you."

"You're most welcome." He kissed her again and for the first time Tess was grateful to Tan, because the situation had led her here to Ed.

*****

About half an hour later, Ed drove the hired four-wheel-drive across the bitumen road and down a rough track. "Are we allowed this way?" Tess asked.

Ed grinned. "Yeah, this is all Ridge land. Brandon owns it."

It was still hard to comprehend one family owned so much. The red dirt was a foreign feature, almost as if she was on another world, but the colour was stunning. They bumped over the rough track for close to half an hour before the crystal clear ocean appeared before them. She squinted at the sun glistening off the water as Ed pulled in near a hitching post.

"It's lovely."

"We like it," Ed agreed. He pushed open the car door and pointed out into the bay. "That's Retribution Island. The ship crashed on the reef surrounding it during a cyclone and stranded people there. When the storm was over, they salvaged what they could, and swam to shore. Not everyone made it."

A long island full of small trees and shrubs lay in the middle of the bay, far enough away to make swimming the distance to the shore a challenge. And when the survivors reached the shore, they would discover mangroves on one side and endless white sand which blended into the red soil on the other. How devastated would they have been?

On such a bright, sunny day, it was difficult to imagine ferocious winds and pelting rain.

"There's a plaque over here, which lists the names of everyone on board."

Tess perked up, and she strode to the metal disc near

the mangroves. It was old and rusted, but the names were clearly visible. "Who erected it?"

"Must have been one of my ancestors. It's incredible it's still here after all these years and cyclones, so maybe someone replaced the original at some stage."

Carefully, she traced the names Lillian and Reginald Stokes. "Are these your ancestors?"

"Yeah."

She read through the names, one by one, not scanning, but giving them the respect they deserved. Dec was written next to the names of the people who had died, presumably during the cyclone. Her heart jumped at the last name on the list. Da Lim. She traced the name, disbelief coursing through her. "That's my ancestor's name." She turned to Ed. "The pearl diver I told you about." Could it be the same person? The dates were right, but she'd never heard of her being shipwrecked.

Ed chuckled. "That's a pretty big coincidence."

She nodded, still studying the name and running through the information she knew of her. "She worked at Cossack. Is that far from here?"

"It's up the coast about six hundred kilometres. It's a ghost town now."

"So she could have been sailing there to work."

Ed nodded. "I guess so. But that means the ship probably left from Fremantle. If Da Lim came from Singapore, why would she go to Freo before coming here?"

Tess shook her head. It was something else to investigate, but her nerves hummed in excitement. She would go back through the scanned journals on her laptop when they got back to the house. But this connection brought a whole other layer to the shipwreck. This land would have been so foreign to Da, so dry and barren. How would they have found water?

Why hadn't the journals mentioned a shipwreck?

"Can I look through your family's trunks when we get back? If there are journals, they probably wouldn't have mentioned Da by name, but maybe they referenced the pearl divers on the ship with them." There were a couple of other Chinese names on the plaque, though most were English or Irish.

"Sure. Do you want to go for a dip before we head back?" His smile was bemused, and she snatched her hand off the plaque where she'd been tracing the names.

Her face flushed. "Sorry."

He slipped his arm around her waist and pulled her close. "No need to apologise." He kissed her. "You get this adorable furrow between your eyes when you're focused, and it makes me want to kiss you." He kissed her forehead.

Tingles spread through her at the intensity of his gaze, and she leaned into him. No one had ever called her adorable before. "Thanks." She pressed her lips against his and the kiss deepened, making her forget all about the plaque and the history.

"We should cool off," Ed said with a self-deprecating grin.

She didn't want to stop, but he was right. She needed to be sensible. They dropped their things on the sand, and she stripped down to her bathers. She'd grown comfortable wearing her bathers during the whale shark tour. Here it was no big deal. Still, she studied the water as she waded in. "I don't have to worry about anything killing me, do I?"

His laugh rang out, making her smile. "No. Occasionally, we'll see a reef shark or a ray, but they ignore us."

"What about those jellyfish?"

"We rarely see them."

Rarely wasn't never. She raised her eyebrows.

"It's fine. I promise. Darce wouldn't let Lara swim

here if he thought it might be dangerous."

That was some comfort. She continued studying the water, searching for any floating, clear balls of jelly.

Ed chuckled. "Chances are you'd feel the Irukandji before you'd see it."

She shuddered. "Not helping."

Ed splashed her as he dived into the warm water. Tess braced herself, then submerged, enjoying the water covering her body. When she surfaced, Ed stood waist deep a few metres from her, his chest glistening. Her worries about jellyfish vanished as her desire increased.

Her nipples puckered as she pressed against his naked chest, and when he pulled her closer, she wrapped her legs around his waist, needing to get as close as possible. She'd spent too long missing out on this, and she wasn't missing a moment more.

"Tess." His groan sent heat to her groin, and his kisses covered her face and her neck. She revelled in his attention, arching her head back so he could access the sensitive area of her throat. In between kisses, he said, "We're supposed to be cooling off."

"Mmm," she agreed. "But this feels so good."

He pulled her close and his warm, hard erection pushed against her. She wanted to touch him, but she hesitated, not sure what to do. She unwrapped her legs and Ed pushed away, ducking his whole body under the water. He took a minute to surface and when he did, his gaze was still intense, but he kept his distance. "Maybe we should get a room in town."

Yes. Her face flushed. How could they explain it to his family? How would they look at her afterwards? "What would your family think?"

"They wouldn't care."

The temptation was strong. Would she be safe in town? The Ridge was a sanctuary, but she'd been able to relax last night at the brewery.

She tried to float as if unconcerned, but sank straight under the water, and came up spluttering. "Can you teach me to float?"

Ed smiled, unconcerned about the change in topic. "I can try."

It would keep both of them distracted. The water was the perfect temperature, not cold, but not warm enough to be unpleasant. She lay on her back, Ed's hands supporting her under her back. "Ready?"

"Yes."

He removed his hands, and she sank, but Ed stopped her before she went under.

"Relax," he said. "Spread your arms and legs like a star, press your hips and stomach towards the surface and tilt your head back."

She did as he suggested, and this time she floated on the surface. She grinned. "I did it!" As she spoke, she turned her head and sank, swallowing a mouthful of water.

Ed helped her surface, chuckling.

"Again," she insisted. This would take some practice.

It took half an hour before she could float and tread water, which Ed insisted on teaching her. "Next time we come, I'll bring goggles, and I'll get you a pool noodle so you can explore the mangroves and reefs over there," Ed said.

Excitement filled her. She wanted to learn to do everything. As she dried herself, she studied the island in the bay. "It doesn't look too far away." Though it was too far for her to swim.

"Brandon swam there once on a dare," Ed said. "He almost didn't make it."

Tess gaped at him. "What?"

"Charlie dared Brandon to swim to the island and promised to do his chores for a month if he did it." Ed shrugged. "Brandon thought it was worth the risk."

"So what happened?"

"Brandon made it, and then Charlie and Darcy went home to get Dad and the dinghy to fetch him. Brandon was preparing to spend the night on the island, because he didn't have the energy to swim back."

She wrapped the towel around her waist. "That would have been scary."

"We camped out a lot as kids," Ed said. "Matt's parents taught us how to make fire, and what things we could eat, so he would have only had a night of discomfort."

So blasé about it. Australians were an interesting bunch.

Something glistened on the island in the morning sun. She shaded her eyes. "What's that?"

Ed joined her. "I don't know. A fisherman might have left rubbish there. Sometimes they come this far down the gulf." He placed his hat on his head. "Or Matt's family might have set something up."

"I thought you said it was your land."

"The island isn't. This entire area is Bayungu land, which is Matt's people."

They sat side by side on the sand and ate lunch. The sun was warm, and Tess slid her T-shirt over her bathers to protect herself. It was funny how comfortable she was with Ed. Perhaps the circumstances of their meeting had wiped away any awkwardness and given them a solid bond. She hoped they could spend more time together in Perth after Tan was arrested.

She shivered despite the heat and scanned the surrounding shoreline. Maybe she was too trusting that she was safe out here. Tan had wanted the station for a reason.

"You OK?" Ed squeezed her knee.

"Just thinking about Tan and wondering where

Salvatore has gone."

"The police will find him, and in the meantime, you're safe here."

She didn't like that they were connected to Tan through the station. If she didn't hear from Dot tomorrow, she would call her parents, and figure out the next step. If the police had her statement and all the details they needed, would Tan and Salvatore still hurt her? She smiled at Ed, pushing away her troubles. Here and now, it was as if it was just the two of them. And the thought brought her a lot of comfort. She could be herself.

She finished her sandwich and sipped from the icy cold thermos Ed handed her.

"You ready to go back?" Ed asked. "We can haul some of those trunks inside and go through them."

The excitement of the investigation pushed her concerns away. She scrambled to her feet. "Absolutely." She held her hand out to pull Ed to his feet.

He chuckled. "Well, I know how to distract you now."

She smiled at him. "Everything about you is a distraction." She kissed him and then gathered their towels and led them over to the ute. "Can I drive?"

Chapter 16

Ed was impressed with the way Tess handled the rough road like a pro. Without gears to worry about, she drove confidently, not concerned about the bumps and soft patches, but slowing when required. Her hands gripped the steering wheel, and a grin covered her face as they jostled their way home. He loved the way she threw herself into learning new things with enthusiasm and determination, and it was a pleasure to teach her. When she drove into the yard, Darcy and Matt were still working the sheep with Brandon's friends. The sharp poke of guilt was normal, but Ed refused to give it any power. They didn't need many people to deal with the lambs. Any more and he'd be in the way. He'd accepted long ago he wasn't cut out to be a farmer.

Tess parked next to the house.

"This way." Ed took Tess over to the machinery shed and she made a beeline to the motorbikes, running her hand over the seat of one.

"I've always wanted to ride a motorbike." The excitement in her eyes was hard to ignore, and Ed fought the urge to cringe. He hadn't ridden since the incident with Charlie, had always made excuses to ride a horse instead, or had come over with a horrible headache any time his father mentioned getting on a bike.

"I'll get Darcy to take you out," he said. "He's a better rider."

She frowned. "Don't you ride?"

"Not much. No opportunity in the city. I never got my bike licence." He led Tess to a small tool shed off the main building, and thankfully she followed without further comment. He inhaled the smell of grease and dirt as he scanned the tidy area. His father had taught all of his children to return items to where they came from. Woe betide anyone who didn't, and the tool was lost. It was far too long a drive into town to buy a replacement.

He pushed open the door to the storage room. A faintly musty odour came out, and he flicked the light on. Directly across from him were clear plastic containers stacked on top of each other, one which had his name on it. Brandon had mentioned something about him having stuff out here, but he'd never got around to checking.

Tess strode over to the old suitcases and trunks stored against the side wall and ran her hand over the top case, her touch reverent.

He wanted her to touch him that way.

Pushing aside his desire, he nudged her out of the way and snapped the clasps which held the suitcase shut. This one was more of a fifties-style case, so probably held things that belonged to his grandparents or great-grandparents.

He grabbed a rag from the tool shed and carefully brushed off the red dust which covered the top. His mother would kill him if he got the things dirty.

The pang of loss hit him. She'd never know.

He took a deep breath to settle himself. He would know, and that's what mattered. Ed passed Tess the cloth, so she could wipe the dust from her fingers, and pried open the lid. A granny square rug lay on top, a black border with squares of different colours. Underneath was the dull white of a wedding dress. Ed hesitated. "Maybe we should do this inside." At least then they could lay the items on a clean table or floor as they explored.

Tess nodded. "Yes. I'd hate to damage anything."

He closed the case again and studied the containers. Four old-fashioned suitcases and two trunks, which were the type he'd seen in historical movies. There should be room in his mother's craft room.

The suitcases weren't heavy, so they each carried one at a time. Darcy called Ed over as they returned to the shed.

"What are you doing?"

"Tess is interested in the family history," he said. "She found the name of her pearl-diving ancestor on the plaque for the Retribution, and she's going to check if there's a journal from Lilian in the stuff."

"Where are you putting it all?"

"Mum's craft room." Perhaps he should have asked Darcy, but he still considered the Ridge his home, even if he hadn't lived there for six years.

Darcy took off his hat and ran a hand through his hair before replacing it. "Can you wait until Lara gets home to go through them? I've been meaning to bring them in for a few weeks, and haven't got around to it. She'll be gutted if you do it without her."

He should have considered Lara. "Sure."

They'd only have to wait a couple of hours, and Ed could imagine Lara's devastation if she caught them going through the trunks. He returned to the storeroom with Tess, and together they carried the rest of the containers over to the house.

"What's in your box?" Tess asked when they returned to the storeroom to check if they'd missed anything.

"I'm not sure. Probably stuff from my childhood." He made no move to open it. His childhood held a few painful memories he didn't want to revisit.

Tess frowned. "You're not curious?"

Not really, but he could tell Tess was. He sighed. Maybe it was time he put it all behind him. His steps drew him over to the clear plastic containers, and he shifted Georgie's to the floor to access his.

Bracing himself, he opened the lid and froze. His black Akubra hat sat on the top, as brilliantly black as the day his parents had bought it. His father had advised against getting black, had said it would attract the sun and heat his head, but Ed had insisted. He'd always felt like the black sheep of the family, and figured it suited him. He'd worn the hat when he went horse-riding with Georgie, or doing his chores, and his father had been right, it was a sun magnet. Not that Ed would have ever admitted it.

"That's like Darcy wears," Tess said.

He placed it on her head. "You can have it."

She grinned. "Does it suit me?"

"Yeah, it does." It made her look as if she belonged here, and Ed's heart gave an uncomfortable tug. He took his phone from his pocket, took a photo and showed it to her.

She took the hat off and tried to give it back to him. "I can't take your hat, Ed."

"It never fit me." It wasn't who he was, it was who he'd tried to be. It made him look the part. "Keep it, please." He pressed it back on her head. She looked cute.

Not wanting to dwell on the past, he pulled out an old biscuit tin. As a kid he'd stored all his treasures in there, but now he couldn't remember what they were. The lid was stiff and rusty from years of disuse and when it finally popped, things flew everywhere. A black lump landed on Tess, and her ear-piercing scream stopped

Ed's heart. His eyes took a moment to focus on the large black spider sitting on Tess's knee. Another second before he registered it was plastic, and that Tess was shaking in terror beside him.

He reached for it.

"No!" She slapped the spider away and pushed herself in front of him—to protect him.

His heart swelled. "It's all right. It's fake." He pulled her trembling into his arms as outside footsteps pounded closer, and then Darcy burst into the room.

"What's wrong? What's happened?"

Ed rubbed Tess's back with one hand as he pointed to where the spider had landed. "Charlie happened."

Darcy blinked and placed a hand to his chest as Matt and the others appeared behind him. "I thought someone was being killed."

Tess still gasped for breath, and Ed scowled. "If Charlie was still here, someone would be being killed." He placed the spider back in the container. "It flew out when I opened the lid."

Darcy's chuckle was full of relief, and he swore. "He's still pranking us from beyond the grave. Why do you have it?"

Ed shrugged, but the memory hurt. Watching his mother pack Charlie's toys away, seeing the spider. Thinking maybe he could take over Charlie's role as prankster in the family, but never having the courage to do so. Tucking the spider away for a day when he was feeling brave.

Tess pulled away from him, brushing the tears from her face. "I'm sorry. I thought it was deadly."

"And yet you protected me. Thank you."

Her tremulous smile warmed him. Behind him, Darcy reassured the other men no one was being murdered.

Darcy smiled at Tess. "Charlie got me with that spider when I was about fourteen. Made it drop from the door frame onto me, and scared the shit out of me. I might have screamed as loudly as you did."

"Good lungs," Matt commented from the doorway.

She blushed. "Thank you for coming to my aid."

"Any time," Darcy said, and with a dip of his hat, they left.

Ed shook his head. He'd never been as suave as his brothers. The one time he'd tried the move on a girl he liked, he'd pulled the hat down so far he couldn't see her anymore. "You OK now?"

She nodded, though her hand shook as she reached for the plastic toy. "It looks so real."

"Charlie terrorised us all with that for weeks just before he died. It's the reason for Georgie's spider phobia."

"He sounds… a little mean."

Ed hesitated. "He was Charlie." How to explain? "He never meant anything malicious by his pranks, he just liked being funny."

"And he thought scaring his siblings was funny?"

"Yeah. He didn't really have an off button. He'd always be doing something—riding horses or motorbikes, learning to drive, going fishing or swimming. If I was reading, and Brandon and Darcy were busy, he'd pester me until I'd do something with him."

"What about Georgie?"

"He adored Georgie, and most of the time he sweet-talked her into anything, but after the spider incident, she wouldn't talk to him for a couple of weeks." And then Charlie had died.

"Sounds like a restless spirit."

It was an apt description. He brushed a kiss on her cheek and then gathered the other items which had fallen from the biscuit tin. A drawing of the Ridge which he'd done sitting beside Dot, a bookmark he'd bought when they'd visited the Carnarvon space museum, and an old coin. He rubbed his thumb over it.

"Where'd you get that?" Tess asked, reaching for it.

He passed it to her. "I found it when I was out riding one day. I figured a prospector must have dropped it."

Tess turned the coin over and squinted. "Have you got a magnifying glass?"

"Probably." He got up and searched the tool shed until he found one hanging up. "Here."

Tess had followed him, and now she tilted the coin to the light and examined it. "Ed, the date on this is 1685."

He jolted and grabbed it from her. "It can't be. Australia wasn't settled by Europeans until 1788." He'd kept the coin a secret knowing Charlie would want it. He hadn't even shown his mother.

"I think it's Dutch. Where exactly did you find it?"

Hell. "I can't remember."

Her eyes shone with excitement. "These types of coins are found in shipwrecks," she said. "And there are a lot of wrecks off the coast."

"But I found it on land."

"Maybe they buried some of their treasure."

Ed chuckled. "Now you're sounding like Lara. She's convinced there's buried treasure at the Ridge. She doesn't believe the story of the cyclone, and has decided it was a lie to hide the true reason they were in the gulf— to search for treasure."

"What time does she get home from school?"

"In about an hour." He loved the idea of buried treasure, but the most likely explanation was a prospector had a lucky coin he'd lost on his journey. Still, he tucked the coin into his pocket to examine later. "Let me put all this stuff back, and then we can make scones for when Lara gets home."

Tess nodded, though he could tell she was dying to get straight into the trunks. Ed had to admit he was keen to see what information they held about his ancestors, but he also knew that after about six generations of Stokes at the Ridge, if there was something to be uncovered, one of them would have undoubtedly already done it.

As he put the biscuit tin back in the crate, a blue folder caught his eye. He hesitated. Had his mum kept it? He slipped the folder out and stared at it for a moment, memories assaulting him. How excited he'd been about the computers at school, and how proud he'd been when he'd coded his first simple game. His father hadn't understood the point, but his mother had showered him in praise.

He flipped the folder open. A pocket in the front cover held a CD with his name on it. The folder also contained his report explaining what the game did, and how he'd created it. He smiled as he read the juvenile words, but he remembered the passion which had filled him when he'd typed the report. This was why he'd studied information technology at university. Not to be help desk and answer the same questions over and over again, but to code and create programs which would bring people joy.

Somewhere along the way, he'd forgotten that. He'd replaced it with his love of astronomy. But maybe he could combine the two.

"Ed, are you all right?" Tess's quiet question made him glance up.

"Yeah. Sorry. I'd forgotten about this." He tucked the folder under his arm and put the lid back on the box. "Something I did as a kid, but I want to take another look." He was fairly sure Darcy's computer still had a CD drive in it.

"We can stay here longer if you want to go through the rest."

"Nah, it's fine." It was enough emotion for one day.

He'd look through the rest later, before he went back to Perth. He slipped his hand into hers. "Let's go make some scones."

Chapter 17

Tess wasn't sure how to read Ed's mood since they'd gone through his things. He seemed a little sad, and he kept glancing at the blue folder he'd brought inside as they made the scones. The third time he did so, she said, "Do you need to do something with that?"

He shook his head. "It's not important."

She cut the scones out of the dough and placed them on the tray. "You keep looking at it."

Ed sighed. "I'm just curious."

"About?"

"What it contains. I remember thinking I was a genius coder, but I imagine it will be simplistic."

"Why don't you look?"

"We're baking."

She rolled her eyes. "We're done." At his nod, she placed the tray into the oven, and Ed set the timer.

"OK. I'll be right back."

Tess understood his curiosity. The thought of going through those trunks was like a constant niggle at the back of her mind, and her ears strained for the sounds of a car engine. Her gaze checked the time as often as Ed glanced at the folder.

He returned with a laptop, and slid the CD into the drive. With his attention fixed on the screen, Tess put the kettle on, and got the butter, jam, and a can of whipped cream from the fridge. Faith would appreciate coming home to afternoon tea on the table after working all day. The men didn't finish on the farm until sunset.

It was a little way she could thank them for taking her in, even if it had been Ed's idea.

A bass beat came from the laptop, one Tess recognised from an old eighties song, and Ed giggled in glee. "I'd forgotten I set it to Queen."

She came around to watch the screen. Ed played a game where a pixelated tractor gobbled up sheep and all the while, the music gave a background beat. "Did you do that?"

He nodded. "It's not bad for a self-taught fourteen-year-old." He laughed as what appeared to be lightning hit his tractor and he died.

Admiration grew. "That's fantastic, Ed."

"I spent hours coding it. Dad threatened to take the computer away from me—he didn't like technology—but because it was for a school assignment, he couldn't." He grinned. "I didn't tell him the assignment was to create something simpler."

Just like he had last night showing her the stars, his face lit up with excitement, and he vibrated enthusiasm. This was what he should do, not feel guilty he didn't enjoy farming. "Do you still code?"

His smile disappeared. "No. I couldn't get a job after uni."

Tess frowned. Ed didn't strike her as someone who would just give up. "But you could have done it in your spare time."

He sighed and pursed his lips. "I submitted a game I designed to a distributor, and they told me it was unrefined and basic." He shrugged. "Kind of killed my joy."

She could understand, but, "It was just one person's opinion."

Ed shrugged as a car pulled up outside the house, and two doors slammed. Moments later, Lara burst through the door, dressed in her yellow and brown uniform, and dumped her school bag to the side. "I'm home. What did I miss?"

Tess chuckled as Lara lifted her nose and sniffed. The oven's timer beeped.

"Perfect timing, La La. Scones are ready." Ed got them out of the oven.

"Awesome." She poured herself a glass of water as Faith came in behind her.

Faith smiled with a shake of her head. "Lara, school bag."

"Right." Lara picked up the bag and disappeared with it down the corridor.

"How was your day?" Ed asked.

"Great. I'm getting more clients all the time." Faith sat at the table with a sigh. "I'll have to hire a receptionist to take phone calls. Advertising at the caravan parks has brought in so much work. There are a lot of grey nomads who don't have up-to-date wills."

Tess frowned. "Grey nomads?"

"Retired people who travel the country in their caravans," Ed explained.

She liked the image. What an adventure, having nowhere you had to be, no expectations, and nothing you had to do.

Lara came back in and helped herself to a hot scone, tossing it from hand to hand and then onto the plate. "So what did you do today?"

"We went to the beach and discovered one of Tess's ancestors was on the Retribution," Ed said.

Lara gaped at her. "Really! Which one? What was he

like? Why was he there?"

Tess chuckled. "*Her* name was Da Lim. I've read one of her journals, but it was written after she returned to Singapore, and only alludes to her time in Australia. She came here to be a pearl diver."

"We thought we'd go through the old chests to see if we can find more information," Ed added.

Lara's face lit up as if they'd told her it was Christmas. She clapped her hands. "Yes! Can we do it now?"

"Do you have any homework?" Faith asked her.

Lara waved her away. "It can wait. This is epic."

Tess glanced at Faith, who pressed her lips together. Her parents would have made her do her homework first. Would she have to wait another couple of hours before they explored the trunks?

"Ple-e-ase," Lara begged.

Ed put his hands together in a prayer, and Tess followed his lead. All three of them waited for Faith's answer.

She laughed. "I don't stand a chance. Go for it, but you're not leaving me out."

Tess grinned as Lara whooped and fist-bumped Ed.

"Let's finish afternoon tea, so we don't have to stop for a snack break," Faith suggested.

Tess grabbed her scone and took a large bite. Next to her, Lara did the same, cream smearing all over her face. They glanced at each other and grinned.

Faith handed Lara a tissue as she spoke to Tess. "It's amazing your ancestor was on the Retribution."

Tess nodded. "All I knew was she worked out of Cossack, so maybe she was on the way there when the cyclone struck."

"Or maybe she was hired to dive on a shipwreck," Lara suggested, her eyes wide. "To bring up sunken treasure."

Tess chuckled, but her pulse accelerated at the

thought. She'd been obsessed by pirate tales as a kid, and Ed had the old coin. "Maybe."

Soon they all stood in the craft room, surrounded by suitcases and trunks. "Which one first?" Faith asked.

Tess eyed the trunks, and Lara pointed to one of them. "That one."

Lara braced herself before she lifted the lid.

It didn't budge.

She frowned and tried again. Nothing. "It's locked."

There was a keyhole in the front. They all turned to Ed.

"Don't look at me. I've got no idea. There might be something in Dad's—Brandon's office." A burst of grief flashed over his face.

Tess squeezed his hand.

"Maybe in the cabinet," Lara suggested, already charging out of the room.

They trailed after her, and Ed opened the cabinet full of old artefacts. Tess's eyes widened. The pearl comb was exquisite, with an engraved pattern on its edge. Next to it stood two old green glass bottles and a brush. On the second shelf were two chunky metal keys. Ed grabbed them both, and they returned to the trunk, where Ed tried the first key. Nothing. Tess held her breath as the next key rotated in the lock.

Lara cheered, and Ed lifted the lid. The scent of mothballs wafted out.

Tess winced as Lara snatched the yellowed cloth on top and pulled it off, dumping it on the ground.

"Hey, La La, not so fast," Ed said. "We've got to take this slowly. These things are really old and if you're not careful, you might damage something."

Lara danced away from the trunk. "I'm sorry. I'm just so excited." She picked up the cloth and held it up. "What is it?"

Tess studied it. "It looks like a tablecloth. Women in

earlier times used to make all the linen for their household. One of your great, great grandmothers might have made this."

The girl lay it reverently over the table in the room. She smoothed it out. "Is it crocheted?"

Tess had no idea, but Ed came over and said, "Yeah. That looks like the lace doilies Mum used to make." He folded it up.

Inside the trunk were clothes, dresses, and suits, which were placed on the table. Then came household items; a mantel clock, its arms showing it stopped at two thirty-five, a porcelain tea set with a delicate rose pattern which had been wrapped in paper, and several books, including a family bible.

Ed carefully turned the pages. "It's from the early nineteen hundreds," he said. "I think this last child might have been my grandpop." He turned to Tess. "Mum was going through the ancestry before she died." He passed the book to her.

The front pages comprised a list of Stokes births, deaths, and marriages, and the first names on the marriage list were Reginald and Lilian. The people who started it all. Perhaps they'd received the bible as a wedding gift. The pen colour changed as more entries were added, and at times the scrawled handwriting was hard to read, but it traced every single Stokes who had lived at the Ridge up until his grandfather. "This is amazing." She glanced at Ed. "This is the Ridge's history."

He grinned. "We should scan it, put it up on social media, and frame it at the reception. Guests would get a real kick out of it."

Faith nodded. "Amy will know exactly what to do."

Lara was looking through the other books. "There's no journal here," she said. "Some of them are novels, and there's a numbers book."

Tess frowned. "Numbers?"

Lara handed it to her.

A ledger of some sort dated from the 1880s. Perhaps it related to stock and supplies for the station. She flicked through the pages to find some context, but couldn't.

"Anything else in there?" Lara asked.

"Nope, it's empty," Ed said.

"What about a false bottom?" Faith asked, and Lara laughed in delight.

Ed snatched a tape measure from the drawer, and measured the interior of the trunk and then the exterior. "It's the same."

Tess smiled at Lara's pout, and then searched the novels in case one had a piece of paper slid inside. Nothing.

Ed photographed everything with his phone before he replaced them. "In case we need to find something again," he explained. "I'll type up an index."

Tess warmed. He had the mind of an archivist. So sexy.

The other key fit the lock of the remaining trunk. This was full of clothes; christening gowns, baby blankets, and wedding dresses. Again they measured the trunk and found no false bottom.

Lara sighed. "I was sure there would be a map or something."

"There are still the suitcases," Faith told her.

"Yeah, but they're not so old."

They went through the cases and found more sentimental items; trophies, certificates, photographs, as well as a few bowls and some more clothes. But the final suitcase revealed a treasure trove of books. Tess's heart rate increased. Not books—journals.

Lara whooped and grabbed the top one, flicking it open. "It's from 1945. Charlotte Stokes."

World War Two era. Several generations after the

Retribution had been wrecked.

"Our great grandmother," Ed said. "She was a tough old bird, by all reports. Dad was scared of her."

It would be interesting to read her view of the Ridge, and her stories relating to the war. Would they have been affected here, so far away from the danger?

"Let's put them in order," Faith suggested. "Then we can read a bit of them each night."

There were twenty journals spanning ten years. Nothing to do with the Retribution, but Tess was still interested. While Faith told a disappointed Lara to do her homework, Tess helped Ed place the journals back into the suitcase in date order. "Would you mind if I read them too?"

He glanced at her. "Be my guest. Do you want to start with the first one?"

She took the journal he handed her, the cover worn and a little loose, as if the bindings were about to give up.

"I'm going to make dinner, but make yourself comfortable."

The book burned her hand, tempting her with its information, with the life it would reveal beneath its cover. "I can help with dinner."

Ed grinned. "I've got it. I can tell how much you want to read it by the way you're gripping it to your chest." He kissed her. "Go. Discover. I'll call if I need your help."

He was the best. "Thank you."

She hurried into their bedroom, ready to discover a new world.

Chapter 18

Dinner was simmering when Brandon and Amy walked into the kitchen. Ed grinned. "How was the honeymoon?" He hugged Amy.

"Amazing," Amy sighed. "We did nothing for two whole days."

Brandon grinned. "Well, not nothing."

She laughed and poked him.

"How were things here?" Brandon asked.

"Darcy and the guys have been doing lambing stuff," Faith said. "And we've been going through the trunks from the shed."

Brandon raised his eyebrows. "Find anything interesting?"

"An old family bible," Ed said. "Amy might be able to use it on social media. It goes back to Lilian and Reginald."

"No treasure maps?" Amy asked with a grin.

"No, but Tess is reading some journals written by Great Granny Stokes." He set the table.

Brandon shuddered. "She always scared me."

Ed had no memory of her. "What was she like?"

"Mean and wrinkled," Brandon said. "I always

thought she was a wicked witch. I wasn't allowed to talk or play when she was here."

Someone knocked on the kitchen door. "Sorry to disturb you," the man called. "Have you got a site free tonight?"

Something about the man's voice made Ed freeze. Amy walked over, blocking Ed's view, and he stepped behind Brandon to hide while Amy answered, "I'll have to check. How many nights do you want?"

"Just the one."

"Come through," Amy invited.

Brandon turned, and Ed clamped a hand on his shoulder to stop him. "Stay there," he hissed. Every nerve in his body shouted danger. That voice was the same as he'd heard in the darkness on the side of the road.

"Thanks." The man entered, and Ed kept his head down, praying Tess wouldn't come in. He shifted, keeping Brandon between him and the guest as he followed Amy out of the room. When they left the kitchen, Brandon said, "What's wrong with you?"

Ed shook his head and moved to the hallway, his muscles tight. The man was the right size. Before he could say anything, Tess appeared holding one of the journals. "Ed, this is fascinating. You need to read this."

Shit.

He grabbed her hand and pulled her into the kitchen, checking behind her. Salvatore met his gaze.

Did he recognise Tess? "What's going on, Ed?" Brandon demanded.

"I'm almost certain that's Salvatore, the guy who threatened us."

"What?" Tess spun around. "Where?"

He dragged her out of the line of sight, but Salvatore was already striding towards them.

Brandon swore. "Laundry. Now. Faith, get the

others."

Faith ran out the back door as Ed backed Tess into the laundry. He pushed her inside as Salvatore entered the room.

Ed shut the laundry door, standing in front of it, his nerves trembling. Brandon stood by the table.

"Is something wrong?" Amy asked, pushing past Salvatore and standing next to Brandon.

"Who's the girl?" Salvatore demanded.

"What girl?" Ed asked, his heart pounding. The man couldn't have known Tess was here, otherwise he wouldn't have been so brazen about asking for a site. Ed didn't think Salvatore had got a good look at him in the darkness, but Tess had said his name then, and again just now.

"The girl you just shoved into that room."

"That's none of your concern," Brandon said, his voice cold. He shifted so he stood in front of Amy.

Amy glanced at Ed, her eyes wide. They had to get her out of harm's way.

"Faith!" Lara called. "I need some help."

Shit. Salvatore stood between them and Lara. Salvatore glanced behind and smiled.

No fucking way would Salvatore hurt his niece. "Lara, hide!"

Salvatore turned back towards the corridor, and Ed and Brandon both sprang into action at the same time, but Brandon was closer.

He slammed into the man, taking them both to the ground. Amy grabbed the phone and slipped past them, running to find Lara.

Brandon had already subdued the big man and Ed found some rope in the kitchen drawer to tie him up.

Footsteps pounded up the steps and Sam burst through the door first, followed by the other military men.

"What's going on?" Sam demanded.

"He attacked me," Salvatore yelled. "Help."

Sam ignored him as Brandon said, "Check for a wallet."

The two of them wrestled Salvatore and retrieved his wallet from his back pocket and then tied him up.

Ed took a photo of his face as Sam checked his driver's licence. "Salvatore. I hear the police are after you."

Amy returned. "Dot's busy, so Nhiari and Colin are on the way."

Ed moved to the laundry and slipped inside. Tess stood at the far end, her hand clenched around a broom.

"Was it him?" she asked, voice shaky.

"Yeah." He showed her the photo.

"That's him. Did he escape?"

"No, Brandon and Sam tied him up. Amy's called the police." He took the broom from her hand and pulled her into his arms. "You're safe."

But it begged the question, what was Salvatore doing here? Ed shifted back and bumped into the bench, knocking the laundry basket and the journal on to the ground. They landed with a hollow thud on the linoleum floor, and Tess jumped.

"It's all right. Just the basket." He picked it up and put it back on the bench, and handed her the journal she'd been reading. "Do you want to go out there and face Salvatore?"

"Does he know I'm here?"

"Not for certain. I don't think he got a good look at you."

"Then I'll stay here until the police come."

Yeah, probably best that Salvatore didn't know for sure.

The door opened and Darcy poked his head inside. "We've moved Salvatore into the lounge room. You can come out."

"Who's with him?" Ed asked as he took Tess's hand.

"All the army guys." Darcy grinned. "They're a scary bunch when they have their game faces on."

"Did they check him for a weapon?" Tess asked.

"Yeah," Ed answered. "They patted him down." Amy, Faith, Lara and Matt sat at the kitchen table. Faith had her arm around Lara, and Matt looked grim. Amy kept glancing towards the corridor where her husband was.

"Anyone want dinner?" Ed asked, moving to turn off the stove.

"I couldn't possibly eat," Lara declared.

"You should, pumpkin," Darcy said. "We all should while we wait for Nhiari to get here."

Ed dished up the curry he'd made, while Faith poured them all drinks. "Did anyone see what Salvatore was driving?"

"A four-wheel drive hire car," Darcy answered. He glanced at Lara. "I saw him arrive and directed him to the house, but before he went inside, he spotted Lee by the campfire and spoke to him."

Tess jolted. "Why?"

Darcy shrugged. "Maybe he was being friendly with another camper."

"But you don't think so," Ed said.

"Lee's reaction had Brandon's buddies paying attention," Darcy said.

Matt added, "Dobby said Lee stiffened harder than a sailor with land leave. Really odd, since Lee's usually so jovial."

"Surely Salvatore's not that stupid," Amy said. "If Lee is working for Stonefish, why would Salvatore blow his cover?"

"Might not have realised we knew about him," Matt said. "They don't know Tess is here, and they don't know

Ed was with her. Maybe he thought we were so isolated, we wouldn't have seen the bulletin about him."

Tess spoke. "He used to do things that irritated Tan. Things he hadn't considered properly, so maybe he is that stupid."

"We'll have to be careful around Lee," Darcy said. "That means no going off with him, pumpkin."

Lara nodded. "OK."

Ed spotted the journal Tess had been carrying when she'd come to see him. "What did you want to tell me about?"

Tess let out a shaky breath and took a moment to answer. "The journal is fascinating. Charlotte was an exacting woman. She used to lock her kids in the cellar if they were naughty."

Ed frowned. "What cellar?"

"The house cellar. They used to keep all the food underground because it was cooler."

Intrigue simmered in his blood. "I never knew the house had a cellar." He glanced at Darcy who shook his head. "Neither did I."

"Does it say how they accessed it?"

Tess flicked through the pages. "Here. She just writes, *Reginald Junior was terribly naughty today, playing with his baby sister instead of doing his chores. I had to lock him in the cellar without dinner to teach him a lesson. But when I fetched him to put him to bed, I discovered he'd opened a jar of preserves and eaten the lot. I made Reginald strap him, and the boy wept in a manner most unbecoming. If only he was as well-behaved as his older brother. Perhaps Reginald's blood isn't as pure as my beloved's.*"

"How old was he?"

"From the details in the family bible, he looks as if he was three."

His grandpop was strapped at three years of age. Charlotte sounded like a bitch. "What else does it say?"

Brandon strode in. "How's everyone?"

Amy stood and hugged him. "We're all right."

Darcy asked, "Did you know the house has a cellar?"

Brandon frowned. "No."

"Apparently Great Granny Charlotte locked Grandpop in it."

"I remember her threatening to do that to me. Mum stopped her." He shook his head. "I'd forgotten about it."

"So where is it?" Ed asked. Could it contain more old stuff?

"Geez, you're testing my memory, Ed. Charlie was a baby, so I can't have been very old." He closed his eyes. "I don't know."

"It's probably close to the kitchen," Tess said. "They'd want easy access to the food."

Lara jumped to her feet, looking at the floor.

Darcy chuckled. "How about we take a look outside? We might see something under the verandah."

"Should we wait until the police come?" Faith asked.

"The guys have him covered," Brandon said. "This might be a nice distraction."

Darcy fetched a torch and headed outside with Lara.

Tess glanced towards the door.

"Come on," Ed said. As they got to their feet, Lara raced inside. "It's under the kitchen."

Darcy followed her more slowly. "Definitely looks as though the brickwork extends lower."

But the kitchen floor was wooden and there was nothing that looked like a hatch in it. His gaze moved to the laundry which had lino flooring.

The hollow thud. "Maybe it's under the laundry. When I dropped the laundry basket, it sounded hollow."

Brandon glanced at him and laughed. "We're pulling up the lino, aren't we?"

"Aren't you the least bit interested in what might be under there?" Ed asked as Lara raced into the laundry.

"Yeah, I am." He sighed. "Let's deal with Salvatore first, then we can search for it."

Ed nodded. Made sense. They would have to move furniture to pull up the lino and that would cause more obstacles to manoeuvre around.

Lara pouted. "Do we have to wait?"

Tess chuckled and whispered, "I'm with Lara."

Ed pulled her closer and kissed her. "It won't be long."

***

After dinner, Tess continued to read Charlotte's journal for clues as to where the entrance to the cellar was, though part of her listened for sounds coming from the lounge room. She still felt incredibly safe surrounded by the Stokes family—particularly Ed.

Almost an hour after Salvatore had walked into the house, the police arrived. Nhiari introduced the man she was with as Constable Colin Lipscombe.

"Where is he?" Nhiari asked.

"The lounge," Darcy answered.

Nhiari scanned the kitchen, her gaze locking on Tess. "Did he see you?"

Tess nodded. "But I'm not sure he saw my face."

"All right. I want you all to go into one of the bedrooms away from the lounge. Wait there until I get Salvatore into the police van. I'll come and get you."

They moved into Lara's room and a few moments later, Salvatore's yells of innocence could be heard from the lounge.

Tess tensed as the shouts moved down the corridor and then faded.

Brandon came to the door. "You can come out. He's in the van."

Tess sighed as Ed hugged her. One less person trying to kill her.

The kitchen table was crowded with Brandon's army buddies, plus all the Stokes and Matt. Nhiari walked in and shut the door behind her. "We'll take him straight to Carnarvon to question him," she said. "Tess, you'll need to formally identify him, but at this stage we've got enough to hold him. Someone will call you in the morning."

"Thank you."

"Good work, sis," Matt said.

Nhiari rolled her eyes at him. "Just doing my job." She left and Brandon locked the door behind her, while Sam closed the kitchen curtains.

Tess frowned. Wasn't the danger past?

"Why are you locking the door?" Ed asked as he sat.

Sam answered. "Because Lee's still out there."

She'd forgotten about him. Was he really involved?

Sam clapped Matt on the shoulder. "Your sister's a bad ass," he said. "You should have heard her shut down Salvatore's complaints."

Dobby nodded. "He tried to get away when we went to put him in the van, and she stopped him in his tracks. Girl's got moves."

Matt grinned. "She practised them all on me."

"She can practise on me any time," Heath said.

Matt scowled at him. "Ew, that's my sister you're talking about."

Heath shrugged.

Tess smiled, enjoying the banter, and asked, "Did Salvatore say anything?"

"He was swearing his innocence, saying we kidnapped him," Sam said. "Then demanding a phone call."

"He'll probably call Tan," Tess said.

"Wouldn't that be nice?" Ed sipped his tea. "Gives the police a direct connection to him."

"So what happens now?" Faith asked.

"I guess we have to see what Salvatore says," Ed

answered. "But it's one less person after Tess."

She would definitely call her parents tomorrow. She'd left it too long as it was. Perhaps Dot could offer her some kind of witness protection, so the Stokes weren't in any danger.

"Thank you for your help," Tess said. "I appreciate it."

Darcy smiled. "Any friend of Ed's is a friend of ours."

Her cheeks heated, and she ducked her head.

Brandon stood to clear the mugs. "So, what do you think? Time to lift the lino in the laundry?"

"You're going to look for the cellar now?" Tess asked, her heart racing.

"These guys go home tomorrow, so I figured we'd use their muscle while they're here."

"What's your plan?" Darcy asked, and the two men went over to the laundry door.

"The most likely place is in the floor—some kind of hatch opening. We'd need to move the washing machine and the old wardrobe so we can lift the lino."

Tess longed to join them, but it was their house. Ed chuckled. "Come on. We'll clear the table and move it to the other side of the room so there's space for them to move the other furniture in here."

Everyone helped to shift things, and Bennet retreated to his bed in the corner, unhappy about all the movement. Finally they were all crowded around the door of the laundry.

"If the lino's stuck down, we can't afford to replace it," Darcy warned.

"I know," Brandon said. "But this is worth it." He pried at the corner, and it peeled back. It lifted easily. Brandon grinned. "It's not even glued down."

"Dad probably wanted to do it on the cheap," Ed said.

He helped Brandon roll back the lino. About halfway

along, Brandon swore. "There's a hatch here."

Lara squealed and clapped her hands. Tess resisted the urge to do the same.

"There's a torch behind you," Darcy said, taking over and rolling the lino towards himself. They cleared out of the room so the lino could be rolled against the wall and the square hatch was clearly visible. A hole about the size of a fifty-cent piece provided a way to raise the hatch.

"Why would they cover it?" Amy asked.

"Charlotte used to lock her children down there when they were naughty," Tess said. "Maybe they were scarred by it."

Brandon lifted the hatch an inch, and it squeaked in protest. Ed helped him, and together they lifted it so it stood open vertically.

Musty air wafted out, and Brandon shone the torch into the cellar. Tess couldn't see anything from where she stood in the doorway, but both men's eyes widened.

"Cool," Ed said, glancing over at her. "You should see this."

"You want to go down first?" Brandon asked, offering Ed the torch.

"Am I the sacrificial canary?"

Brandon chuckled. "No. I figured since you discovered its existence, you deserve to go down first."

"I'll go!" Lara called.

Ed laughed. "I can at least wipe the cobwebs away, La La."

Tess shivered. Suddenly the cellar wasn't quite as appealing.

Darcy handed Ed a cobweb duster from the shelf, and Ed stepped on the first stair, testing his weight. The wood creaked but held.

He made his way down, cautiously testing each step. "There's a lightbulb in the ceiling," he said. "Must be a switch somewhere."

Darcy pointed to the light switch next to the door. "Try the bottom switch. It's never worked for anything."

Amy flicked the switch, and light shone out of the cellar hole.

"Holy crap," Ed called. "This is amazing."

Lara danced from foot to foot as Brandon descended. "Look at all this stuff."

Tess clutched her hands together and fought not to emulate Lara in her excitement.

"Can we come down?" Darcy called.

"Yeah, there's plenty of room. Must cover the entire kitchen area."

Darcy grabbed Lara as she sprang for the hatch. "Slowly, pumpkin. Those steps haven't been used in years."

"But Ed and Brandon were fine."

She had a point, but still Darcy went first, examining each step. At the bottom he announced, "They seem safe." He gestured to Lara, who trotted down. "Awesome!"

The others surged forward. Matt joined Tess, waiting for her turn. "Georgie's going to be mad she missed this."

He was right. "Should you call her?" Tess asked.

He hesitated and then sighed, pulling out his phone. He took a photo of the hatch and then typed a message.

Almost immediately, his phone rang. His eyes lit up, but when he answered, all he said was, "What do you want, Freckles?"

Tess could hear Georgie's voice from where she stood. "What's going on?"

"Tess discovered the farmhouse has an old cellar. The others are down there now."

"Show me."

He sighed as if he was suffering. "I'll video call you back."

His entire body language shifted from excited to bored as he phoned her back and then entered the cellar. Georgie's cry of surprise was loud.

Ed poked his head above the floorboards. "Are you coming?"

Tess smiled. "I didn't want to get in the way."

"You're the reason we're all down here. Come on." He waved her over.

The lightbulb was weak, but it threw enough light to see the walls of the area, all lined with wooden shelves. The floor was paved with stone and a little uneven, and several posts helped to support the floor above. One post had a rope around the base. Had Charlotte tied her children in there? Tess wrapped her arms around herself. It was cold and musty. With the light off and the hatch closed, it would be pitch black and scary. Those poor children.

Dust coated everything, and Amy wiped it off a jar. "This looks like jam or preserves."

"Any date on it?" Faith asked.

Amy held it up to the light. "1960."

So maybe Ed's parents hadn't known of the cellar's existence.

Tess wandered over to the far wall where a desk sat and pulled open a drawer. Inside were a stack of papers and a book.

"Take a look," Ed said.

The papers were building designs.

"They're the extensions to the house," Ed said. "When they put the bathroom inside and added a couple of bedrooms."

The other book appeared to be a ledger with details of stock and feed in them. Next to the desk was an old trunk, and the other shelving contained tins, old toys, and other odds and ends that old houses collected.

"Let's open the trunk," Lara said.

"Not until I get there," Georgie replied. "I'm on my way."

"Geor-gie," Lara complained.

Matt shrugged. "She's hung up, La La. You're going to have to wait."

Brandon and Darcy carried the trunk upstairs, and the others followed. Tess walked along the shelving, studying what was there. Some of the stuff had a really old feel to it, the glass jars with more intricate mouldings, and the tin containers were the type which sold well in vintage shops. "This is really cool," she said to Ed. "Do you think Lilian and Reginald built it?"

"I don't know. It's got to be pretty old if Charlotte was using it. Maybe there're more details in her journals."

Tess wanted to stay up all night reading them. They were a fascinating look into the life of a woman who was miserable living in such an isolated location. She'd been forced to marry again after the war because her husband had died, and she had a young baby to support.

Tess trailed her fingers over the cool, rough rock wall, and one wobbled under her fingers. The light bulb flickered and went out, plunging them into darkness, with only a glow coming from the stairs.

"We should have another bulb upstairs," Ed said, taking her hand.

Tess was torn. Part of her wanted to examine every inch of this cellar and see what information the papers contained, what kind of history the bottles told, but the other part was just as interested in the trunk they'd carried upstairs.

In the laundry, Ed grabbed a spare bulb, and Tess flicked the light switch off so he could replace it.

"Ready," Ed called.

She flicked the switch, but no light came from the cellar. Ed swore. "Must be the wiring."

Disappointment filled her as Ed returned. "I'll call

someone tomorrow. Do you want to use the torch?"

In the kitchen behind her, the others sat around the table, discussing what they thought would be in the trunk. She could wait a night. She wanted to add her own theories. "Let's join the others."

"It's pretty old," Brandon was saying. "The top is a little rotted."

"It's got to be a treasure chest," Lara said. "Maybe no one has been able to open it."

Darcy chuckled. "I'm pretty sure someone would have opened it before now, pumpkin."

She pouted. "Not if there was no key."

"Could be it's the signed confession of the mutineers," Sam said. "Along with details of their gruesome exploits." He winked at Lara.

"The other trunks had clothing in them," Faith said.

"But why wouldn't they have moved it into the shed with the rest of them before they closed the cellar?" Ed asked.

"We could see if there's anything in Charlotte's journals," Tess suggested.

"Yes!" Lara said, leaping to her feet. "Where are they?"

"In my room. Do you want to help me get them?" Tess asked.

Lara nodded and tucked her hand into Tess's. "This is *so* exciting. I'm so glad you came."

Tess's heart squeezed at the little girl's acceptance of her. "Me too." Her gaze caught on the backpack her mother had bought her before she'd come to Australia. Her mother would be horrified about her climbing into dusty cellars and being so involved in what was private Stokes business. She sighed. Her mother was probably anxious she hadn't called. It was time Tess toughened up and faced her.

She needed answers.

Chapter 19

Ed took the journal Tess handed him, and soon there was silence as they all tried to decipher Charlotte's scratchy, hard to read handwriting. Her displeasure about the dust, the isolation, and her three children who wouldn't behave was clear, and he felt sorry for his grandpop. "Not a happy woman."

"I don't remember her," Darcy said. "She was what—our great grandmother?"

"Yeah," Brandon said. "I have only vague memories of having to be quiet and behave myself when she visited. Our grandparents brought her up here."

"Are they still alive?" Tess asked.

Ed shook his head. "Grandpop died of cancer before I started uni, and Nanna died not long after. They lived in Perth."

"Dad said Grandpop never liked the station, which is why he was happy for Dad to take over as soon as he was old enough," Darcy said.

"If he was locked in the cellar regularly, I can understand why he had such awful memories," Faith said.

Ed didn't have many memories of his grandparents.

They'd visited less than once a year, and his Grandpop had always been sombre. But now it made sense. He would have associated this land with a crappy childhood. Ed was surprised he hadn't sold it the moment he inherited, but maybe by then, Bill had fallen in love with the land.

"Charlotte mentions the mess in the cellar here," Amy said. "All sorts of old rubbish; trunks, papers, clothes. Her plan is to burn the lot."

Tess stiffened beside him as Amy flicked through the pages to find out what happened. "Her husband forbade it, but she says she'll wait until he's away for a few days, and do it anyway."

"What a witch," Lara exclaimed.

Ed chuckled and nodded.

Outside, a car pulled up, and Matt stood to unlock the kitchen door. Georgie hurried inside, frowning at Matt holding the door open for her. "What are you doing?"

"Being a gentleman."

She grunted and continued inside, her eyes darting to the trunk, and then to her family. "Someone better tell me what's going on."

"We went through the trunks in the shed," Ed told her. "Found some journals which Tess read, and she saw reference to a cellar. So we pulled up the lino in the laundry and found a hatch."

"I want to see for myself." She disappeared into the laundry, and Matt trailed after her.

"Don't you go locking me in here," Georgie told him.

"I wouldn't dream of it, Freckles."

Ed grimaced. It was just as well Charlie had never known about the cellar, otherwise he would have tricked them in there, and then switched off the light. Ed closed his eyes. But Charlie also would have come up with the most amazing adventures revolving around the cellar as well. He'd always had the best imagination. Ed smiled.

He'd forgotten that.

A few minutes later, Georgie was back. "That's so cool."

"Can we open the trunk now?" Lara pleaded.

"Yes," Georgie said, striding over to it. She tried to lift the lid, but it was stuck. "Anyone got a key?"

It was a different style of trunk from the ones they'd opened earlier, older, with more water damage. It would make Tess's day if it was the trunk Lilian had owned, and if it contained information about the Retribution. "I'll check Dad's office." On his way, he grabbed the keys which fit the other trunks, and then scanned the display cabinet in case he'd missed something. No other keys. Back in the kitchen, he handed the keys to Georgie, but they didn't turn the lock.

"Sam's an expert at locks," Brandon said. "Think you can pick it?"

"Maybe." He examined the lock. "Let me get my gear." He headed outside.

"He brings lock picking gear with him to a wedding?" Amy asked.

Brandon laughed. "He likes to be prepared for anything."

Sam walked in a couple of minutes later. "Lee is gone."

Ed jolted. "What?"

"His tent and car are gone. I'm guessing he wasn't supposed to check out yet." Sam glanced at Amy.

"He was booked in for another fortnight."

Brandon swore. "He must have been working for Stonefish."

"Maybe he got bad news and had to leave," Lara said, twisting her hands together.

"It doesn't look good, pumpkin," Darcy said. "He would have at least come over and said he had to leave early."

Amy got out her phone. "No email or missed call."

"I'll call Dot," Brandon said.

"What's this about Lee?" Georgie asked.

Ed told her about Salvatore. Was Tess in danger? Surely Lee would have said something to Stonefish if he recognised her.

Georgie swore. "I thought he was a decent guy."

"Does this mean Tan knows where I am?" Tess whispered to Ed.

"Maybe." But why would Salvatore blow Lee's cover, if that was the case? "We'll see what Dot has to say."

Sam picked the lock on the trunk while Brandon spoke with Dot. He whooped as the lid lifted a crack, and Georgie hugged him. "My hero." She reached for the lid, and Sam kept his hand on it, preventing her from opening it.

"Hold your horses," he said. "Wait for Bran."

Georgie scowled. "I take that praise back."

Tess vibrated next to him, and whether it was from fear of Tan, or excitement for the contents of the trunk, Ed didn't know. He slid his arm around her waist. "Everything will be fine. I'll protect you."

She leaned into him. "I know."

He closed his eyes, buoyed by her faith in him. With her he felt like a superhero. Her trust gave him confidence. He pressed a kiss on her hair.

Brandon hung up. "Salvatore has been singing all the way to the station. He's placing all the blame on Tan, and mentioned Lee was their contact up here."

Amy paled. "I trusted him."

Ed felt for his sister-in-law. He had taken Lee stargazing the last time he'd been here and had enjoyed spending time with the intelligent and interesting man. Ed wished he'd taken more photos at the wedding. "What do we do now?"

"She wants Tess to come in tomorrow and officially

identify Salvatore. They'll have people arrest Tan in Perth."

Tess exhaled, and Ed hugged her.

"They'll put a bulletin out for Lee, but he's probably gone to ground," Brandon continued. "He knows his way around the bush."

Matt nodded. "I'll call my parents and ask them to keep an eye out for him."

"I doubt he'll come back," Faith said. "We all know him. He'd have to be desperate."

"Should I ring my brother-in-law?" Tess asked. "They're cousins, and he might find out where he is."

"Let's ask Dot and Nhiari tomorrow," Brandon said.

Silence filled the room as they contemplated Lee's betrayal. There was nothing they could do about it tonight, and they had the best form of distraction sitting next to Sam and Georgie. Ed gestured to the trunk. "I think everyone's dying to see what's inside."

Lara clapped her hands and Georgie said, "Finally!"

Tess smiled, though she bit her lower lip, her mind obviously elsewhere. They crowded around the trunk, and Georgie and Lara lifted the lid.

Damn. Tess slumped next to him.

The inside was lined with floral paper, and it was empty.

"Well, that explains why they left it down there," Darcy said.

Lara turned to Ed. "Where's the tape measure?"

"In Granny's craft room."

She ran out and returned shortly after with the tape measure. The others had returned to the table, but Ed helped her measure the inside and then the outside. There was about an inch difference, but the thick bottom accounted for that.

"We should rip the paper," Lara said.

"No," Darcy said. "It's bedtime. You've got school

and pony club tomorrow."

Lara turned pleading eyes to Ed.

"I'll do some research tonight, La La. We don't want to damage the trunk, but I'll see if I can find references to trunks with false bottoms and how to find them."

"If you find anything, you'll wait for me?"

"Of course."

She hugged him. "Thanks, Ed." She followed Darcy and Faith out of the room to get ready for bed.

"That wasn't worth the trip out here," Georgie groused.

"We've been reading your great grandmother's journals." Tess handed her the one they'd been reading. "You might find them interesting."

Georgie smiled. "Thanks."

"What time are you working tomorrow?" Ed asked her.

She nibbled on her nail. "It's my day off."

What was she worried about? "You going to stay the night?"

"I might as well. Can I look through the other trunks?"

Damn. He'd been looking forward to sleeping in the same room with Tess again. "They're in the craft room."

"We'll do a lap of the grounds," Sam said. "Make sure Lee didn't leave us a parting gift."

"I'll join you," Brandon said. "Lock the door behind us. I'll take a key."

Ed stared at the closed door, his muscles stiff. Was his brother walking into danger? He'd never considered it before, probably because they'd never been close, but he disliked the tension filling him. Although Ed still hadn't forgiven him for leaving after Charlie died, he didn't want to lose any more of his family.

"Do you two want more tea?" Amy asked.

Ed checked with Tess, then shook his head. "You

want to explore the cellar some more?"

Tess hesitated, and then sighed. "We might miss something in the dark. Let's wait for morning and we can go through it systematically."

He smiled as she gathered up the journals the others had left on the table. "I need to talk to Georgie about where she's sleeping," he said. "Why don't you take those to our room, and I'll join you in a minute?"

"All right."

Amy sat with a mug of tea clenched in her hands, glancing towards the door. Even more worried than him. Ed placed a hand on her shoulder and put as much confidence in his voice as he could. "They'll be fine, Ames."

She smiled up at him. "I know, but I can't go to bed until Brandon's back."

"I'll wait up with you. Just let me have a word with Georgie." Ed found Georgie hunched over one of the trunks. She looked up. "This is fascinating. Why didn't we ever do this before?"

Ed shrugged. "As kids, we wouldn't have cared."

"True."

"Is there anything up with you?" he asked.

She twisted her hair around her finger. "No. Why?"

He took hold of her hand. "Because earlier you were biting your nail, and now you're twirling your hair."

She sighed. "You're annoying."

Ed smiled. "So what gives?"

"I applied for a job with Parks and Wildlife Services," she said. "I've got an interview on Friday."

"That's great." He hugged her. "Why are you nervous?"

"Because I want it so badly."

"You'll rock the interview, Mermaid. Everyone loves you."

She squeezed him. "Thanks, Astro Boy. I needed to

hear that." She turned back to the trunks.

Now he needed to address why he was here. Ed picked up the mantel clock and turned it over in his hands. It was made of some dark wood, and the craftmanship was excellent. "Can you sleep in the shearers' quarters tonight?"

She looked up, surprised. "Oh, Tess is in our room, right?"

He nodded.

"Do you think we can trust her? If Lee was a spy..."

"She isn't." His reaction was instant. He wouldn't believe that, he couldn't. "We can trust her."

"You're not letting her doe eyes seduce you, are you?"

He rolled his eyes. "Give it a rest, Georgie."

"I just don't want you to be hurt."

Was it so hard to believe Tess could like him for himself? "When you've womaned up about your love life, then you can lecture me on mine."

She frowned at him. "What are you talking about?"

"Matt."

Her eyes narrowed and her gaze darted to the door. "Shut up. I told you that in a moment of weakness."

He didn't push her. "Do you need to grab any clothes from the room before we go to bed?"

She clambered to her feet. "Yeah." She patted him on the shoulder. "I hope you're right about Tess."

So did Ed.

He returned to the kitchen where Amy waited, hands still clasped around her tea, which hadn't been drunk. "Lee's long gone," Ed said.

"I can't help worrying."

"Brandon and his mates can handle anything." Ed had no clue if it was true, but it sounded good.

She nodded.

Ed hugged her, glad Brandon had left the army, and she wouldn't have this constant fear when he was away.

"Drink your tea." Though he loved Amy like a sister, part of him was jealous that she'd been enough to bring Brandon home, and his family hadn't been. Pushing aside the old feelings, he wandered over to the door and unlocked it, opening it a crack to see outside. Dobby and Heath stood on the verandah of the shearers' quarters with bottles of beer. Ed frowned and opened the door wider, stepping out. Sam handed Brandon a beer, and they clinked bottles.

You've got to be kidding me.

Brandon was drinking with his mates, while Amy sat inside, worrying. Ed clenched his hands. "Brandon's fine," he called to Amy. "They're by the shearers' quarters. I'm going to have a word."

Amy relaxed and sipped her tea. "Thanks, Ed."

Ed barely heard her as he strode across the hard ground, old resentments simmering to the surface, his gaze on his older brother. It was just like him not to let his loved ones know he was fine. When he got close enough, he called, "I guess you didn't find anything."

Brandon turned and smiled. "No, everything's fine."

"So you're going to stand here, having a beer with your mates, while your wife is inside worried out of her mind?" Ed knew his brother was inconsiderate, but this was next level. "I thought you cared for Amy, but you don't give a shit about anyone but yourself, do you?"

Brandon swore and stepped towards the house.

Ed slapped a hand against Brandon's chest. "Don't worry, I've told her you're fine. You can continue getting pissed with your mates." He clenched his hand, resisting the sudden urge to punch his brother. Where had all this fury come from? He'd thought he'd dealt with Brandon's abandonment years ago. His whole body vibrated, and he forced himself to stride away, lest he do something he'd regret.

"Ed, wait."

Ed kept walking, away from the sheds, away from the house. The dark called to him.

Footsteps behind him, and then Brandon placed a hand on his shoulder, pulling him up short. Ed whirled to him. "Fuck off, Bran."

Brandon stepped back, hands raised, his face just visible in the light. "What's your problem?"

Disbelief made Ed snort. "You're such a dick."

"I was going to the house to tell Amy after I took the beer."

"Yeah, sure you were." Ed turned to go.

"If you've got a problem with me, Ed, just spit it out." Annoyance tinged Brandon's tone now.

Slowly, Ed turned back to him, every childhood fear and misery battering to get out. "Where do I start?" Ed asked. "When you abandoned your family without a single word? How you didn't give a shit about Mum or Dad, but returned the moment you could get something? How you slotted back in here, taking over the farm as if it was your right, even though you didn't care about us enough to stay in touch?" Tears wet his eyes, and he blinked to get rid of them. He wasn't giving his brother that satisfaction. "When Charlie died, we needed you, Bran. Mum was out of her mind with grief, Dad rarely came in from the farm before we went to bed, and Georgie was so scared." His voice broke. "I wrote to you, Bran, begging you to come home. Did you even get the letter?"

Brandon was silent, and then he swore quietly. "You don't know the whole story, Ed."

"I know plenty. I know you didn't care enough about us to come back." He'd prayed every day for over a year that Brandon would return, and everything would be all right again. Disgusted at himself that he was still this upset after over fifteen years, he turned to go.

"Wait." Brandon swore again. "I need to tell you the

truth. Please, Ed, give me a second." The anguish in Brandon's voice made Ed hesitate. Brandon ran a hand through his hair and exhaled noisily. "Charlie's death was my fault."

Ed jolted. Of all the things he'd expected Brandon to say, that was not one of them. "What?"

He cleared his throat. "I caused the stampede which killed Charlie."

Ed's mind whirled. "How? Why?"

"I don't know how much you remember, but Charlie was going through a stage where he was trying to scare us. He had this black plastic spider…"

The one that had terrified Tess. "I remember."

"So I wanted to get him back. I bought a plastic snake, set it up outside the cattle yard, so Charlie would spring it when I asked him to check the water trough."

A good idea. Charlie wouldn't expect to be pranked outside the house, not near the new cattle they were trialling. "What happened?"

"Gertie sprang it instead. It flew into the cattle yard and startled the cattle. Charlie was at the gate."

Gertie had been their old blue heeler. "Fuck." Brandon's absence made so much more sense now. What a horrific thing to live with. Ed's anger vanished, and he stepped forward. "Bran…" What could he say? "It was an accident. If it hadn't gone bad, you would have been our hero for getting Charlie back."

Brandon shifted away. "Well it did go bad."

Hell. Ed's insides felt raw. "I blamed myself for Charlie's death for years as well."

"Why?"

"We had a fight that morning. I wished Charlie would go away… and then he did."

Brandon squeezed his shoulder. "I'm sorry. At the time I was so caught up in my guilt, I didn't consider how anyone else was coping. I figured you were all better off without me."

He would have been so lonely. "I'm sorry I never asked. I figured you didn't care."

His brother's smile was sad. "I missed the family and this land every single day. I didn't think I'd ever be able to come back."

Shit. "We missed you too." He hugged his brother, wishing he could take back the years of hurt. "Sorry for yelling at you."

"I deserved it," Brandon said, hugging him back.

They separated, and Ed smiled at him. "For what it's worth, I'm glad you're home."

"Me too."

Ed cleared his throat and behind Brandon, he caught sight of Sam and the others still on the verandah. How much had they heard? Heat filled his cheeks. "I'd better check on Tess. Enjoy your beer."

He hurried inside.

Chapter 20

Tess stared at the ceiling of the bedroom the next morning, comforted by Ed's heavy breathing in the bed next to hers. After Ed had told her about his altercation with Brandon, they'd stayed up late reading Charlotte's journals. But Ed's pain at something which had happened years ago made her realise she had to face her own family issues before they got out of control. She needed to call her parents. First, she switched on her laptop to check her emails, in order to gauge how frantic her parents were.

Two hundred messages when normally she was lucky to get ten a week.

She tensed at those from Tan with the subject *Call me* and ignored them in case they came with some kind of tracking malware. Instead, she clicked on the first one from her mother.

It was full of concern. Tan had said she'd run away, where was she? Had she run off with a boy?

Tess smiled and glanced at Ed.

The next dozen were increasingly frantic and demanding. *Call immediately.* No mention of Joy telling them she had called, but her sister must have done.

The last was written yesterday, and said they would call the Australian police and report her missing if she didn't contact them right away.

She grabbed her phone. Time to be brave. She'd go outside, so she didn't wake Ed, and call them right now.

Tess picked up the black Akubra on the side table and rubbed her thumb over the thick felt. Ed had given it to her, and wearing it, even for a minute yesterday had made her feel powerful and in control.

Decided, she placed it on her head and walked out the door.

In the kitchen, Sam, Heath and Dobby were saying goodbye to Georgie and Amy. Brandon was driving them to the airport to catch their flight back to the city. Matt and Darcy must already be working, and Faith would have taken Lara to school.

Heath grinned at her. "I was hoping you'd be up before we left." He swept her up and hugged her. "Nice hat."

"Thanks." Tess's heart pinched as she hugged him back. He'd been so kind to her. "I'll miss you."

"Don't be a stranger," Heath said. "You need anything, you call. You've got my number?"

She nodded. "You be careful wherever you're going." She'd never known anyone who worked in the armed forces and hated the thought they might go somewhere dangerous.

"Always am," he assured her.

"We keep him out of trouble," Sam said. "You try to do the same from now on."

She smiled. A week ago, being in a room full of large men would have intimidated her, but these guys had shown her she didn't always have to be afraid. She waved as they drove away, and then excused herself from Georgie and Amy to call her parents, her muscles tense.

"Hello?" Her mother always sounded uncertain when

she answered the phone.

Annoyance filled her. Tess would never be that timid again. "Mum, it's Tess." She moved towards the sand dunes, the red dirt and peace calling to her.

A sharp inhalation. "Where are you? Why did you run away? Why didn't you answer any of my messages?"

Tess railed against the feeling of being suffocated. She was an adult, she didn't need to tell her parents everything she did. "I'm safe, Mum. Didn't Joy tell you?" She inhaled the fresh air, the scent of eucalyptus, and the openness of the country, dissolving the suffocation.

"She didn't tell me where you were."

"That's because she didn't know." Tess took a deep breath. Her mum was going to be horrified. "I left Tan's place because I saw him kill someone."

Silence.

"Mum?"

"You haven't told anyone, have you?" Her mother's voice wavered.

Tess frowned. "What?"

"They won't believe you. Tan is an important person. If you tell anyone what you saw, they'll think you're lying. You mustn't say a word."

Not the response she'd expected from her mother. "Mum, he had me followed. Someone tried to kill me."

She gasped. "No. You misunderstood. You must come home immediately."

"I can't. He has my passport."

"Then go back to him. He'll forgive you as long as you haven't told anyone."

Had someone put her into an alternative reality? Why was her mother defending Tan? Tess shook her head, the confusion giving way to annoyance. "Mum, I can't."

"You must. His people have your father. They'll kill him."

She froze, staring at the red dirt. A beetle rolled a ball

of dung along the ground in front of her, oblivious to her shock. "What?"

"They have your father," her mother sobbed.

"What? How?" Nothing made sense anymore.

Her mother sniffed, and just as Tess was about to scream with frustration, she said, "It's a long story."

"Well, start telling it."

Her mother gasped as if affronted by Tess's tone, but Tess didn't care. She needed answers.

"It started about ten years ago. Your father got a job at the docks and was approached by one of his colleagues. They would give him some money if he didn't pay any attention to what was in a container coming in. We were struggling back then, and it was supposed to be a once-off occurrence, so he agreed."

Tess closed her eyes. She could guess the rest. "What was in the shipment?"

"They never said. The next time a shipment came in, he refused, but this organisation had evidence of him agreeing to the previous shipment, and so they blackmailed him. He's been trapped for years."

"Tan's part of this organisation?"

"Yes."

"Why did you send me to stay with him then?" Surely they should have protected her.

"Because he found out you were going to Australia and demanded it. Your father was trying to get out, and this was a way of controlling him. We tried to talk you out of going, but you insisted."

She refused to feel guilty. They should have told her the truth, or at least warned her. "Mum, you need to go to the police."

"No! They'll kill your father."

"The police have a warrant for Tan's arrest."

Her mother wailed. "No! You must stop them. Tell them you lied."

It was too late. Salvatore was in gaol, and he'd talked. They had probably already arrested Tan. Would her father be killed? Tess wanted to be sick.

"They said if you don't go back to Tan within six hours of calling us, they'll kill your father. They're monitoring our calls."

The nausea swirled like a cyclone in Tess's stomach. Maybe the police could help her save her father. "I'll call you back, Mum." It was eight o'clock. The first thing she needed to do was find out where Tan was. She strode back into the house, the fly screen door slamming behind her.

"Everything OK?" Amy asked.

Nothing was. She shook her head. "Do you have Dot's phone number?"

"What happened?" Georgie asked.

"I called Mum. She said Stonefish have taken Dad and will kill him if I go to the police."

Ed walked in, hair dishevelled and his T-shirt and shorts crinkled. "What did I miss?"

Just the sight of him calmed her rapid heartbeat. "I need to find out if they've arrested Tan. They've got my dad." Her voice quivered.

He snapped to attention and whipped out his phone. "I'll call Dot."

Tess paced the kitchen. At some stage they had returned the washing machine and the cupboard to the laundry and set the table back in its proper position.

Ed put the phone on speaker. "Dot, did they arrest Tan?"

"Not yet. He didn't return to his house last night and wasn't at the restaurant."

Ed swore.

"What's happened?"

He gestured for Tess to speak.

"I called my parents. Mum said Stonefish are holding

Dad. They'll kill him if I don't return to Tan."

"Where are your parents?"

"In Singapore."

Dot cursed. "I'll need to make some calls. Stay there, and I'll contact you as soon as I know more."

Tess glanced over at the door. Was here safe anymore? Tan was out there somewhere, as was Lee. Was her brother-in-law involved as well? How far did Stonefish's influence spread?

Ed touched her arm, and she flinched.

"They'll do what they can."

Trite words. How much could the Australian police do from here? Her father was somewhere in Singapore. She could imagine him tied to a chair like that woman had been. Someone pointing a gun at his head.

She could end this. If she called Tan, she could arrange for her father to be freed.

"Tess, you can't do anything, but wait." Ed pulled her into his arms.

She closed her eyes, hugging him back. She could do something, if she was brave enough. But would it make a difference? Would she be risking everything she'd gained—Ed, these wonderful friends, her newfound confidence—by trying to negotiate?

Georgie spoke. "Ed's right, Tess. The police will sort it out. They're probably tracking Tan now. Give them a couple of hours."

Her father didn't have that much time. "They were monitoring Mum's calls. I've got six hours to turn myself in."

"You can't get to Perth that quickly."

"Yes, I can." There might be room on the army guys' flight home. She ran to her room and shoved her things in her backpack.

"What are you doing?" Ed stood at the doorway.

"I need to get on Heath's flight."

"No, Tess. It's too dangerous."

"I have to."

Her phone beeped with a message. *Call me.*

She froze. Only Ed and her mother had her number, but this wasn't a phone number she recognised. She glanced at Ed.

"Who's it from?"

"I don't know." But it had to be related to her father.

He strode over. "Show me." He frowned as he read the message. "Dot might be able to trace it."

She nodded to him, and he rang Dot back. Quickly, he explained the situation, and then put Dot on speaker. "She wants you to call the number so she can listen in."

"You'd better tell Amy and Georgie what we're doing." The last thing they needed was for one of them to make too much noise and give away where Tess was.

Ed handed his phone to Tess and left the room.

"Tess, if it is Tan, you need to keep him talking," Dot said. "Try to find out where he is. If he wants you to go somewhere, ask who will meet you, that kind of thing. Listen carefully, there might be background noises that will give away where he is."

"Can you protect my dad?"

Dot sighed. "I've rung people, but I don't know how good their contacts are. Is there somewhere the rest of your family can go in the meantime?"

Was there? No, she couldn't call her mother back if they were monitoring the calls.

Ed returned with Amy and Georgie. Tess stiffened. She didn't want an audience, but perhaps they'd hear something she didn't. "I'll call the number."

She put her phone on speaker. Every muscle in her body tensed as she waited for someone to answer. Finally, just as Tess thought the call would go to voice mail, a male answered. "Where are you, Tess?"

Her heart raced. "You don't need to know, Tan."

"I disagree." His tone was calm, as if discussing the weather. "The fate of your father depends on where you are."

"Where are you?"

He laughed. "Safe. Don't you worry about me."

Was that the sound of waves in the background?

"I want you to be in Hyde Park in an hour. Someone will pick you up."

She glanced at Ed. "I don't know where that is."

"It's just north of the CBD."

"You know I'm not in the city."

"You might have returned after your little jaunt."

He was testing her. She stayed silent. Let him do the talking. It was more opportunity to get the information Dot needed.

"I'm sure wherever you are, I can have someone with you within the hour."

Her hand trembled. Surely he couldn't. Unless he already knew where she was. Lee could have told him. "Australia's a big country."

"It is, but I know you're still in the state, and north of the Tropic of Capricorn."

Could he be tracing her new phone? She hadn't thought to ask Dot if it was possible. "What will you do if I come to you?"

"I'll set your father free."

"How do I know you'll keep your promise? You might kill us both."

Tan chuckled, a most unpleasant sound. "I might, but I'll definitely kill him if you don't. Tell me where you are."

Her skin prickled, and her stomach lurched. She couldn't let that happen. Her family needed her father more than they needed her. Ed shook his head, his eyes wide. She turned away, her heart aching. "I'm in Retribution Bay."

"How convenient. I know a few people there. I'll send you a map. Be at that location within the hour." He hung up.

"Tess—" Ed began.

"No. I can't let anything happen to my father. I have to go."

"Dot, did you get anything?" Georgie asked.

"He's in the area, too. He might meet you himself. Have you got the map yet?"

Tess's knees went weak and she glanced towards the door half expecting Tan to walk in, gun in hand. "No." She stared at the phone, willing the map to arrive quickly, yet not wanting it to come. She should leave now, before the others knew. That way, none of them would be in any danger. Her phone beeped and her hand shook as she clicked on the image. She frowned, enlarging it, trying to figure it out.

"Where is it?" Dot asked.

Tess handed her phone to Ed. "I don't know."

Ed swore. "The gulf. The bastard wants to meet on our land, near Retribution Island."

Another text came with instructions to steal a four-wheel drive to get there.

Dot swore. "If he's already in the area, he'll see us coming." She ordered some of her people to suit up.

"We've got motorbikes," Amy said. "If you dress like Darcy and Bran, you could get close enough, and pretend you're checking troughs or something."

Georgie shook her head. "There aren't any sheep in the area. But a group of horse riders might not cause much notice." She swore. "There's not enough time to get there though."

It was kind of them to be brainstorming options, but there was one solution. "I'll go on my own," Tess said. "If you give me a radio, I'll tell you where he came from."

"No," Ed said. "I won't let you go alone."

"We don't have a lot of choice, Ed. The police can't get there in time. Not without Tan seeing them."

"I'll go with you. I'll take the rifle."

No! She wouldn't risk him.

"Ed, don't be stupid," Dot said.

He walked out of the room, Georgie following close behind, her voice raised in protest.

"Ed," Dot repeated.

"He's gone," Tess said. She eyed her backpack on the bed and spotted the hire car keys on the bedside table. Wherever the rifle was, she might get to the four-wheel drive before Ed could stop her. She knew how to get to the beach, and there were no other four-wheel drives here. He couldn't follow her. She could keep him safe.

Dot swore. "Give me ten minutes to come up with a plan. I'll call you back."

Amy turned to Tess. "We'll work this out. I'll call Brandon." She left the room, and Tess snatched the keys from the bedside table and slung her bag over her shoulder. She had little time. Her heart thumping, she went through to the kitchen where Amy was on the phone.

"I'm going to find Ed," Tess said and headed out the door. Her fingers fumbled as she pressed the button to unlock the hire car and threw her bag on the front seat. She started the car, shifted the gear lever into drive, and accelerated away from the house, her pulse pounding in her ears. A glance in the rear-view mirror showed no one was coming after her.

Good. It might be a while before they noticed she was gone.

Chapter 21

"Ed, you're not going." Georgie shoved her way in front of the gun safe, blocking Ed's access.

He clenched his hands to stop himself from thrusting her aside. "I'm not letting Tess go on her own. Tan will kill her."

"It's not your problem. The police will sort out something."

His mouth dropped open, and he stared at his sister. How could she say that? "I love her." The statement resonated through him with truth. He couldn't let Tess face this alone.

Georgie's face crumpled. "And I love you. Please, Ed. Don't go. I can't lose anyone else."

Her fear tore at his heart. Every now and then Georgie would revert to the scared little girl he remembered after Charlie had died. He hugged her. "I'll be careful, Mermaid. I promise."

She clung to him.

"If Matt was in Tess's position, would you let him go alone?"

She stiffened. "That's not fair."

He kissed her forehead. "No, it's not. We'll work out

a plan. I can hide in the dunes as backup. You know I never miss."

"That's when you were shooting beer bottles. Could you really shoot a person?"

If the person was threatening Tess, he could. "Let's hope it doesn't come to that." He nudged her away from the gun safe and opened it, checking the rifle to make sure the chamber was empty, and then slung it over his shoulder. He grabbed a box of bullets. "Come on, Dot will have a plan by now."

He stalked over to the house. Something was wrong, out of place. He frowned, and then it clicked. "Where's my car?" Fear spiked, and he raced inside. "Where's Tess?"

Amy turned to him. "She went to find you."

"The car's gone." He ran into his bedroom, but neither she nor the keys were there. Damn it. He dialled her phone, but it went straight to voice mail. She was already out of range. Why had she gone without him? He'd promised to help her.

He shoved his phone in his pocket and stormed back to the kitchen. "I need a car."

"Wait a second, Ed," Georgie said. "Let's call Dot back. And if you're going, wear something more protective."

He glanced down. He still wore the shorts he'd slept in and was barefoot. Damn it. "Call her." He lay the rifle on the table and headed to his room.

A minute later, he was back in the kitchen and putting on his boots. Dot was on speaker. "I've arranged a plane to fly over the area to track Tan," she said. "My team is getting into position now."

Ed shook his head. "They'll hear you a mile away—literally. You can't sneak up."

"We've got time."

"Tess has already left," Ed said. "If Tan's in position

early…"

Dot swore. "I told her to wait."

"Brandon's on his way," Amy said. "He turned around as soon as I called. He might get there in time."

"I'm going to arrest the idiot," Dot growled.

But they were unarmed. "I'm going after her." He picked up the rifle, daring Georgie to say something. She closed her eyes and then nodded.

"Ed, don't you dare," ordered Dot. "I don't need multiple civilians to deal with."

"You'll have to take a bike." Amy grabbed a backpack, and threw water and a radio in it before thrusting it at him.

Shit. Nausea welled up as he added the box of bullets to the backpack. "Fine." He strode to the shed to one of the motorbikes. Every inch of him resisted closing the distance, but he did it. This was for Tess. He'd be in complete control. He swallowed past the fear. With the rifle secure against his back, he rode out of the shed as Darcy sped back towards the house in the ute. The urge to stop and wait for the ute was strong, but his brother would only try to stop him.

He twisted the throttle and accelerated, flying along the flat ground. His hands gripped the handle bars as he sped across the bitumen road to the track to the beach. Tess had left the gate open, and he roared through. Maybe he'd catch her before she reached the beach. He wished he hadn't taught her how to use the four-wheel drive.

Ed increased his speed, remembering his father's instructions—*relax, be loose, let the bike wriggle over the bumps.* He'd always felt out of control riding a motorbike, and his crash with Charlie hadn't helped matters.

Dust floated in the air before him, but he couldn't see the car. Tess couldn't be too far in front now.

The gulf was just up ahead. If he raced over the hill

into sight, anyone watching would know he was there.

Ed slowed and pulled off the track, riding across to a clump of shrubs. Hopefully it was far enough off the main track so no one would spot it. He broke a few branches off to cover the white mudguards, and then grabbed some bullets from the backpack and shoved them in his pocket, leaving the backpack with the bike. He crept closer to the beach, sticking to the bushes. Charlie had never been patient enough for tracking and hunting, but Ed had tagged along when Matt had tried to teach him, and Ed had loved the stealth of it.

He reached the hill and crouched low, scanning the area. Tess was parked next to the hitching post and trough about twenty metres away. She sat in the car, waiting, the black Akubra on her head like she was some kind of bad ass. Should he tell her he was there? Maybe, but first he had to work out whether anyone else was around.

Aside from the road he'd taken, there was another track coming from the west, which ended on the far side of the beach, past the mangroves. Dot would use it. But if Tan was staying in or near town, he might come from that direction as well.

Ed hadn't been further east in a long time, but there wasn't a track. Their neighbours used the road on Ridge land if they wanted to go to the beach.

He kept low, and slowly scanned his surroundings, looking for an odd colour or shape on the landscape. Or a movement. It had now been an hour since Tan had called, and chances were high he would have someone in place by now. He wouldn't have expected Tess to arrive so early.

A hum reached his ears. He stared up, searching the sky for a drone or plane. Clear, but drones were difficult to spot. The hum grew louder. It was more of an engine—a boat engine.

Ed shifted to view the gulf. Sure enough, a silver dinghy motored towards the shore from Retribution Island with one person inside. Was it Tan? Would he risk being out here by himself? Surely he'd have some kind of backup—Lee?

Ed wished he'd brought binoculars. Dot wouldn't be here for another half an hour. Taking his time, he studied all the places where someone could monitor the beach. The mangroves in front of him would make it difficult, but the rise over by Ed's right was the perfect spot. As he watched, something moved about thirty metres away, its brown colour at odds with the red surroundings. The wrong colour for a racehorse goanna, and too low to the ground for a kangaroo, but it reminded Ed of an Akubra hat.

Someone was there.

The dinghy was still halfway across the bay. Ed crept backwards and, keeping low, he shuffled closer to his target, taking the rifle from his back and holding it in position. Inserting a bullet would make too much noise, but whoever was watching from the hill wouldn't know the gun was unloaded.

His heart pounded and his hands sweated around the rifle. The mid-morning sun wasn't hot but was high enough in the sky not to mess with his vision. He placed his feet noiselessly, and soon he was parallel to where he'd seen the figure. He clenched the rifle and moved closer. The dinghy's tone changed to announce it was slowing. Not much time.

Ed immediately recognised the figure lying in the sand, eyes to a set of binoculars. He gritted his teeth, crouched, and shoved the rifle into the man's side. "Don't move, Lee."

Lee barely flinched. "Ed, you shouldn't be here."

"I won't let anyone kill Tess."

"I'm not planning on it," Lee replied, lowering the

binoculars, and glancing at him. "I want to protect her."

Ed frowned. Not what he'd expected Lee to say. He hesitated. "Why?"

Lee moved slowly, reaching for a pistol lying in the grass.

"Don't move."

"You take it," Lee said. "Quickly now. Tan won't mess around for long."

Ed shuffled forward as Tan got out of the dinghy. When he glanced back at Lee, he found himself looking down the barrel of the pistol.

He froze.

"Get down, set up your rifle," Lee said. "Tan will have a gun in a holster under his jacket."

Ed blinked, confused. Lee wasn't going to shoot him? He did as Lee ordered, lying down, adding two bullets to the rifle, and getting into position, all the while hyper aware of Lee and his gun.

"Aren't you working for Tan?" Ed murmured.

Silence. "I work for Stonefish."

Ed wanted to ask more, but Tess was getting out of the car. He prayed Lee could be trusted and aimed for Tan. Would he be able to pull the trigger if it came down to it?

***

Tess trembled as she shut the car door, the sound like a gunshot across the quiet landscape. What was she doing here? It had seemed like a good idea when she'd taken the car, but she'd had plenty of time to second-guess herself on the drive here, and during the long wait. She'd never expected Tan to arrive via boat, but at least he was alone.

"I want to know my father is alive," Tess called.

Tan laughed. "You should have asked your mother if you could speak to him."

Huh? "Your people have kidnapped him."

"That's what I told her to say, and she's so obedient. She knows what happens to people who disobey Stonefish."

Tess stared at him. Her mother had lied to her? But she must know Tan would kill Tess. She couldn't breathe. "No! I don't believe you."

"I don't care. It's the truth, but you won't ever know."

His words brought her attention back to him. "What are you going to do?"

"I'll make sure you can't testify, and then I'm getting the hell out of Australia."

She blinked. "Why kill me if you're leaving?"

"Because my boss doesn't like loose ends."

His boss. So he wasn't in charge. "I've already told the police everything. They have my statement on record, plus Salvatore talked as well. It's enough for a court case." She hoped. She had no idea how the legal system worked in Australia.

"Salvatore will be dealt with." He scowled. "When did you get so confident? What happened to the mouse who was working for me?"

She squared her shoulders. "You don't know me."

Tan moved closer and Tess fought the urge to back up. What would he do to her? She couldn't see a gun or any other weapon.

"It's interesting you should end up here when for the past few months I've been trying to buy this property."

Tess shifted. "If I'd known, I wouldn't have come. The couple I hitched a ride with were coming here on holiday."

"Couple? Salvatore said you were with a guy."

"His wife hid in the back with me."

Tan was getting closer, so she moved away from the car, back towards the track. "Is this a property?" she asked. "Looks like bush to me. Why would you want it?"

"None of your business."

If she kept him talking, maybe the police would arrive in time. She should have waited. "So, are you planning to take the dinghy to Singapore?"

He scowled. "No. If I go to Singapore, I'm as good as dead."

She jolted. Interesting. "Why?"

"Because I screwed up. You did this to me." He reached inside his jacket, drew out a gun and pointed it at her.

Shit. Her heart raced, and she couldn't drag her gaze from the end of the gun, waiting for the shot.

"I might have worked out a solution if you hadn't seen me kill Charmaine."

Her hands trembled as she raised them.

"You need to pay."

Chapter 22

Tess backed away from the car, moving closer to Ed, but still too far away. With Lee next to him, he didn't dare make himself known. "You got any backup here?"

"It's just me I think, but Stonefish don't tell me everything."

That was in line with everything else they'd learnt about the consortium. Their pawns only knew what they needed to. Beyond the car, something moved. No, someone. Brandon. The cavalry had arrived, but would Lee shoot them? Ed scoured the area behind him and saw Sam sneaking around the opposite side, closing in, but it didn't appear as if Sam had seen him. Which meant Dobby and Heath would be nearby as well.

"Ed, when this is over, make sure the police check the island."

Ed frowned at Lee. "Why?" Had he seen the others?

"Just do it. I can't say more."

It was weird lying next to a man he'd drunk a beer with, and who had pointed a gun at him. Who had been potentially spying on his family for months now, and maybe even sabotaging the place. Yet part of him wanted to trust Lee. "Did you kill our sheep?"

Silence.

"Why do Stonefish want the land so badly?"

Lee was silent for so long, Ed didn't think he would get an answer, but then the man said, "Multiple reasons. If those trunks you carried into the house the other day are as old as they looked, you might find some answers there. The island might hold others."

He glanced towards Retribution Island. Before Ed could ask for more information, Tan pulled a gun on Tess.

He stiffened.

"Take it easy. Aim for his hand," Lee said.

Was he crazy? Tan's hand was the smallest target. "What are you going to do?"

"Aim for his head."

Ed jerked, but didn't dare take his eyes off Tess to look at the man lying next to him. "Why?"

"Because he's made many people's lives hell." The grim statement resonated with determination.

Ed didn't want Tess to witness that. "Let me distract him."

He prayed Lee could be trusted, and Brandon wouldn't get caught in the crossfire. He stood, rifle to his eye, and called, "Drop the gun, Tan."

Lee swore and hissed, "You idiot. Brandon had it covered."

So Lee had seen Brandon. Something weird was going on.

Tan stretched his arm, pointing the gun at Tess. "You think you can shoot before I can?" Then Tan frowned. "You're one of the Stokes." He swore. "She was at the Ridge all this time, and no one told me?"

Ed kept his gaze steady as he stepped towards Tan so Lee could get a clear shot. Then the implication hit him. Lee hadn't told Tan Tess was there. Why not?

"Ed, you need to go," Tess called. "Please."

His gaze flicked to her fear-filled eyes and then focused back on Tan. Brandon sneaked out from around the bonnet of the car, moving towards Tan.

Bang.

Ed flinched at the gunshot as Brandon slammed into Tan. Tess screamed.

No! Ed ran towards her, frantically looking for blood. Sam reached her first and hauled her out of the way, dragging her around the other side of the car. Brandon had Tan's gun and pointed it at the man, but there was no point.

Blood was sprayed across the ute and there was a hole in the back of his head.

Ed glanced over his shoulder but couldn't see Lee.

"Lower the gun, Ed," Brandon shouted.

He did so and ran towards Tess. He shoved the rifle at Heath, who had appeared next to Sam, and dragged Tess into his arms. "Are you all right?"

She nodded. "He didn't shoot me."

Ed inhaled the frangipani scent of her hair and trembled. "I thought he was going to kill you. I told you to wait. I told you I'd help."

She shook her head, pressed away from him. "I couldn't let you get hurt."

He wanted to shake her. "Don't you understand, I'd do anything to protect you?" He closed his eyes, as fear and relief clashed together, but over both emotions flooded one which was far stronger. "I love you, Tess."

She gasped, staring up at him.

He adjusted her hat so he could see her better. "You're amazing—so brave and smart, so full of passion—"

That's all he got before she kissed him, fierce and possessive. "I love you too."

Ed closed his eyes, holding her against him, needing to reassure himself she was fine.

Brandon's call broke through the magic. "Anyone got a radio? We need to call Dot."

"There's one in my backpack." Which he'd left with the bike.

"This one?" Dobby asked, holding up the backpack.

"Yeah."

Dobby handed it to Ed, and he switched the radio on. "Ames, are you there?"

"Yes. Is everyone all right?"

"Yeah, but we need the police."

"I'll tell Dot she can move in."

Ed winced. Dot was going to be mad.

"Is Tan going to live?" Tess asked, walking around the car. Heath moved to block her view.

"No, he's dead," Brandon said.

"You didn't have to shoot him, Ed," Heath said. "We were right here."

Ed jolted. "I didn't. It was Lee."

Brandon stared at him. "What?"

"Lee was with me watching everything." He pointed, and Sam took off in that direction. "I swear, the bullet won't match the rifle."

In the distance, the sound of a car engine grew louder.

Ed drew Tess away from the body.

"I need to call my parents," she said.

He checked his phone, but there was no reception. "You can as soon as we get back to the house."

She shook her head. "Tan said my father hadn't been kidnapped. He said Mum was told to lie. I need to know the truth."

The hurt radiated from her, and Ed pulled her into his arms again. "We'll find out the truth. I promise." He kissed her forehead, needing to touch her still.

A police car roared down the road and braked. Dot and Nhiari leapt out, hands on their guns.

"Tan was shot in the head," Ed said.

Dot swore.

Dobby pointed to Tan's gun lying in the sand, out of reach. "He carried that."

"You guys should all be on a plane right now," Nhiari stated as she grabbed a camera from the car and started photographing the scene.

Dot crouched by Tan and examined the exit wound. "Fuck," she said, running a hand through her hair. "All of you away from the body." She pointed towards the police four-wheel-drive. She spotted Tess, and her eyes narrowed. "I told you we would handle this."

Tess stiffened beside Ed. "I didn't want anyone I cared about getting hurt."

"Right. Who shot him?"

Ed hesitated. Lee had saved Tess's life, and there might have been other Stonefish people out here he hadn't seen. "We don't know for sure."

Dot frowned and scanned those who were there as Sam came jogging back.

"Lee got away," Sam said, panting. "His four-wheel drive was parked on a track about a kilometre away."

"What was he doing here?" Dot asked.

"He said he wanted to protect Tess," Ed told her. "Said something about Tan making too many people's lives miserable."

Dot sighed. "All right. We're going to need statements from everyone, and I'm going to need more of my team."

Another police car drove down the shore from the west.

"There's water in the back seat," Dot continued. "Take a bottle and find somewhere in the shade. No one's going anywhere until we've sorted this mess."

***

The sun was wickedly hot by the time Dot gave them

all leave to go. Tess took Ed's hand so he could help her to her feet from where she'd been sitting in the meagre shade. They'd both been interviewed extensively by Nhiari and Dot, and the adrenaline of the morning was well and truly gone. Tess stumbled, too tired to watch where she was going, but Ed stopped her from falling.

"I've got you."

She smiled. Her hero. "I know."

They followed Heath, Sam and Dobby to where they'd parked their vehicle. Brandon was going to ride the motorbike back, and the police wanted to keep the hire car a little longer.

All these people had come to her rescue. The thought warmed Tess and reduced the hurt about what her mother had done.

Perhaps she'd made the wrong decision by going to Tan by herself, but she wouldn't regret it. Not if it meant Tan was dead.

She climbed into the back seat, sandwiched between Ed and Heath. It wasn't over yet. The police had confiscated Ed's rifle and would keep it until they cleared him of any wrongdoing. They'd found the bullet next to the four-wheel drive, and it was the wrong size for the rifle, so they hadn't arrested Ed. The hire car company wouldn't be thrilled about the dent in the paint work.

Tess glanced across at Ed as Sam drove them back to the homestead. He hadn't said a lot while they'd waited to be interviewed, but he had held her close, which had helped.

She still couldn't believe how quickly everything had happened. One minute she believed Tan was going to kill her, the next she was terrified for Ed's life, and then Brandon had appeared, and men had swarmed around her and she hadn't had a second to think. But the gun shot had stopped her heart.

For a split second she'd thought Ed had been shot,

and she'd never known such terror. She squeezed his knee to reassure herself he was fine.

They drove into the yard, and Darcy charged down the steps of the house, Georgie right behind him. Before they'd come to a complete stop, Darcy had Ed's side door open. "Are you completely fucking crazy?"

"No." Ed unbuckled the seat belt and Darcy dragged him out of the car and wrapped him in a bear hug.

"You stupid idiot. You had us all terrified."

Tess smiled. She slid out of the opposite side of the car after Heath. Georgie hugged Ed now, and Darcy stalked towards Tess.

"And you," he said.

Tess's back hit the door, but Darcy dragged her into his arms. "Thank you for trying to stop my brother from doing something stupid, but you didn't have to go alone. We're here for you too."

Tess's heart ached as tears ran down her cheeks. She squeezed him back, unable to speak. Her own family didn't care about her this much.

When Darcy let her go, Georgie was next. "I get why you did what you did, but you obviously didn't realise my brother is stubborn." She hugged her. "I'm glad you're both all right."

Tess swallowed hard. "Thank you."

"Come inside," Amy called from the porch. "I've made lunch, and we can all find out what happened."

Ed joined Tess, slipping his hand into hers. Always there for her. She hesitated. The urge to follow them inside was strong, but there was one thing she had to deal with first. "I have to call my parents."

"Of course."

She didn't want to bring such potential ugliness into the house. "Can I borrow your phone?" She wanted to video call her parents. She needed to see if they were lying. Her pulse fluttered as she dialled the number.

"Tess!" Her mother appeared on the screen. "You're all right! Did you speak to Tan?" Behind her, Joy moved into the frame, concern in her eyes.

Tess nodded, wandering towards the shed where Maggie lay in the shade. "Where's Dad?"

Her mother hesitated, glancing at Joy.

Tess's stomach clenched. "Mum, where is he?"

"He's at work," Joy said.

Did Joy not know? "Mum?"

Her mother nodded. "He left for work this morning."

Tess couldn't read her expression—defiant, determined, scared? "You lied to me."

"I said what I was told to say." There was no apology in her expression.

"I need to speak to him. I'll call you back." She hung up and with trembling fingers, she called her father.

Ed squeezed her hand.

Would her father answer? He might not be able to depending on where he was. She met Ed's gaze, and he said, "I'm right here."

That made all the difference.

"Hello?" Tess could faintly hear her father's voice over the sounds of machinery in the background, but he was dressed in his work clothes and appeared as healthy as the last time she'd spoken to him. Behind him were several large shipping containers.

Nausea rose in her stomach. "Dad. You're all right?"

"Tess? What's happened? Where are you?"

She closed her eyes as the betrayal washed over her. She couldn't speak over the lump in her throat.

"Tess? You need to call Tan."

She inhaled deeply. "Mum told me you'd been kidnapped. She said Stonefish would kill you if I didn't turn myself in." It had never occurred to her to call her father, that her mother would lie to her about something so serious.

Silence.

"Well, I'm glad you were smart enough to call me first."

Disbelief made her speechless. Tears blurred her vision. "I almost died," she whispered. "If not for some friends, Tan would have killed me." She hung up, unable to look at him any longer. Both her parents had spouted the lie without hesitation.

Ed gathered her into his arms and held her as she sobbed. What would she have done in the circumstances? Had her mother really believed Tess would call her father to confirm what she'd said? Had she trusted Tan's word that Tess wouldn't be harmed? Or had she simply put her life above her daughter's?

"I'm sorry, Tess." Ed rubbed her back and pressed kisses against her head.

She clung to him, needing the touch, needing to know someone cared about her. Her phone rang, but she ignored it. She couldn't deal with more right now.

It took a couple of minutes before the wave of grief passed. She leaned away from him. "I have to call Mum back." She didn't want to, but she needed answers.

Ed moved away, but she placed a hand on his arm. "I need you here."

He nodded and slid a hand around her waist. Her support. Nearby, the sheep, Flotsam and Jetsam, were being patted by a couple of kids staying at the campground. Such a normal day for most people.

This time her mother was sitting on the couch with Joy beside her. Her mother's eyes widened. "Who's with you?"

Tess squeezed Ed's hand. "This is Ed. He saved my life—twice."

Her mother's mouth dropped open as Ed smiled. "Hi, Mrs Lim."

"That's my sister, Joy."

Ed waved.

All so normal, as if she was introducing her family to her boyfriend. But they had almost got her killed. "I spoke to Dad. He's fine."

Her mother nodded. "I told you he was at work."

"So why did you also tell me he'd been kidnapped, and was going to be killed?"

Joy gasped and looked at her mother in horror. "What? Why would you say that?"

"Because Tan told me to. He said if I didn't, he would ensure your father was actually taken and killed."

Tess shook her head. "Why didn't you go to the police? Or warn me?"

"They were monitoring our calls."

"Are they monitoring this app?"

A look of horror crossed her face. "I don't know." She reached for the screen, but Joy swatted her away, snatching the phone from her grasp.

"Will someone tell me what's going on?" Joy demanded.

Tess waited for her mother to speak, but she kept her lips pressed together. "I saw Tan murder someone last week. I escaped, and he's been chasing me since." Joy's mouth dropped open. "Today when I called Mum, she told me Dad had been kidnapped, and if I didn't go back to Tan, they would kill him. So I risked my life to meet with Tan in the middle of nowhere, and he pulled a gun on me. But someone killed him before he could hurt me." Should she mention Lee? Could her brother-in-law be involved?

Her mother shook. "He said nothing would happen to you. He simply had to explain what had happened."

"How long have you been dealing with Stonefish, Mum—ten years? Have they ever told you the whole truth?"

"They enabled this lifestyle you've had," her mother

retorted. "They paid for your education, this house, your trip to Australia. We owe them."

"But not at the price of Tess's life," Joy said.

Tess glanced at her sister. "Joy, you need to talk to Dylan. Find out if he's involved with Stonefish."

Her sister gaped at her.

"His cousin is, Mum and Dad are. I don't know how far Stonefish's influence spreads."

Joy clutched her necklace. "I will."

"You must come home," her mother said. "I'll arrange your flight."

Ed stiffened.

"No, Mum. I'm staying here. I'm finishing my education." As if she could return home to her parents now. She could barely look at her mother.

"You have no place to stay. We won't pay for your accommodation."

"Tess can stay with me for as long as she likes," Ed said. "I'll support her."

Tess jolted. Did he mean it? He'd done so much already. "You don't have to, Ed." She'd get another job, figure something out. She would make it work.

"I want to, Tess." His love showed on his face.

Tess's heart hitched, and she flung her arms around him, almost knocking the phone out of her hand. "I love you."

"No," her mother said. "You can't live with a man, without being married."

Tess had had enough. "You can't control me any longer, Mum. You lost that right when you almost had me killed." She looked at her sister. "Be careful talking to Dylan. Let me know how it goes."

Joy nodded. "Take care. And you take care of my sister, Ed."

"I will," he promised.

Tess ended the call and turned to Ed. "Did you really

mean it about me moving in with you?" If she could do that, she could use the money she'd saved to go towards her university fees.

"Yeah, I did." He kissed her. "I like having you around. But I have to warn you, I have a house mate who's a little odd."

She chuckled. "As long as he doesn't try to kill me, he'll be much better than my previous house mate." She could deal with anything now.

She kissed him and for the moment everything felt right. Tess would figure out her fractured relationship with her parents at some stage, but that was for another day.

"Come on. The others will be waiting to hear the full story." Ed tugged her back towards the house.

This time there was no uncertainty as she walked into the kitchen, where everyone sat around the table. They turned to her, making her the centre of attention, but all she felt was their overwhelming support. This was what family was supposed to be like, and Ed was right by her side.

Chapter 23

"You could both do with one of these." Brandon handed Ed and Tess a shot of whisky each as they entered the kitchen, and Ed drank it in one gulp. The burn felt good after the terror of the morning, and the warmth mellowed him. He was still reeling from the news Tess's mother had put her in harm's way on purpose. He'd wanted to tell her what a miserable excuse for a mother she was, but it wouldn't have been a great first impression, and Ed was mindful he planned to be in Tess's life for a long time.

Ed pulled out a chair for her to sit.

"So what happened?" Georgie demanded.

Ed exchanged a glance with Tess. "Do you want to start?"

"There's not much to tell. Tan arrived by boat, told me my mother had lied, and my father was fine, and he was going to kill me before he left Australia."

Georgie blinked. "What now? Your dad wasn't in danger?"

Tess shook her head.

"Tan told her mum that Tess wouldn't be hurt, he just needed to talk to her," Ed explained.

"And she believed him?" Amy stared at her, wide-eyed.

Tess shrugged.

Ed took over, wanting to take the attention off Tess's family's questionable actions. "When I arrived, I spotted Lee lying in the grass watching." He handed Tess the salad bowl and explained his conversation with Lee. "It was weird. Lee admitted to working for Stonefish, but not Tan. He didn't know if Tan had any other backup there."

"If he killed Tan, why didn't he hurt you?" Darcy asked.

"I got the feeling he didn't want Tess or me to be hurt," Ed told him. "He said the police should check out Retribution Island when all this was done."

Sam picked up his mug. "What's out there?"

"I don't know."

"You got a boat?" Dobby asked Brandon.

"There's an old dinghy in the shed."

Ed smiled. "Dot said if anyone goes near the island, she'll arrest the lot of us."

"Only if she finds out about it," Heath said.

Ed was curious, too. "Lee also said the trunks we brought inside the other day might have answers as to why Stonefish want the Ridge."

"But they didn't," Tess said.

"We haven't had a good look in the cellar yet." Something else occurred to him. "How long has the new track been there?"

Darcy frowned. "What new track?"

He gestured for Sam to speak.

"Lee took off on a track which ran almost parallel to the beach."

Darcy glanced at Matt. "Do you know about it?"

Matt shook his head. "I'll ask my folks, but they normally chat to you about that kind of thing."

"When the police are finished, we can go for a drive," Brandon said.

"Did Lee admit to any of the sabotage?" Amy asked tentatively.

"I asked about the sheep, but he didn't answer," Ed replied. "Georgie, how much do scenic flights cost?"

She blinked at him. "Huh?"

He'd been thinking about Lee's words on the way home. "Lee said the island might hold answers, and there's a new track to the gulf. They don't want the Ridge for the sheep, so it has to be the location. We can't cover all our land easily, but a plane can. Maybe Darcy and Matt should charter a flight, see if they can spot any anomalies from the air."

Dobby nodded. "Great idea."

"I'll call them." Georgie reached for her phone. "When do you want to go up?"

"As soon as possible," Darcy answered.

"We should read the rest of those journals, and go through the trunks again," Brandon added.

"And the cellar," Tess said.

Dobby sighed. "I need to get us on the afternoon flight home," he said. "Otherwise the Major is going to have a fit."

"Thanks for your help, mate." Brandon clapped him on the shoulder.

"Any time. Keep us in the loop. We're all invested now." He went outside to make the call.

Ed ate his lunch while Brandon told the others how they'd parked at a distance and sneaked up to the gulf to take out Tan. Tess was silent until the end. "Thank you for coming after me," she said. "All of you. I didn't expect you to risk your lives for me."

"We've been through some stuff recently," Brandon said. "We wouldn't let anyone go through that alone— particularly not someone who is special to Ed."

She ducked her head, cheeks red, but then straightened and looked Brandon in the eye. "Thank you."

Ed grinned. Tess had come a long way since he'd met her as a bedraggled shell a week ago. He was so proud of her, and it made him love her all the more.

"I've got you a flight this afternoon," Georgie announced, placing her phone on the table. "He can take you up in two hours."

Dobby walked in. "That works. Our flight is in three hours."

"All right," Darcy said. "Matt and I will take the guys to the airport, and then see if we can spot anything unusual from the air. You can search for historical clues here."

It felt good to finally do something active against Stonefish. Perhaps soon they would find the way to stop them completely. But in the meantime, at least Tan and Salvatore were no longer a threat to Tess.

And if Tan was one of the head people in Western Australia, maybe Stonefish would stop bothering the Stokes for a while.

Even though Lee was still out there, Ed got the feeling he wouldn't be a threat to them.

But talking about Tess and the future reminded Ed of something. "Be right back."

He went into his room and called his roommate.

"How's the Ridge?" Sheridan answered. "Tell me you're hating it, and you're coming home early to help with this roll out."

"Nope." Ed chuckled. That was something else he needed to address. It was time to find a new job, one he enjoyed. "Actually, I need to run something by you." He was fairly sure Sheridan wouldn't have a problem with Tess moving in, but nerves still tickled his skin. "Remember how I mentioned I was carpooling with a woman?"

"Yeah. Don't tell me you've fallen in love and got married?"

Ed grinned. "You're half right."

Sheridan grunted. "What?"

"Tess is amazing. You'll love her," Ed said. "Thing is, there was a bit of an issue with the place she was staying—"

"She's moving in with us?"

Ed relaxed. "If you're all right with it."

"The more the merrier," Sheridan said. "As long as you give me some notice when you want me to move out. The rental market sucks at the moment."

"Thanks, mate."

"Don't sweat it. See you when you get back."

As Ed returned to the kitchen, Amy's phone beeped with a text message. She gasped and dashed out of the room. Brandon frowned and followed her.

What now?

Amy returned, carrying her laptop. "Give me a second, Brandon." Her fingers shook as she pressed some buttons, and then her hand covered her mouth. "They're here."

What was going on? Ed, Tess, and Georgie all moved so they could see the laptop screen. It was full of professional photos from Brandon and Amy's wedding.

"Lee sent them," Amy explained. She clicked on her email. The message said, *Words can't express how sorry I am.*

"Do you think he's as trapped as the others have been?" Ed asked.

"Maybe," Brandon said, as Amy clicked to download the folder from an online sharing platform.

"I'm glad you got your photos," Tess said. "They're lovely."

Amy's eyes shone. "They are, aren't they?"

Ed hugged his sister-in-law and then took Tess's

hand. "Can I talk to you for a moment?"

He took her into their bedroom. "Tess, I was serious about everything I said to your family. I will support you with whatever you choose to do." He squeezed her hands. "I've just called Sheridan and he's cool with you moving in. You can live with me as long as you want and study whatever you like, and I'll pay your university fees. I want you in my life."

"I hadn't considered changing my major." She blinked. "I want to be in your life, but I won't let you do everything. I'll find another job. I want to contribute to us."

"Us." Ed smiled. "I like the sounds of that.

She kissed him. "So do I."

Thank you for reading!

I hope you enjoyed reading Escape to Retribution Bay. If you did like it, and want to show your support, there are a couple of things you could do. The first is to leave a review wherever you bought it. I love reading my reviews and it gives me a real boost when I'm having a difficult writing day.

If you're not comfortable with that, you could always recommend the book to friends, add it to lists over on GoodReads, or ask your library to buy a copy. Every little bit helps more people discover my books so I can keep writing them.

Acknowledgements

I was fortunate to go on a research trip to Exmouth while writing this book. A big thanks to the Department of Local Government, Sport and Cultural Industries who provided a grant to fund some of the trip.

Exmouth, WA is the town Retribution Bay is based on, and for those of you who have been there, you'll recognise a few actual locations in this story. Some very kind locals have allowed me to interview them to create a more authentic story. For this particular story I need to thank Jimmy Small who owns Ocean Eco Adventures, and told me what I need to know about whale shark tours. I also spoke to Sergeant Craig Carter of the Exmouth Police who helped answer a few questions I had about police procedure. There were others I spoke to, but I can't tell you who yet, without giving away what will happen in future stories.

I have to also thank Michelle Diener for hiring the van which was the inspiration behind this story. We drove across Australia on our way to the Romance Writers of Australia conference in Melbourne in 2019 in a dodgy van just like Ed and Tess's. At the time I knew it would have to appear in a story and this was the perfect story for that van.

Finally I must thank my team, Ann Harth, Teena Raffa-Mulligan and Mayhem Cover Creations for their editing and cover design.

Secrets in Retribution Bay

Aussie Heroes: Retribution Bay #4

Georgie and Matt's story is coming in 2022.